The King of Diamonds

A Tale of Mystery and Adventure

Louis Tracy

The King of Diamonds: A Tale of Mystery and Adventure

Copyright © 2019 Indo-European Publishing

The present edition is a reproduction of previous publication of this classic work. Minor typographical errors may have been corrected without note, however, for an authentic reading experience the spelling, punctuation, and capitalization have been retained from the original text.

ISBN: 978-1-64439-213-3

CONTENTS

Chapter I

No. 3, Johnson's Mews

"Is there no hope, doctor?"

"Absolutely none—now."

"If she had gone to the—the workhouse infirmary—would she have lived?"

The doctor paused. The gulp before that hateful word was not lost on him. He tried professional severity, and bestowed some care on the buttoning of a glove.

"I am surprised," he said, "that an excellent woman like your mother should encourage your feelings of—er—repugnance toward—er—Confound it, boy, have you no relatives or friends?"

"No, sir. We are alone in the world."

"And hard up, eh?"

The boy dug a hand into a pocket with the stolid indifference of despair. He produced two shillings and some pennies. He picked out the silver, and the man reddened in protest.

"Don't be stupid, Philip. That is your name, is it not? When I want my fee I will ask for it. Your mother needs a nurse, wine, chicken broth. You are old enough to realize that a doctor practicing in a neighborhood like this might want such things himself and whistle for them. But in the—er—infirmary they are provided by the State."

"Would my mother have lived had she consented to be taken there a month ago?"

Again the man wondered at the stony persistence of the questioner, a fearless-looking, active boy of fifteen, attired in worn clothes too small for him, and wearing an old pair of boots several sizes too large. The strong, young face, pinched with vigils and privation, the large, earnest eyes, heavy with unshed tears, the lips, quivering in their resolute compression over a chin that indicated great strength of character, appealed far more to the doctor than the whimpering terror with which the children of the poor usually meet the grim vision of death.

The wrestle with the glove ceased and a kindly hand rested on Philip's shoulder.

"No," came the quiet answer. "May God help you, she would not have lived."

"God does not help anybody," was the amazing retort.

The doctor was shocked, visibly so.

"That is a foolish and wicked statement," he said, sternly. "Do not let your mother hear such awful words. She has lived and will die a true Christian. I have never met a woman of greater natural charm and real piety. She has suffered so much that she merits the life eternal. It is a reward, not a punishment. Cast away these terrible thoughts; go, rather, and kneel by her side in prayer."

For an instant the great brown eyes blazed fiercely at him.

"Am I to pray that my mother shall be taken from me?"

"Even that, if it be God's will."

The gleam of passion yielded to utter helplessness. The boy again brought forth his tiny store of money.

"Surely," he said, "I can buy some small amount of wine. In the shops they sell things in tins that make chicken broth, don't they? I have a fire and a kettle. Would you mind telling me—"

"There, there! You go to your mother, and endeavor to cheer her up. I will see what I can do. What! Would you argue with me? Go at once; I insist. Listen, she is calling for you!"

In that poor tenement there were no secrets. A rickety staircase, crudely built against the retaining wall of the only living room on the ground floor, led steeply to an apartment above, and culminated in an opening that suggested a trapdoor. The walls, roughly paneled, were well provided with shelves and pegs. The back door was fastened with a latch, a contrivance rarely seen in the London of to-day. The front window looked out into a badly-paved court girt by tumbledown stables. A smaller window at the back revealed a dismal yard darkened by lofty walls. Although little more than a stone's throw removed from the busy Mile End Road, the place was singularly quiet. It was already dead, and only waited the coming of men with pickaxes and crowbars to sweep away the ruins.

The boy heard his name whispered rather than spoken. The sound galvanized him into vivid consciousness.

"Doctor," he said, earnestly, "you will come back?"

"Yes, yes; within half an hour. Tell your mother to expect me."

Philip ran up the stairs. Long practice had enabled him to move with a minimum of noise. It was pitiful to see the manner in which he emerged, with stealthy activity, into the creaking loft above. Here, at first glance, there was an astonishing degree of comfort. Odd pieces of worn carpet, neatly joined, covered the floor. The two windows, facing only to the front of the dwelling, were curtained. The whitewashed walls were almost hidden by cuttings from the colored periodicals published during the previous Christmas season. A screen divided the room into two compartments, each containing a tiny bed. On one of these, propped up with pillows, lay the wasted figure of a woman over whose face the shadows were falling fast. The extreme thinness, the waxen pallor, the delicate texture of debilitated skin and unnatural brilliancy of the eyes, gave her a remarkably youthful appearance. This fantastic trick of death in life accentuated the resemblance between mother and son. The boy, too, was sharply outlined by hunger, and, in the fading light of a March day, the difference between the dread tokens of approaching collapse and the transient effects of a scanty regimen on a vigorous youth was not readily distinguishable.

"Do you want anything, mother dear?" said the boy, laying his hand tenderly on the clammy forehead.

"Only to ask you, Phil, what it was that the doctor told you."

The voice was low and sweet—the diction that of an educated woman. The boy, too, though his tones were strong and harsh, spoke with the accent of good breeding. His manner and words gained some distinction from a slight touch of French elegance and precision. This was only noticeable in repose. When excited, or moved to deep feeling, the Continental veneer acquired at the Lycée in Dieppe instantly vanished, and he became the strenuous, emphatic Briton he undoubtedly was by birth and breeding.

"He said, dearest, that what you wanted was some good wine—nice things to eat. He is an awfully fine chap, and I am afraid I was rude to him, but he didn't seem to mind it a bit, and he is coming back soon with chicken broth and port wine, and I don't know what."

His brave words were well meant, but the mother's heart understood him too well to be deceived. A thin hand caught his wrist and feebly drew him nearer.

"You say you were rude to him, Phil? How can that be possible? What did you say or do to warrant such a description?"

He hesitated for a moment. With rare self-control in one so young, he fiercely determined not to communicate his own despair to his mother. So he laughed gently.

"We are so jolly hard up, you know, and it sounded strange in my ears to talk about expensive luxuries which I could not buy. He has often told us, dear, that you would be better cared for in the infirmary. I am afraid now he was right, only we couldn't bear—to be parted. Could we, mother?"

Not all his valor could control his tremulous lips. A beautiful smile illumined the face of the invalid.

"So you are trying to hoodwink me, Phil, for the first time. I know what the doctor said. He told you that I could not recover, and that I had not long to live; in a word, that I am dying."

Then the boy gave way utterly. He flung himself down by the side of the bed and buried his face in the coverlet.

"Oh, mother, mother!" he wailed, and his passionate sobs burst forth with alarming vehemence. The poor woman vainly strove to soothe him. She could not move, being paralyzed, but her fingers twined gently in his hair, and she gasped, brokenly:

3

"Phil, darling, don't make it harder for me. Oh, calm yourself, my dear one, if only for my sake. I have so much to say to you, and perhaps so little time. Be strong, Philip. Be strong and brave, and all will be well with you. I know you will miss me—we have been all in all to each other since your father's death. But my memory must be sweet, not bitter to you. When you think of me I want the recollection to inspire you to do that which is right regardless of consequences, to strive always for honor and for the approbation of your own conscience. My own dear boy, we must bow to the will of God. We have indeed been sorely tried, you far more than I, for I can look back on years of perfect happiness with a loving husband and a delightful child, whereas you have been plunged into poverty and misery at an age when life should be opening before you with every promise of a successful career. Perhaps, Phil, your trials have come to you early, as mine have found me late. I trust I have borne reverses of health and fortune with patience and resignation. My present sufferings will be a lasting joy to me if, in the life to come, I can know that my example has been a stimulus to you amidst the chances and changes of your career. Promise me, darling, that you will resign yourself to the decrees of Providence even in the bitter hour of our parting."

Her voice failed. Tears stood in her eyes. The knowledge came to her anew that natural emotions can at times conquer all restraints. The maternity strong within her clamored for the power to shield her offspring from the dangers that would beset him. There was a maddening pain in the thought that a few brief hours or minutes might unclasp her arms from him forever.

It was Phil who first gave utterance to the wild protest in their souls.

"Mother," he mourned, bitterly, "I don't want to live without you. Let us die together. If you cannot stay with me, then I swear—"

But a scream of terror, so shrill and vehement that it seemed to be almost miraculous from so frail a form, froze the vow on his lips.

"Phil! What are you saying? Oh, my son, my son, do not break my heart before I die. Kiss me, dearest. I am cold. I can scarce see you. Come nearer. Let me look once more into your brave eyes. You will be a great man, Phil. I know it. Who should know your character like your mother? But you must have faith in God always. I have prayed for you, and my prayers will surely be granted. I will watch over you. If you are in danger my spirit will come back to you across the void. We cannot be parted. Oh, God, it is impossible! You are the life of my life. I am not dead while you still live."

Even as she spoke, her left hand and arm, hitherto untouched by the cruel blight which had made her a helpless invalid during many weary months, became numb and rigid. She was dying now, not with the struggle against the king of terrors which often marks the passing of humanity, but with a slow torpidity more akin to sleep.

4

Her brain was clear, but the stock of nervous force had sunk so low that her few remaining words were spoken with difficulty. They were mostly endearing expressions, appeals to her loved one to hope and pray, to trust steadfastly in the all-wise power that would direct his destiny. With the last flicker of existence the maternal instinct became dominant again and she asked him not to forget her.

The boy could only murmur agonized appeals to the merciless unseen not to rob him of the only being he held dear on earth, but even in that awful moment he had the strength to cease his frantic protests when they seemed to cause her pain, and he forced himself to join her in prayer.

When the doctor brought a nurse and some small store of the much-needed delicacies, Mrs. Anson was already unconscious.

The boy, aroused from frenzy by the steps on the stairs, shrieked incoherently:

"I have killed my mother. See! She is dead. I killed her. I made her cry. You told me to look after her until you returned. She cried and screamed because I spoke so wildly. It is all my fault. I—"

"Hush! Your mother is not dead, but dying. Not all the skill of man can save her. Let her die in peace."

No other words could have checked the wild torrent of lament that surged from that wounded heart. So she still lived. There remained a faint flicker of life. Not yet had she passed the dreadful barrier of eternity. Through his blinding tears he thought he could discern a smile on the worn face. The doctor watched Phil more narrowly than the sunken frame on the bed. It was best that the paroxysm of grief should go untrammeled. The nurse, a young woman unused as yet to the inevitableness of death, moved timidly toward the windows and adjusted the curtains to admit more light.

At last, when Phil's strength yielded to the strain of his sorrow and the very force of his agony had spent itself, the doctor leaned over the inanimate form and looked into the eyes.

"It has ended, Phil," he whispered. "Your mother is in heaven!"

In heaven! What a tocsin of woe in a message of faith! The boy suddenly stood up. Hope was murdered within him. His tears ceased and his labored breathing came under control with a mighty effort. He stooped and kissed the pale cheeks twice.

"Good-by, mother," he said, and the dull pain in his voice was so heartrending that the nurse's sympathies mastered her. She burst out crying. Professional instinct came to the doctor's aid. He sharply reprimanded the half-hysterical woman and sent her off on an errand to bring those whose duty it is to render the last services to frail mortality. The boy he led downstairs. He was a busy man, with many claims on his time, but this strange youngster interested him, and he resolved to turn the boy's thoughts forcibly away from the all-absorbing horror of his mother's death.

"Have you a tumbler or a cup?" he said, sharply.

Phil handed him a tumbler. The doctor poured out some wine taken from the nurse's basket, soaked a piece of bread in the liquor, and gave it to the boy with an imperative command to eat it instantly.

Somewhat to his surprise, he was obeyed. While Phil was devouring the food of which he stood so greatly in need, the doctor reviewed the circumstances of this poverty-stricken household so far as they were known to him. Mr. and Mrs. Anson had occupied a fairly good position in Dieppe, where Philip's father was the agent of an old-established London firm of coal shippers. About two years earlier, both husband and wife were seriously injured in a motor car accident. Mr. Anson sustained concussion of the brain, and practically never regained his senses, though he lingered for some weeks and was subjected to two operations. Mrs. Anson's spine was damaged, with the result that she changed from a bright and vigorous woman into a decrepit invalid doomed to early death from slow paralysis.

When the great expenses attendant on these mishaps were paid, she found herself not only absolutely poor, but rendered incapable of the slightest effort to turn her many and varied talents to account in order to earn a livelihood. She came to London, where her late husband's employers generously gave her rent-free possession of the tenement in which she was lying dead, helped her with funds to furnish it modestly, and found a clerkship for Philip with a promise of early promotion.

But the cup of sorrow is seldom left half filled. Barely had the widow settled down to a hopeful struggle on behalf of her beloved son than a quarrel between partners led to the sale of the firm's business to a limited liability company. Economies were effected to make way for salaried directors. Philip was dismissed, with several other junior employees, and the stable yard was marked out as a suitable site for the storage of coal required by the local factories.

This development took place early in the New Year, and the new company allowed Mrs. Anson to occupy her tiny abode until the last day of March. It was now March 5th, and how the widow and her son had lived during the past two months the doctor could only guess from the gradual depletion of their little store of furniture.

It was odd that such an intelligent and well-bred woman should be so completely shut off from the rest of the world, and his first question to Phil sought to determine this mystery.

"Surely," he said, "there is some one to whom you can appeal for help. Your father and mother must have had some relatives—even distant cousins—and, if they are written to, a friendly hand may be forthcoming."

Philip shook his head. The mere taste of food had provoked a ravenous appetite. He could not eat fast enough. The doctor stayed him.

"Better wait a couple of hours, Phil, and then you can tackle a hearty meal. That's the thing. I like to see such prompt obedience, but you certainly have wonderful self-control for one so young. I may tell you, to relieve present anxieties, that a few employees of your father's firm have guaranteed the expenses of your mother's funeral, and they also gave me a sovereign to tide you over the next few days."

Funeral! The word struck with sledge-hammer force. Phil had not thought of that. He remembered the dismal pomp of such events in this squalid locality, the loud sobbing of women, the hard-faced agony of men, the frightened curiosity of children. His mother, so dear, so tender, so soft-cheeked—the bright, beautiful, laughing woman of their life in Dieppe—to be taken away from him forever, and permitted to fade slowly into nothingness in some dreadful place, hidden from the sunshine and the flowers she loved! For the first time he understood death. When his father was killed his mother was left. Anxious tending on her dispelled the horror of the greater tragedy. Now all was lost. The tears that he hated were welling forth again, and he savagely bit his lip.

"You have been—very good—to us, doctor," he forced himself to say. "If ever—I can repay you—"

"There, there, not a word! Bless my soul, yours is a difficult case."

Again the doctor tackled his glove. He glanced at his watch.

"Four o'clock! I am an hour late on my rounds. No, Phil. Don't go upstairs. There are some women coming. Wait until they have tended your mother. And—one last word. It will do you no good to keep vigil by her side. Best think of her as living, not dead. You will be grateful for my advice in after life."

The women arrived, coarse but kindly-hearted creatures. One of them gave the boy a packet of letters.

"I found 'em under the dear lydy's pillow," she said. Neither poverty nor death robbed Mrs. Anson of the respect paid to her by all who came in contact with her.

He sat down, untied a string which bound the letters together, and looked at the address on the first envelope. It bore his mother's name and a recent postmark. Wondering dolefully what correspondence she could have had during these later months that demanded such careful preservation, he took out the letter. Suddenly he hesitated. Perhaps these documents alluded to something which his mother did not wish him to know. For an instant his impulse was to consign the packet to the fire. No; that might be wrong. He would glance at their general purport and then commit them to the flames if he thought fit.

The letter in his hand was headed: "The Hall, Beltham, Devon," and dated about a month earlier. It read:

7

"Dear Madam: I am requested by Sir Philip Morland to ask you not to trouble him with further correspondence. This is the fourth time I have been desired by him to write in these terms, so please note that your letters will in future remain unanswered.

"Yours truly,
"Louisa Morland"

The curt incivility of the note brought an angry flush to the boy's face. Who was Sir Philip Morland that he should dare to offer this insult to a lady? Evidently a relative, and a near one, for Morland was his mother's name, and his own Christian name suggested a family connection. Yet she had never spoken of any such person.

Three other letters, of preceding dates, showed that "Louisa Morland" kept accurate reckoning. There were half a dozen more, from a firm of solicitors. Some of these were merely formal acknowledgments of letters received and forwarded, but one stated that they "were instructed by Lady Morland to inform Mrs. Anson that Sir Philip Morland declined either to see or hear from her."

That was all. Philip sprang up with face aflame. He was alone in the house now, alone with his dead mother.

He went upstairs, with the letters crushed in his right hand as though he would choke a reptile which had stung the only being he loved. He bent over the shrunken form, so placid, so resigned, so angelic in the peace of death, and his hot tears fell unchecked.

"You poor darling," he murmured, "I believe you humbled yourself even to beg from these people for my sake. What can I do to show my love for you?"

Chapter II

On the Edge of the Precipice

On Friday evening, March 19th, a thunderstorm of unusual violence broke over London. It was notably peculiar in certain of its aspects. The weather was cold and showery, a typical day of the March equinox. Under such conditions barometric pressure remains fixed rather than variable, yet many whose business or hobby it is to record such facts observed a rapid shrinkage of the mercury column between the hours of six and seven. A deluge of rain fell for many minutes, and was followed, about 7.30 P. M., by a mad turmoil of thunder and an astounding electrical display not often witnessed beyond the confines of the giant mountain ranges of the world.

So violent and unnerving was the outburst that the social life of London was paralyzed for the hour. Theater parties, diners in the fashionable restaurants, the greater millions anxious to get away from offices and shops, those eager alike to enter and leave the charmed circle of the four-mile radius, were ruthlessly bidden to wait while the awesome forces of nature made mad racket in the streets. All horseflesh was afraid. The drivers of cabs and omnibuses were unable to make progress. They had sufficient ado to restrain their maddened animals from adding the havoc of blind charges through the streets to the general confusion caused by the warring elements. Telegraph and telephone wires became not only useless but dangerous, and the suburban train service was consequently plunged into a tangle from which it was not extricated until midnight.

So general was the confusion, so widespread the public alarm, that the sudden cessation of the uproar at eight o'clock caused more prayers of thankfulness to be uttered in the metropolis than had been heard for many a day. But worse remained. Thus far the lightning had been appalling, brilliantly lurid, but harmless. At ten o'clock the storm raged again, this time without the preliminary downfall of rain, and the lightning, though less sensational in appearance, was demoniac in effect, levying a toll on human lives, causing fires and general damage to property, accounts of which filled many columns of the newspapers next morning. This second outburst was succeeded by heavy and continuous rain. At the hour when the theaters emptied their diminishing audiences into the streets London wore its normal rain-sodden aspect. It was not until the following day that people fully understood the magnitude and terrifying results of the later display.

About a quarter to eight, while the first storm was at its height, a carriage and pair dashed into a fashionable West End square and pulled up outside a mansion cast in the stereotyped mold of the early Victorian period. The horses, overfed and underworked, had been rendered frantic by the drive through the park from the further west. Fortunately, they knew this halting place, or the coachman would never have succeeded in stopping them. As it was, they sweated white with fear, and the footman, shouting to the occupants of the carriage that he could not attend to the door, ran to their heads after giving a vigorous tug at the house bell.

A boy, tall and thin, and scantily attired for such weather, who had taken shelter in the dark portico of the mansion, ran forward to offer his services at the carriage door. A bundle of evening papers, covered with a piece of sacking, somewhat impeded the use of his left hand, and, as it happened, in his right he held a large bun on which he had just commenced to dine.

Before he could turn the handle the carriage door opened from the inside. A man sprang out.

"Get out of the way," he said, impatiently, and the newsboy obeyed, glad that he had not followed his first impulse and flung away the bun.

A vivid flash of lightning made the horses rear and plunge.

"Look sharp, Elf," cried the stranger, in no more cordial tone. "Gather your wraps and jump out. On a night like this these nervous brutes—"

A peal of thunder that rattled the windows interrupted him. The two animals reared and backed with one accord. The plucky footman, hanging onto the crossbars of the bits, was lifted off his feet and banged violently against the pole. He was forced to let go, and fell, staggering backward some yards before he dropped. There was a smash of iron and wood, and the near hind wheel of the carriage jammed against the curb. A slight scream came from the interior. Certain that the vehicle would turn over instantly, the man who had alighted slammed the door and sprang clear. In doing so he tripped over the newsboy and fell heavily on the pavement. The boy, quicker to note that the breaking of the pole had given a momentary respite, rushed into the roadway, throwing away both precious bun and still more precious stock of unsold papers.

He wrenched the other door open, and shouted:

"This way, madam! Quick!"

"Madam" was quick. She sprang right into his arms, and proved to be a girl of twelve or thereabouts, dressed all in white, and wrapped in an ermine cloak.

Over went the carriage with a fearful crash. The coachman managed to jump from the box into the roadway. He retained the reins and whip in his grasp, and now, losing his temper, lashed the struggling horses savagely. This cowed them, and they ceased their antics.

10

The boy and the girl found themselves standing on the sidewalk, close to the ruined vehicle.

"You have saved my life!" said the girl, sweetly, and without any trace of the nervousness which might naturally be expected after such a narrow escape from a serious accident.

The boy noted that her eyes were large and blue, that she wore a great shining ornament in her hair, and that she appeared to be dressed in somewhat fanciful manner, though the big cloak she wore concealed the details.

The door of the mansion opened, and servants came running out.

Suddenly the boy received a violent blow on the side of the head.

"Confound you!" shouted the man who had fallen on the pavement, "why didn't you get out of the way when I told you?"

The boy, astounded by such recognition of his timely help, made no reply, but the girl protested vehemently.

"Oh, uncle," she cried, "why did you strike him? He got me out of the carriage just before it turned over. He did, indeed!"

Another vivid flash of lightning illumined the scene. It lit up the group with starling brilliancy. The boy, still somewhat shaken by the vicious blow, was nevertheless able to see clearly the pale, handsome, but dissipated features of his enraged assailant, whose evening dress and immaculate linen were soiled by the black mud of the pavement. The girl, dainty and fairy-like, a little maid of aristocratic type, and of a beauty that promised much in later years, was distressed now and almost tearful.

Through the crowd of frightened servants, augmented by a few daring pedestrians, a burly policeman, gigantic in waterproof overalls, was advancing with official bluster.

"What has happened?" he demanded. "Is anybody hurt?"

The man answered:

"My horses were startled by the storm. I jumped out and was endeavoring to extricate my niece when this wretched boy got in the way."

"Uncle," protested the girl, "you closed the door on me, and the boy—"

"Shut up!" he growled, curtly. "Go inside the house!"

But his niece shared with him at least one characteristic. She possessed the family temper.

"I will not go away and let you say things which are untrue. Listen to me, Mr. Policeman. Lord Vanstone did close the door because he thought the carriage would turn over on top of him. For some reason the accident did not happen immediately, and the boy ran round to the other side and helped me out just in time."

"Confound the brat! I think he was the real cause of the whole affair. Why was he hiding in my doorway?"

11

Lord Vanstone was more enraged than ever by the girl's obstinate defense of her rescuer and her insistence on his own seeming cowardice.

"I was not hiding. I only took shelter from the storm. I tried to help you because the footman was struggling with the horses. I do not claim any credit for simply opening a door and helping the young lady to alight, but I lost both my dinner and my papers in doing so."

Everyone experienced a shock of surprise at hearing the boy's elegant diction. The policeman was puzzled. He instantly understood the facts, but dared not browbeat an earl.

"You do not bring any charge against him, my lord?" he said.

But his lordship deigned no reply. He told the coachman to arrange for the removal of the carriage, grasped his niece by the arm and led her, still protesting, into the house.

The policeman saw the bundle of papers scattered over the roadway, and, near them, the partly-eaten bun. After a wrench at his garments he produced a penny.

"Here," he said to the boy. "Buy another bun and be off. It's a good job for you the young lady spoke up the way she did."

"She merely told the truth. That man was a liar."

Refusing the proffered penny, the boy turned on his heel. The policeman looked after him.

"That's a queer kid," he thought. "Talked like a regular young gent. I wonder why he is selling papers. Poor lad! He lost a bob's worth at least, and small thanks he got for it."

Passing out of the square by the first eastward street, Philip Anson, with his head erect and hands clinched in his pockets, strode onward at a rapid pace. The lightning was less frequent now, and the thunder was dying away in sullen rumblings. He was wet and hungry. Yet, although he had three halfpence, the remaining balance of the only sales effected that evening, he passed many shops where he could have bought food.

In Piccadilly, where the cessation of the storm created a rush of traffic, he was nearly run over, by reason of his own carelessness, and received a slash from a whip, accompanied by a loud oath from an angry cabman. He shivered, but never even looked around. Crossing Trafalgar Square, he plunged through the vortex of vehicles without troubling to avoid them in the slightest degree. Once the hot breath of a pair of van horses touched his cheek while a speechless driver pulled them back onto their haunches. Again, the off-wheel of an omnibus actually grazed his heel as he sped behind the statue of Charles the First.

At last he reached the comparative seclusion of the Embankment, and stood for a moment to gaze fixedly at the swirling, glinting river.

"Not here," he muttered, aloud. "I must be nearer to mother—dear old mother! She is there, waiting for me."

He trudged steadily away, through Queen Victoria Street, Cornhill, Leadenhall Street, and so on to Johnson's Mews, in the Mile End Road. Pausing at a marine store dealer's shop, kept by an army pensioner, an Irishman, with whom he had a slight acquaintance, he entered. An elderly man was laboriously reading a paper of the preceding day's date.

"Good-evening, Mr. O'Brien," he said. "Can you oblige me with a piece of rope? I want a strong piece, about three or four yards in length. I can only spare three halfpence."

"Faix, I dunno. They use nails on the crates mostly nowadays. If I have a bit it's at yer sarvice. I wouldn't be afther chargin' the likes o' you."

Philip's story was known in that humble locality, and the old soldier sympathized with the boy. "He has rale spunk an' no mistake," was his verdict when others said Philip was proud and overbearing. O'Brien moved rheumatically about the squalid shop. At last he found some portion of a clothesline.

"Will that do?" he inquired.

Philip tested it with vigorous pulling against his knee.

"Excellently," he said. "Let me pay you for it."

"Arrah, go away wid ye. And, be the powers, isn't the poor lad cowld an' famished. Luke here, now. In five minutes I'm goin' to have a cup o' tay—"

"I am awfully obliged to you, but I could not touch a morsel. I am in a hurry."

"Are ye goin' a journey? Have ye got a job?"

"I think so. It looks like a permanency. Good-by."

"Good-by, an' good luck to ye. Sure the boy looks mighty quare. 'Tis grief for his mother has turned his head entirely."

No words could more clearly express Philip's condition than this friendly summing up. Since his mother's burial he had been half demented. His curt, disconnected answers had lost him two places as an errand boy, which he could easily have secured. His small stock of money, ridiculously depleted by the generosity with which he met the open hints of the undertaker's assistants, barely sufficed to keep him in food for a week. Then he sought employment, but with such stiff upper lip and haughty indifference to success that he unknowingly turned those against him who would have assisted him.

For two days he was chosen to act as van boy for a parcel delivery firm. He earned a few meals, but in a fit of aberration induced by the sight of a lady who was dressed in a costume similar to one he remembered his mother wearing at Dieppe, he allowed a ham to be stolen from the rear of the van. This procured his instant dismissal, with threats. Then he sold newspapers, only to find that every good site was jealously guarded by a gang of roughs who mercilessly bullied any newcomer. Personal strength and courage were unavailing against sheer numbers. His face was still swollen and his ribs sore as the result of being knocked down and kicked at Ludgate Circus; at Charing Cross next day he was hustled under the wheels of an omnibus and narrowly escaped death. So he was driven into the side streets and the quiet squares, in which, during three or four days, he managed to earn an average of eightpence daily, which he spent on food.

Each night he crept back to the poor tenement in Johnson's Mews, his bleak "home" amidst the solitude of empty stables and warehouses. The keeper of a coffee stall, touched one night by his woe-begone appearance, gave him some half-dried coffee grounds in a paper, together with a handful of crusts.

"Put 'arf that in a pint of water," he said, looking critically at the soddened mess of coffee, "an' when it comes to a bile let it settle. It'll surprise you to find 'ow grateful an' comfortin' it tastes on a cold night. As for the crusts, if you bake 'em over the fire, they're just as good as the rusks you buy in tins."

This good Samaritan had repeated his gift on two occasions, and Philip had a fairly large supply of small coal, sent to his mother by the colliery company, so his position, desperate enough, was yet bearable had he but sought to accustom himself to the new conditions of life. There was a chance that his wild broodings would have yielded to the necessity to earn a living, and that when next a situation was offered to him he would keep it, but the occurrences of this stormy night had utterly shaken him for the hour. He was on the verge of lunacy.

As he passed through the dark archway leading to his abode, the desolate stable yard was fitfully lit by lightning, and in the distance he heard the faint rumble of thunder. The elemental strife was beginning again. This was the second and more disastrous outbreak of the evening of March 19th.

Although wet to the skin he was warm now on account of his long and rapid walk. When he unlocked the door another flash of lightning revealed the dismal interior. He closed and locked the door behind him. On the mantelpiece were a farthing candle and some matches. He groped for them and soon had a light. On other occasions his next task was to light a fire. By sheer force of habit he gathered together some sticks and bits of paper and arranged them in the grate. But the task was irksome to him. It was absurd to seek any degree of comfort for the few minutes he had to live. Better end it at once. Moreover, the storm was sweeping up over the East End with such marvelous speed that the lightning now played through the tiny room with dazzling brilliancy, and the wretched candle burned with blue and ghostlike feebleness. The cold of the house, too, began to strike chilly. He was so exhausted from hunger that if he did not eat soon he would not have the strength left to carry out his dread purpose.

He sprang erect with a mocking little laugh, picked up the candle and the piece of rope, and climbed the stairs. He paused irresolutely at the top, but, yielding to overwhelming desire, went on and stood at the side of the bed on which his mother had died. He fancied he could see her lying there still, with a smile on her wan face and unspoken words of welcome on her lips.

A flood of tears came and he trembled violently.

"I am coming to you, mother," he murmured. "You told me to trust in God, but I think God has forgotten me. I don't want to live. I want to join you, and then, perhaps, God will remember me."

He stooped and kissed the pillow, nestling his face against it, as he was wont to fondle the dear face that rested there so many weary days. Then he resolutely turned away, descended four steps of the ladder-like stairs, and tied the clothesline firmly to a hook which had been driven into the ceiling during the harness-room period of the room beneath. With equal deliberation he knotted the other end of the cord round his neck, and he calculated that by springing from the stairs he would receive sufficient shock to become insensible very quickly, while his feet would dangle several inches above the floor.

There was a terrible coolness, a settled fixity of purpose far beyond his years, in the manner of these final preparations. At last they were completed. He blew out the candle and stood erect.

At that instant the room became absolutely flooded with lightning, not in a single vivid flash, but in a trembling, continuous glare, that suggested the effect of some luminous constellation, fierce with electric energy. Before his eyes was exhibited a startling panorama of the familiar objects of his lonely abode. The brightness, so sustained and tremulous, startled him back from the very brink of death.

"I will wait," he said. "When the thunder comes, then I will jump."

Even as the thought formed in his mind, a ball of fire—so glowing, so iridescent in its flaming heat that it dominated the electric waves fluttering in the over-burdened air—darted past the little window that looked out over the tiny yard in the rear of the house, and crashed through the flagstones with the din of a ten-inch shell.

Philip, elevated on the stairway, distinctly saw the molten splash which accompanied its impact. He saw the heavy stones riven asunder as if they were tissue paper, and, from the hole caused by the thunderbolt, or meteor, came a radiance that sent a spreading shaft of light upward like the beam of a searchlight. The warmth, too, of the object was almost overpowering. Were not the surrounding walls constructed of stone and brick there must have been an immediate outbreak of fire. As it was, the glass in the windows cracked, and the

15

woodwork began to scorch. In the same instant a dreadful roll of thunder swept over the locality, and a deluge of rain, without any further warning, descended.

All this seemed to the wondering boy to be a very long time in passing. In reality it occupied but a very few seconds. People in the distant street could not distinguish the crash of the fallen meteor from the accompanying thunder, and the downpour of rain came in the very nick of time to prevent the wood in the house and the neighboring factories from blazing forth into a disastrous fire.

The torrent of water caused a dense volume of steam to generate in the back yard, and this helped to minimize the strange light shooting up from the cavity. There was a mad hissing and crackling as the rain poured over the meteor and gradually dulled its brightness. Pandemonium raged in that curiously secluded nook.

Amazed and cowed—not by the natural phenomenon he had witnessed, but by the interpretation he placed on it—the boy unfastened the rope from his neck.

"Very well, mother," he whispered, aloud. "If it is your wish I will live. I suppose that God speaks in this way."

Chapter III

What the Meteor Contained

Philip descended the stairs. He was almost choking now from another cause than strangulation. The steam pouring in through the fractured window panes was stifling. He took off his coat, first removing from an inner pocket the bundle of letters found under Mrs. Anson's pillow, and carefully stuffed the worn garment into the largest cavities. By this means he succeeded somewhat in shutting out the vapor as well as the lurid light that still flared red in the back yard.

The lightning had ceased totally, and the improvised blind plunged the room into impenetrable darkness. He felt his way to the stairs and found the candle, which he relighted. The rain beating on the roofs and on the outer pavements combined with the weird sounds in the inclosed yard to make a terrifying racket, but it was not likely that a youth who attributed his escape from a loathsome death, self-inflicted, to the direct interposition of Providence in his behalf, would yield to any sentimental fears on that account. Indeed, although quite weak from hunger, he felt an unaccountable elation of spirits, a new-born desire to live and justify his mother's confidence in him, a sense of power to achieve that which hitherto seemed impossible.

He even broke into a desultory whistling as he bent over the hearth and resumed the laying of the fire abandoned five minutes earlier with such sudden soul-weariness. The candle, too, burned with cheery glimmer, as if pleased with the disappearance of its formidable competitor. Fortunately he had some coal in the house—his chief supply was stored in a small bin at the other side of the yard, beyond the burial place of the raging, steaming meteor, and consequently quite unapproachable.

Soon the fire burned merrily, and the coffee-stall keeper's recipe for using coffee grounds was put into practice. Philip had neither sugar nor milk, but the hot liquid smelled well, and he was now so cold and stiff, and he had such an empty sensation where he might have worn a belt, that some crusts of bread, softened by immersion in the dark compound, earned keener appreciation than was ever given in later days to the most costly dishes of famous restaurants yet unbuilt.

After he had eaten, he dried his damp garments and changed his soaked boots for a pair so worn that they scarcely held together. But their dryness was comforting. An odd feeling of contentment, largely induced by the grateful heat of the fire, rendered his actions leisurely. Quite half an hour elapsed before he thought of peeping through the back window to ascertain the progress of external events. The rain was not now pelting down with abnormal fury. It was still falling, but with the quiet persistence that marks—in London parlance—"a genuine wet day." The steam had almost vanished. When he removed his coat from the broken panes he saw with surprise that the flagstones in the yard were dry within a circle of two feet around the hole made by the meteor. Such drops as fell within that area were instantly obliterated, and tiny jets of vapor from the hole itself betrayed the presence of the fiery object beneath. His boyish curiosity being thoroughly aroused, he drew an old sack over his head and shoulders, unlocked a door which led into the yard from a tiny scullery, and cautiously approached the place where the meteor had plowed its way into the ground. The stones were littered with débris, but the velocity of the heavy mass had been so great that a comparatively clean cut was made through the pavement. The air was warm, with the hot breath of an oven, and it was as much as Philip could bear when he stood on the brink of the hole and peeped in. At a good depth, nearly half his own height he estimated, he saw a round ball firmly imbedded in the earth. It was dully red, with its surface all cracks and fissures as the result of the water poured onto it. Much larger than a football, it seemed to him, at first sight, to be the angry eye of some colossal demon glaring up at him from a dark socket. But the boy was absolutely a stranger to fear. He procured the handle of a mop and prodded the meteor with it. The surface felt hard and brittle. Large sections broke away, though they did not crumble, and he received a sharp reminder of the potency of the heat still stored below when the wood burst into sudden flame.

This ended his investigations for the night. He used the sacking to block up the window, replenished the fire, set his coat to dry, and dragged his mattress from the bedroom to the front of the fire. The warmth within and without the house had made him intolerably drowsy, and he fell asleep while murmuring his prayers, a practice abandoned since the hour of his mother's death.

In reality, Philip was undergoing a novel sort of Turkish bath, and the perspiration induced thereby probably saved him from a dangerous cold. He slept long and soundly. There was no need to attend to the fire. Long ere the coal in the grate was exhausted, the presence of the meteor had penetrated the surrounding earth, and the house was far above its normal temperature when he awoke.

The sun had risen in a cloudless sky. A lovely spring morning had succeeded a night of gloom and disaster, and the first sound that greeted his wondering ears was the twittering of the busy sparrows on the housetops. Of course he owned neither clock nor watch. These articles, with many others, were represented by a bundle of pawn tickets stuffed into one of the envelopes of his mother's packet of letters. But the experience of even a few weeks had taught him roughly how to estimate time by the sun, and he guessed the hour to be eight o'clock, or thereabouts.

His first thought was of the meteor. His toilet was that of primeval man, being a mere matter of rising and stretching his stiff limbs. While lacing his boots he noticed that the floor was littered with tiny white specks, the largest of which was not bigger than a grain of bird seed. These were the particles which shot through the broken window during the previous night. He picked up a few and examined them. They were hard, angular, cold to the touch, and a dull white in color.

On entering the yard he saw hundreds of these queer little rough pebbles, many of them as large as peas, some the size of marbles and a few bigger ones. They had evidently flown on all sides, but, encountering lofty walls, save where they forced a way through the thin glass of the window, had fallen back to the ground. Interspersed with them he found pieces of broken stone and jagged lumps of material that looked and felt like iron.

By this time the meteor itself had cooled sufficiently to reveal the nature of its outer crust. It appeared to be an amalgam of the dark ironlike mineral and the white pebbles. Through one deep fissure he could still see the fiery heart of the thing, and he imagined that when the internal heat had quite exhausted itself the great ball would easily break into pieces, for it was rent in all directions.

His first exclamation was one of thankfulness.

"I am jolly glad that thing didn't fall on my head," he said aloud, forgetting that had its advent been delayed a second or two, the precise locality selected for its impact would not have mattered much to him.

"I wonder what it is," he went on. "Is it worth anything? Perhaps if I dig it out, I may be able to sell it as a curiosity."

A moment's reflection told him, however, that he would not be able to disinter it that day, even if he possessed the requisite implements. On its lower side it was probably still red-hot. Through the soles of his boots, broken as they were, he could easily feel the heat of the ground, so the experiment must be deferred for twenty-four hours, perhaps longer. At any rate, he was sure that his mysterious visitor represented a realizable asset, and the knowledge gave him a sudden distaste for coffee grounds and stale crusts. He resolved to spend his remaining three halfpence on a breakfast, and at the same time, make some guarded inquiries as to the nature and possible cash value of the meteor itself. Evidently, its fall had attracted no public attention. The fury of the elements and the subsequent heavy rain were effectual safeguards in this respect, and Johnson's Mews, marked out for demolition a fortnight later, were practically deserted now day and night. Philip did not then know that London had already much to talk about in the recorded incidents of the two storms. The morning newspapers were hysterical with headlines announcing fires, collapse of buildings, street accidents, and lamentable loss of life in all parts of the metropolis. As the day wore, and full details came to hand, the list of mishaps would be doubled, while scientific observers would begin a nine days' wrangle in the effort to determine the precise reason why the electrical disturbance should have been wholly confined to the metropolitan area. Philip Anson, a ragged boy of fifteen, residing in a desolate nook of the most disheveled district in the East End, possessed the very genesis of the mystery, yet the web of fate was destined to weave a spell that would deftly close his lips.

Meanwhile he wanted his breakfast. He gathered thirty fair-sized, white pebbles and a few jagged lumps of the ironlike material. These he wrapped in a piece of newspaper, screwed up the small package tightly, and placed it in his trousers' pocket. Thinking deeply about the awesome incidents of the previous night, he donned his coat and did not notice the packet of letters lying in the chair. Never before had these documents left his possession. The door was locked and the key in his pocket before he missed them. It was in his mind to turn back. In another second he would have obeyed the impulse, had not a mighty gust of wind swept through the yard and carried his tattered cap into the passage. That settled it. Philip ran after his headgear, and so was blown into a strange sea of events.

"They are quite safe there," he thought. "In any case, it will be best not to carry them about in future. They get so frayed, and some day I may want them."

Emerging from the haven of the mews, he found the untidy life of the Mile End Road eddying in restless confusion through a gale. The gaunt, high walls surrounding his secluded dwelling had sheltered him from the blustering, March wind that was now drying the streets and creating much ill-temper in the hearts of carters, stall owners and girls with large hats and full skirts. In a word, everything that could be flapped or shaken, or rudely swept anywhere out of its rightful place, was dealt with accordingly. In one instance a heavy tarpaulin was lifted clean off a wagon and neatly lodged over the heads of the driver and horses of a passing omnibus. They were not extricated from its close embrace without some difficulty and a great quantity of severe yet cogent remarks by the wagoner and the driver, assisted by the 'bus conductor and various passengers.

Philip laughed heartily, for the first time since his mother's death. He waited until the driver and the wagoner had exchanged their farewell compliments. Then he made off briskly toward an establishment where three halfpence would purchase a cup of coffee and a bun.

In ten minutes he felt much refreshed, and his busy mind reverted to the mysterious package he carried. Thinking it best to seek the counsel of an older head, he went to O'Brien's shop. The old man was taking down the shutters, and found the task none too easy. Without a word, Philip helped him, and soon the pensioner was wiping his spectacles in the shelter of the shop.

"I dunno what the weather is comin' to at all at all," he grumbled.

"Last night was like the takin' uv the Redan, an' this mornin' reminds me uv crossin' the Bay o' Biscay."

"It certainly was a fearful thunderstorm," said Philip.

"Faix, boy, that's a thrue word. It was just like ould times in the hills in Injia, where the divil himself holds coort some nights. But what's the matter? Didn't you get that job?"

Philip laughed again. "I am not sure yet," he replied. "I really came in to ask you what this is."

With his hand in his pocket, he had untwisted the paper and taken out the white pebbles, which he now handed to O'Brien.

The old man took it, smelt it and adjusted his glasses for a critical examination.

"It ain't alum," he announced.

"No. I think not."

"An' it ain't glass."

"Probably not."

"Where did yer get it?"

"I found it lying on the pavement."

O'Brien scratched his head. "'Tis a quare-looking objec', anyhow. What good is it?"

"I cannot tell you. I thought that possibly it might have some value."

"What! A scrap of white shtone like that. Arrah, what's come over ye?"

"There is no harm in asking, is there? Some one should be able to tell me what it is made of."

Philip, from his small store of physical geography, knew that meteors were articles of sufficient rarity to attract attention. And he was tenacious withal.

"I suppose that a jeweler would be the best man to judge. He must understand about stones," he went on.

"Maybe; but I don't see what's the use. 'Tis a sheer waste of time. But if y're set on findin' out, go to a big man. These German Jews round about here are omadhauns. They don't know a watch from a clock, an' if they did they'd chate ye."

"I never thought of that, yet I ought to know by this time. Thank you; I will go into the city."

He took the pebble, which he placed in his waistcoat pocket. Walking briskly, he traversed some part of the sorrowful journey of barely twelve hours earlier. What had happened to change his mood he did not know, and scarcely troubled to inquire. Last night he hurried through these streets in a frenzied quest for death. Now he strode along full of hope, joyous in the confidence of life and youth. His one dominant thought was that his mother had protected him, had snatched him from the dark gate of eternity. Oddly enough, he laid far more stress on his escape from the meteor than on the accident that prevented his contemplated suicide. This latter idea had vanished with

21

the madness that induced it. Philip was sane again, morally and mentally. He was keenly anxious to justify his mother's trust in him. The blustering wind, annoying to most wayfarers, only aroused in him a spirit of resistance, of fortitude. He breasted it so manfully that when at last he paused at the door of a great jewelry establishment in Ludgate Hill, his face was flushed and his manner eager and animated.

He opened the door, but was rudely brought back to a sense of his surroundings by the suspicious question of a shop-walker.

"Now, boy, what do you want here?"

The unconscious stress in the man's words was certainly borne out by the contrast between Philip, a social pariah in attire, and the wealth of gold and precious stones cut off from him by panes of thick glass and iron bars. What, indeed, did this outcast want there?

Confused by the sudden demand, and no less by its complete obviousness, Philip flushed and stammered:

"I—er—only wished to obtain some information, sir," he answered.

Like all others, the shopman was amazed by the difference between the boy's manners and his appearance.

"Information," he repeated, in his surprise. "What information can we give you?"

The wealth of the firm oppressed this man. He could only speak in accents of adulation where the shop was concerned.

Philip produced his white pebble.

"What is this?" he said.

The directness of the query again took his hearer aback. Without a word, he bent and examined the stone. Professional instinct mastered all other considerations.

"You must apply to that department." He majestically waved his hand toward a side counter. Philip obeyed silently, and approached a small, elderly personage, a man with clever, kindly eyes, who was submitting to microscopical examination a number of tiny stones spread out on a chamois leather folding case. He quietly removed the case when his glance rested on the boy.

"Well?" he said, blankly, wondering why on earth the skilled shop-walker had sent such a disreputable urchin to him. Philip was now quite collected in his wits. He held out the pebble, with a more detailed statement.

"I found this," he said. "I thought that it might be valuable, and a friend advised me to bring it here. Will you kindly tell me what it is?"

The man behind the counter stared at him for a moment, but he reached over for the stone. Without a word he placed it beneath the microscope and gave it a very brief examination. Then he pressed it against his cheek.

"Where did you get it?" he asked.

"I found it where it had fallen on the pavement."

"Are you sure?"

"Quite sure."

"Strange!" was the muttered comment, and Philip began to understand that his meteor possessed attributes hitherto unsuspected.

"But what is it?" he inquired, after a pause.

"A meteoric diamond."

"A meteoric diamond?"

"Yes."

"Is it worth much?"

"A great deal. Probably some hundreds of pounds."

Philip felt his face growing pale. That dirty-white, small stone worth hundreds of pounds! Yet in his pocket he had twenty-nine other specimens, many of them much larger than the one chosen haphazard for inspection, and in the back yard of his tenement lay heaps of them, scattered about the pavement like hailstones after a shower, while the meteor itself was a compact mass of them. He became somewhat faint, and leaned against the glass case that surmounted the counter.

"Is that really true?" was all he could say.

The expert valuer of diamonds smiled. His first impulse was to send for the police, but he knew that meteoric diamonds did fall to earth occasionally, and he believed the boy's story. Moreover, the thing was such a rarity and of such value that the holder must be fully able to account for its possession before he could dispose of it. So his tone was not unkindly as he replied:

"It is quite true, but if you want to ascertain its exact value you should go to a Hatton Garden merchant, and he, most probably, would make you a fair offer. It has to be cut and polished, you know, before it becomes salable, and I must warn you that most rigid inquiry will be made as to how it came into your hands."

"It fell from heaven," was the wholly unexpected answer, for Philip was shaken and hardly master of his faculties.

"Yes, yes, I know. Personally, I believe you, or you would be in custody at this moment. Take it to Messrs. Isaacstein & Co., Hatton Garden. Say I sent you—Mr. Wilson is my name—and make your best terms with Mr. Isaacstein. He will treat you quite fairly. But, again, be sure and tell the truth, as he will investigate your story fully before he is satisfied as to its accuracy."

Philip, walking through dreamland, quitted the shop. He mingled with the jostling crowd and drifted into Farringdon Road.

"A diamond—worth hundreds of pounds!" he repeated, mechanically. "Then what is the whole meteor worth, and what am I worth?"

Chapter IV

Isaacstein

The keen, strong, March wind soon blew the clouds from his brain. He did not hurry toward Hatton Garden. He sauntered, rather, with his right hand clinched on the tiny parcel in his pocket, the parcel which had suddenly been endowed with such magic potentialities. It was the instinct to guard a treasure of great value that led to this involuntary action. He was preoccupied, disturbed, vaguely striving to grasp a vision that seemed to elude his exact comprehension.

What did it all mean? Was it really possible that he, Philip Anson, orphaned, beggared, practically a starving tramp, should have the riches of Golconda showered upon him in this mad fashion. If the small stone he had shown to the jeweler were worth hundreds, then some of those in the paper were worth thousands, while as for the stone in the back yard of his house—well, imagination boggled at the effort to appraise it. The thought begot a sense of caution, of reserve, of well-reasoned determination not to reveal his secret to anybody. Perhaps it would be best not to take Messrs. Isaacstein & Co. wholly into his confidence. He would simply show them the stone he had exhibited to Mr. Wilson and take the best price they offered. Then, with the money in his possession, he could effect a much needed change in his appearance, visit them again, and gradually increase his supply of diamonds until he had obtained more money than he could possibly spend during many years.

Above all else was it necessary that his meteor should be removed to a safer place than Johnson's Mews. Philip had no scruples about appropriating it. Lords of the Manor and Crown rights he had never heard of.

His mother, watching his every action from some Elysian height, had sent the diamond-loaded messenger as a token of her love and care. It was his, and no man should rob him of it. It behooved him to be sparing of explanations and sturdy in defense of his property.

A good deal depended on the forthcoming interview, and he wished he could convert a small fraction of the wealth in his pocket into a few honest pennies with the king's head on them. The excitement and exercise had made him hungry again. His breakfast was not of ample proportions, and his meals of yesterday had been of the scantiest. It would be well to face the diamond merchants with the easy confidence that springs from a satisfied appetite. Yet, how to manage it? He was sorry now he had not borrowed a sixpence from O'Brien. The old soldier would certainly have lent it to him. He even thought of returning to the Mile End Road to secure the loan, but he happened to remember that the day was Saturday, and it was probable that the Hatton Garden offices would close early. It was then nearly eleven o'clock, and he could not risk the delay of the long, double journey.

At that instant a savory smell was wafted to him. He was passing a small restaurant, where sausages and onions sizzled gratefully in large, tin trays, and pork chops lay in inviting prodigality amid rich, brown gravy. The proprietor, a portly and greasy man, with bald head and side whiskers, was standing at the door exchanging views as to business with his next-door neighbor, a greengrocer. Philip, bold in the knowledge of his wealth, resolved to try what he could achieve on credit.

He walked up to the pair.

"I have not got any money just now," he said to the restaurant keeper, "but if you will let me have something to eat I will gladly come back this afternoon and pay you double."

Neither man spoke at first. Philip was always unconscious of the quaint discrepancy between his style of speech and his attire. He used to resent bitterly the astonishment exhibited by strangers, but to-day he was far removed above these considerations, and he backed up his request by a pleasant smile.

The fat man grew apoplectic and turned his eyes to the sky.

"Well, I'm—" he spluttered.

The greengrocer laughed, and Philip blushed.

"Do you refuse?" he said, with his downright manner and direct stare.

"Well, of all the cool cheek—" The stout person's feelings were too much for him. He could find no other words.

"It is a fair offer," persisted the boy. "You don't think I mean to swindle you, surely?"

"Well, there! I never did!"

But the greengrocer intervened.

"You're a sharp lad," he guffawed. "D'ye want a job?"

"No," was the short reply. "I want something to eat."

"Dash my buttons, an' you're a likely sort of kid to get it, too. In you go. I'll pay the bill. Lord lumme, it'll do me good to see you."

"Mr. Judd, are you mad?" demanded his neighbor, whose breath had returned to him.

"Not a bit of it. The bloomin' kid can't get through a bob's worth if he bursts himself. 'Ere, I'll bet you two bob 'e pays up."

"Done! Walk in, sir. Wot'll you be pleased to 'ave, sir?"

Philip's indignation at the restaurant keeper's sarcasm yielded to his wish to see him annihilated later in the day. Moreover, the sausages really smelt excellently, and he was now ravenous. He entered the shop, and gave his orders with a quiet dignity that astounded the proprietor and hugely delighted the greengrocer, who, in the intervals of business, kept peeping at him through the window. Philip ate steadily, and the bill amounted to ninepence, which his ally paid cheerfully.

The boy held out his hand.

"Thank you, Mr. Judd," he said, frankly. "I will return without fail. I will not insult you by offering more than the amount you have advanced for me, but some day I may be able to render you good service in repayment."

Then he walked off toward the viaduct steps, and Mr. Judd looked after him.

"Talks like a little gentleman, 'e does. If my little Jimmie 'ad lived 'e would ha' bin just about his age. Lord lumme, I 'ope the lad turns up again, an' not for the sake of the bloomin' ninepence, neither. Tomatoes, mum? Yes'm. Fresh in this mornin'."

After crossing Holborn Viaduct, Philip stood for a little while gazing into the showroom of a motor agency. It was not that he was interested in Panhard or De Dion cars—then but little known to the general public in England—but rather that he wished to rehearse carefully the program to be followed with Mr. Isaacstein. With a sagacity unlooked for in one of his years, he decided that the meteor should not be mentioned at all. Of course, the diamond merchant would instantly recognize the stone as a meteoric diamond, and would demand its earthly pedigree. Philip resolved to adhere to the simple statement that it was his own property, and that any reasonable inquiry might be made in all quarters where meteoric diamonds were obtainable as to whether or not such a stone was missing. Meanwhile he would obtain from Mr. Isaacstein a receipt acknowledging its custody and a small advance of money, far below its real worth, leaving the completion of the transaction until a later date. The question of giving or withholding his address if it were asked for was a difficult one to settle offhand. Perhaps the course of events would permit him to keep Johnson's Mews altogether out of the record, and a more reputable habitation would be provided once he had the requisite funds.

Thinking he had successfully tackled all the problems that would demand solution, Philip wasted no more time. He entered Hatton Garden, and had not gone past many of its dingy houses until he saw a large, brass plate, bearing the legend: "Isaacstein & Co., Diamond Merchants, Kimberley, Amsterdam and London."

He entered the office and was instantly confronted by a big-nosed youth, who surveyed him through a grille with an arched opening in it to admit letters and small parcels.

"Is Mr. Isaacstein in?" said Philip.

"Oah, yess," grinned the other.

"Will you kindly tell him I wish to see him?"

"Oah, yess." There was a joke lurking somewhere in the atmosphere, but the young Hebrew had not caught its drift yet. The gaunt and unkempt visitor was evidently burlesquing the accent of such gentle people as came to the office on business.

Philip waited a few seconds. The boy behind the grille filled in the interval by copying an address into the stamp book.

"Why do you not tell Mr. Isaacstein I am here?" he said at last.

"Oah, yess. You vil be funny, eh?" The other smirked over the hidden humor of the situation, and Philip understood that if he would see the great man of the firm he must adopt a more emphatic tone.

"I had better warn you that Mr. Wilson, of Messrs. Grant & Sons, Ludgate Hill, sent me here to see Mr. Isaacstein. Am I to go back to Mr. Wilson and say that the office boy refuses to admit me?"

There was a sting in the description, coming from such a speaker.

"Look 'ere," was the angry retort. "Go avay und blay, vil you? I'm pizzy."

Then Philip reached quickly through the little arch, grabbed a handful of shirt, tie and waistcoat, and dragged the big nose and thick lips violently against the wires of the grille.

"Will you do what I ask, or shall I try and pull you through?" he said, quietly.

But the boy's ready yell brought two clerks running, and a door was thrown open. Phil released his opponent and instantly explained his action. One of the clerks, an elderly man, looked a little deeper than the boy's ragged garments, and the mention of Mr. Wilson's name procured him a hearing. Moreover, he had previous experience of the youthful janitor's methods.

With a cuff on the ear, this injured personage was bidden to go upstairs and say that Mr. Wilson had sent a boy to see Mr. Isaacstein. The added insult came when he was compelled to usher Philip to a waiting room.

Soon a clerk entered. He was visibly astonished by the appearance of Mr. Wilson's messenger, and so was Mr. Isaacstein, when Philip was paraded before him in a spacious apartment, filled with glass cases and tables, at which several assistants were seated.

"What the deuce—" he began, but checked himself. "What does Mr. Wilson want?" he went on. Evidently his Ludgate Hill acquaintance was useful to Philip.

"He wants nothing, sir," said Philip. "He sent me to you on a matter of business. It is of a private nature. Can you give me a few minutes alone?"

Isaacstein was a big-headed, big-shouldered man, tapering to a small point at his feet. He looked absurdly like a top, and surprise or emotion of any sort caused him to sway gently. He swayed now, and every clerk looked up, expecting him to fall bodily onto the urchin with the refined utterance who had dared to penetrate into the potentate's office with such a request.

Kimberley, Amsterdam and London combined to lend effect to Isaacstein's wit when he said:

"Is this a joke?"

All the clerks guffawed in chorus. Fortunately, Isaacstein was in a good humor. He had just purchased a pearl for two hundred and fifty pounds, which he would sell to Lady Somebody for eight hundred pounds, to match another in an earring.

"It appears to be," said Philip, when the merriment had subsided.

For some reason the boy's grave, earnest eyes conquered the big little man's amused scrutiny.

"Now, boy, be quick. What is it?" he said, testily, and every clerk bent to his task.

"I have told you, sir. I wish to have a few minutes' conversation with you with regard to business of an important nature."

"You say Mr. Wilson sent you—Mr. Wilson, of Grant & Sons?"

"Yes, sir."

Isaacstein yielded to amazed curiosity.

"Step in here," he said, and led the way to his private office, surprising himself as well as his assistants by this concession.

Philip closed the door, and Isaacstein turned sharply at the sound, but the boy gave him no time to frame a question.

"I want you to buy this," he said, handing over the diamond.

Isaacstein took it, and gave it one critical glance. He began to wobble again.

"Do you mean to say Mr. Wilson sent you to dispose of this stone to me?" he demanded.

"Not exactly, sir. I showed it to him, and he recommended me to come to you."

"Ah, I see. Sit down, there—" indicating a chair near the door. The diamond merchant himself sat at his desk, but they were both in full view of each other.

"Where did you get it?" he asked.

"I found it."

"Quite so. But where?"

"At this moment I do not wish to go into details, but it is mine, mine only, and I am quite willing that you should make every inquiry to satisfy yourself that it was not stolen. I suppose that is what you fear?"

Sheer wonder kept the Jew silent for a space.

"Do you know its value?" he said, with a sudden snap.

"Mr. Wilson told me it was worth several hundreds of pounds."

"Did he, really?"

"Yes. He said you would treat me quite fairly, so I wish you to advance me a few pounds until you have decided upon its real price. You see, sir, I am very poor, and my present appearance creates an unfavorable impression. Still, I am telling you the absolute truth, and I show my confidence in you and in my own case by offering to leave the diamond with you on your receipt, together with a small sum of money."

Philip thought he was getting on very well. Isaacstein's large eyes bulged at him, and speech came but slowly. He leaned forward and rummaged among some papers. Then he opened a drawer and produced a magnifying glass, with which he focused the diamond.

"Yes, it is worth six or seven hundred pounds," he announced, "but it will be some time before I can speak accurately as to its value. I think it may be flawless, but that can only be determined when it is cut."

Philip's heart throbbed when he heard the estimate.

"Then I can have a few pounds—" he commenced.

"Steady. You are not in such a hurry; eh? You won't tell me where you got it?"

"I may, later, if you continue to deal with me as honestly as you have done already."

Isaacstein moved on his seat. Even in a chair he wanted to wobble. There was a slight pause.

"Have you any more like this stone? I suppose not, eh?"

"Yes, I have many more."

"Eh? What? Boy, do you know what you are saying?"

"No doubt you are surprised, sir, but not more than I am myself. Yet, it is true. I have some—as big again."

Philip, in his eagerness, nearly forgot his resolution to advance slowly. How the diamond merchant would shake if only he could see some of the white pebbles in the meteor.

"As big again! Where are they?"

The chair was creaking now with the rhythmic swaying of its occupant.

"Where this one came from, Mr. Isaacstein."

Philip smiled. He could not tell how it happened, but he felt that he was the intellectual superior of the man who sat there glowering at him so intently. Already the boy began to grasp dimly the reality of the power which enormous wealth would give him. Such people as the Jew and his satellites would be mere automata in the affairs of his life, important enough in a sense, with the importance of a stamp for a letter or a railway ticket for a journey, but governed and controlled utterly by the greater personage who could unlock the door of the treasure house. For the first time, Philip wished he was older, bigger, more experienced. He even found himself beginning to wonder what he should do until he reached man's estate. He sighed.

Isaacstein was watching him closely, trying to solve the puzzle by the aid of each trick and dodge known in a trade which lends itself to acute roguery of every description. The look of unconscious anxiety, of mental weariness, on Philip's face, seemed to clear away his doubts. He chuckled thickly.

29

"How many, now," he murmured. "Ten, twenty—of assorted sizes, eh?"

"Far more! Far more! Be content with what I tell you to-day, Mr. Isaacstein. I said my business was important. When you are better acquainted with me, I think you will find it sufficiently valuable to occupy the whole of your time."

Philip was ever on the verge of bursting out into confidences. His secret was too vast, too overpowering for a boy of fifteen. He wanted the knowledge and the trust of an older man. He did not realize that the Jew, beginning by regarding him as a thief, was now veering round to the opinion that he was a lunatic. For it is known to most men that the values of diamonds increase out of all proportion to their weight. While a one-carat stone is worth, roughly speaking, ten pounds, a twenty-carat gem of the same purity is worth any sum beyond two thousand pounds, and the diamond Philip had submitted for inspection would probably cut into ten or twelve carats of fine luster. To speak, therefore, of an abundance of larger and finer stones, was a simple absurdity. The De Beers Company alone could use such a figure of speech, and even then only at isolated dates in its history.

The boy, with his eyes steadfastly fixed on the Jew's face and yet with a distant expression in them that paid slight heed to the waves of emotion exhibited by the heavy cheeks and pursed-up mouth, awaited some final utterance on the part of his questioner. Surely he had said sufficient to make this man keenly alive to the commercial value of the "business" he offered. Under the conditions, Isaacstein could not refuse to give him sufficient money to meet his immediate wants.

The Jew, seemingly at a loss for words, bent again over the stone. He was scrutinizing it closely when a heavy tread crossed the outer showroom and the door was flung open.

A policeman entered, and Isaacstein bounced out of his chair.

"I have sent for you, constable, to take this boy into custody," he cried, excitedly. "He came here ten minutes ago and offered for sale a very valuable diamond, so rare, and worth so much, that he must have stolen it."

Philip, too, sprang up.

"It is a lie!" he shouted. "How dare you say such a thing when I have told you that it is mine!"

The policeman collared him by the shoulder.

"Steady, my young spark," he said. "Mr. Isaacstein knows what he is about, and I don't suppose he is very far wrong this time. Do you know the boy, sir?" he went on.

Isaacstein gave a voluble and accurate summary of Philip's statements. Each moment the policeman's grip became firmer. Evidently the boy was the mere agent of a gang of thieves, though it was beyond comprehension that anyone short of an idiot should choose an emissary with broken boots and ragged clothing in order to effect a deal with the leading house in Hatton Garden.

Philip listened to the recital in dumb agony. His face was deathly pale, and his eyes glowed with the rage and shame that filled his soul. So the Jew had been playing with him, merely fooling him until some secret signal by an electric bell had sent a messenger flying for the police. His dream of wealth would end in the jail, his fairy oasis would be a felon's cell. Very well, be it so. If he could help it, not all the policemen in London should rend his secret from him. With a sudden glow of fiery satisfaction, he remembered that his clothing contained no clew to his address, and he had not given his name either at Ludgate Hill or Hatton Garden. How long could they keep him a prisoner? Would others find his meteor and rob him of his mother's gift? In less than a fortnight men would come to tear down the buildings in Johnson's Mews. Well, it mattered not. The courage of despair which nerved him the previous night came to his aid again. He would defy them all, careless of consequence.

The policeman was saying:

"It's a queer affair, sir. Did he really say he had lots more of 'em?"

"Yes, yes! Do you think I am romancing? Perhaps they are in his possession now."

"Have you any more of these stones, boy?"

Philip, with lips tensely set, was desperately cool again. He moved his arm, and the constable's grasp tightened.

"You are hurting me," said the boy. "I merely wish to put my hand in my pocket. Are you afraid of me, that you hold me so fast?"

The policeman, like the rest, did not fail to notice Philip's diction. The scornful superiority of his words, the challenge of the final question, took him aback. He relaxed his grip and grinned confusedly.

Philip instantly produced his paper of diamonds and opened it widely, so that all the stones could be seen. He handed the parcel to the policeman.

"Take good care of them, constable," he said. "Judging from results, they would not be safe in that man's hands."

But Isaacstein did not hear the insult. When he saw the collection he nearly lost his senses. What had he done? Was he or the boy mad? Veins stood out on his forehead, and he wobbled so fearfully that he clutched the desk for support. A scarecrow of a boy wandering about London with thousands of pounds' worth of diamonds in his pocket, wrapped up in a piece of newspaper like so many sweets! There were not any meteoric diamonds of such value in all the museums and private collections in the world. He began to perspire. Even the policeman was astounded, quite as much at being called "constable" by Philip as by the mean appearance of articles presumably of great value.

"This is a rum go. What do you make of it, Mr. Isaacstein?" he said.

The query restored the Jew's wits. After all, here was the law

31

speaking. It would have been the wildest folly for a man of his position to dabble in this mysterious transaction.

With a great effort he forced himself to speak.

"Lock him up instantly. This matter must be fully inquired into. And do be careful of that parcel, constable. Where do you take him? To the Bridewell station? I will follow you in a cab in five minutes."

So Philip, handcuffed, was marched down the stairs past the gratified office boy and out into the street.

As for Isaacstein, he required brandy, and not a little, before he felt able to follow.

Chapter V

Perplexing a Magistrate

In after years Philip never forgot the shame of that march through the staring streets. The everlasting idlers of London's busiest thoroughfares gathered around the policeman and his prisoner with grinning callousness.

"Wot's 'e bin a-doin' of?"

"Nicked a lydy's purse, eh?"

"Naw! Bin ticklin' the till, more like."

"Bli-me, don't 'e look sick!"

They ran and buzzed around him like wasps, stinging most bitterly with coarse words and coarser laughter. An omnibus slowed its pace to let them cross the road, and Philip knew that the people on top craned their necks to have a good look at him. When nearing the viaduct steps, the policeman growled something at the pursuing crowd. Another constable strode rapidly to the entrance and cut off the loafers, sternly advising them to find some other destination. But the respite was a brief one. The pair reached Farringdon Street, and had barely attracted attention before they passed the restaurant where Philip had lunched. The hour was yet early for mid-day customers, and the bald-headed proprietor saw them coming. He rushed out. The greengrocer, too, turned from his wares and joined in the exclamations of his friend at this speedy dénouement of the trivial incident of twenty minutes earlier.

The restaurant keeper was made jubilant by this dramatic vindication of the accuracy of his judgment.

"The thievin' young scamp!" he ejaculated. "That's right, Mr. Policeman. Lock 'im up. 'E's a reg'lar wrong 'un."

The constable stopped. "Hello!" he said. "Do you know him?"

"I should think I did. 'E kem 'ere just now an' obtained a good blowout on false pretences, an'—"

"Old 'ard," put in the greengrocer, "that's not quite the ticket. 'E asked you to trust 'im, but you wouldn't."

The stout man gurgled.

"Not me. I know 'is sort. But 'e 'ad you a fair treat, Billy."

"Mebbe, an' mebbe not. Ennyhow, two bob won't break me, an' I'm sorry for the kid. Wot's 'e done, Mr. Policeman?" Mr. Judd was nettled, yet unwilling to acknowledge he was wholly wrong.

"Stole a heap of diamonds. Do either of you know him?"

"Never saw him afore this mornin'."

"Never bin in my 'ouse before."

"Then come along," and Philip was tugged onward, but not before he found courage to say:

"Thank you once more, Mr. Judd. I will keep my word, never fear."

"What are you thanking him for?" said the constable.

"For believing in me," was the curt answer.

The policeman tried to extract some meaning from the words, but failed. He privately admitted that it was an extraordinary affair. How came a boy who spoke like a gentleman and was dressed like a street Arab to be wandering about London with a pocketful of diamonds and admitted to the private office of the chief diamond merchant in Hatton Garden? He gave it up, but silently thanked the stars which connected him with an important case.

At last Philip's Via Dolorosa ended in the Bridewell police station. He was paraded before the inspector in charge, a functionary who would not have exhibited any surprise had the German Emperor been brought before him charged with shoplifting.

He opened a huge ledger, tried if his pen would make a hair stroke on a piece of paper, and said, laconically:

"Name?"

No answer from the prisoner, followed by emphatic demands from inspector and constable, the former volunteering the information that to refuse your name and address was in itself an offense against the law.

Philip's sang-froid was coming to his aid. The horror of his passage through the gaping mob had cauterized all other sentiments, and he now saw that if he would preserve his incognito he must adopt a ruse.

"Philip Morland," he said, doggedly, when the inspector asked him his name for the last time before recording a definite refusal.

"Philip Morland!" It sounded curiously familiar in his ears. His mother was a Miss Morland prior to her marriage, but he had not noticed the odd coincidence that he should have been christened after the "Sir Philip" of the packet of letters so fortunately left behind that morning.

"Address?"

"Park Lane."

The inspector began to write before the absurdity of the reply dawned on him. He stopped.

"Is your mother a caretaker there, or your father employed in a mews?"

"My father and mother are dead."

"Then will you kindly inform us what number in Park Lane you live at?"

"I have not determined that as yet. I intend to buy a house there."

34

Some constables lounging about the office laughed, and the inspector, incensed out of his routine habits, shouted, angrily:

"This is no place for joking, boy. Answer me properly, or it will be worse for you."

"I have answered you quite properly. The constable who brought me here has in his possession diamonds worth many thousands of pounds belonging to me. I own a hundred times as many. Surely I can buy a house in Park Lane if I like."

The inspector was staggered by this well-bred insolence. He was searching for some crushing legal threat that would frighten the boy into a state of due humility when Mr. Isaacstein entered.

The Hatton Garden magnate again related the circumstances attending Philip's arrest, and the inspector promptly asked:

"What charge shall I enter? You gave him into custody. Do you think he has stolen the diamonds?"

Isaacstein had been thinking hard during a short cab drive. His reply was unexpectedly frank.

"He could not have stolen what never existed. There is no such known collection of meteoric diamonds in the world."

"But there must be, because they are here."

By this time the parcel of dirty-white stones was lying open on the counter, and both Jew and policeman were gazing at them intently. There was a nettling logic in the inspector's retort.

"I cannot answer riddles," said Isaacstein, shortly. "I can only state the facts. If any other man in the city of London is a higher authority on diamonds than I, go to him and ask his opinion."

"Mr. Isaacstein is right," interposed Philip. "No one else owns diamonds like mine. No one else can obtain them. I have robbed no man. Give me my diamonds and let me go."

The inspector laughed officially. He gazed intently at Philip, and then sought illumination from the Jew's perturbed countenance, but Isaacstein was moodily examining the contents of the paper and turning over both the stones and the scraps of iron with an air of profound mystification.

"I'll tell you what," said the inspector, jubilantly, after a slight pause. "We will charge him with being in unlawful possession of certain diamonds, supposed to have been stolen. He has given me a false name and a silly address. Park Lane, the young imp said he lived in."

"A man in your position ought to be more accurate," interposed Philip. "I did not say I lived in Park Lane. I told you I intended to buy a house there."

Seldom, indeed, were the minor deities of the police station bearded in this fashion, and by a callow youth. But the inspector was making the copperplate hair strokes which had gained him promotion, and his brain had gone back to its normal dullness.

35

"I will just see if we cannot bring him before a magistrate at once," he said, addressing Mr. Isaacstein. "Can you make it convenient to attend the court within an hour, sir? Then we will get a week's remand, and we will soon find out—"

"A week's remand!" Philip became white again, and those large eyes of his began to burn. "What have I done—"

"Silence! Search him carefully and take him to the cells."

The boy turned despairingly to the Jew.

"Mr. Isaacstein," he said, with a pitiful break in his voice, "why do you let them do this thing? You are a rich man, and well known. Tell them they are wrong."

But Isaacstein was wobbling now in a renewed state of excitement.

"What can I do, boy!" he vociferated, almost hysterically. "You must say where you got these stones, and then, perhaps, you can clear up everything."

Philip's lips met in a thin seam.

"I will never tell you," he answered, and not another word would he utter.

They searched him and found nothing in his pockets save a key, a broken knife, some bits of string neatly coiled, and a couple of buttons. He spent the next hour miserably in a whitewashed cell. He refused some coffee and bread brought to him at twelve o'clock, and this was the only sentient break in a wild jumble of conflicting thoughts. The idea came to him that he must be dreaming—that soon he would awaken amidst the familiar surroundings of Johnson's Mews. To convince himself that this was not so, he reviewed the history of the preceding twenty-four hours. At that time yesterday he was going to Fleet Street with a capital of ninepence to buy a quire of newspapers. He remembered where he had sold each of the five copies, where he bought a penny bun, and how he came to lose his stock and get cuffed into the bargain for rescuing a girl from an overturning carriage.

Then his mind reverted to his fixed resolve to hang himself, and his stolid preparations for the last act in his young life's tragedy. Was that where the dream started, or was the whole thing a definite reality, needing only a stout heart and unfaltering purpose to carry him through triumphantly? Yes. That was it. "Be strong and brave and all will be well with you." Surely his mother had looked beyond the grave when she uttered her parting words. Perhaps, if he lay down and closed his eyes, he would see her. He always hoped to see her in his dreams, but never was the vision vouchsafed to him. Poor lad, he did not understand that his sleep was the sound sleep of health and innocence, when dreams, if they come at all, are but grotesque distortions of the simple facts of everyday existence. Only once had he dimly imagined her presence, and that was at a moment which his sane mind now refused to resurrect.

Nevertheless, he was tired. Yielding to the conceit, he stretched himself on the wooden couch that ran along one side of his narrow cell.

Some one called to him, not unkindly.

"Now, youngster, jump up. The van is here."

He was led through gloomy corridors and placed in a receptacle just large enough to hold him uncomfortably in a huge, lumbering vehicle. He thought he was the only occupant, which was true enough, the prisoners' van having made a special call for his benefit.

After a rumbling journey through unseen streets, he emerged into another walled-in courtyard. He was led through more corridors, and told to "skip lively" up a winding staircase. At the top he came out into a big room, with a well-like space in front of him, filled with a huge table, around which sat several gentlemen, among them Mr. Isaacstein, while on an elevated platform beyond was an elderly man, who wore eyeglasses and who wrote something in a book without looking up when Philip's name was called out.

A police inspector, whom Philip had not seen before, made a short statement, and was followed by the constable who effected the arrest. His story was brief and correct, and then the inspector stated that Mr. Wilson, of Grant & Sons, Ludgate Circus, would be called at the next hearing, as he—the inspector—would ask for a remand to enable inquiries to be made. Meanwhile, Mr. Isaacstein, of Hatton Garden, had made it convenient to attend that day, and would be pleased to give evidence if his worship desired to hear him.

"Certainly," said Mr. Abingdon, the magistrate. "This seems to be a somewhat peculiar case, and I will be glad if Mr. Isaacstein can throw any light upon it."

But Mr. Isaacstein could not do any such thing. He wound up a succinct account of Philip's visit and utterances by declaring that there was no collection of meteoric diamonds known to him from which such a remarkable set of stones could be stolen.

This emphatic statement impressed the magistrate.

"Let me see them," he said.

The parcel was handed up to him, and he examined its contents with obvious interest.

"Are you quite sure of their meteoric origin, Mr. Isaacstein?" he asked.

"Yes."

"Can you form any estimate of their probable value?"

"About fifty thousand pounds!"

The reply startled the magistrate, and it sent a thrill through the court.

"Really! So much!" Mr. Abingdon was almost scared.

"If, after cutting, they turn out as well as I expect, that is a moderate estimate of their worth."

"I take it, from what you say, that meteoric diamonds are rare?"

Isaacstein closed his throat with a premonitory cough and bunched up his shoulders. A slight wobble was steadied by his stumpy hands on the rail of the witness box. He was really the greatest living authority on the subject, and he knew it.

"It is a common delusion among diamond miners that diamonds fall from the skies in meteoric showers," he said. "There is some sort of foundation for this mistaken view, as the stones are found in volcanic pipes or columns of diamantiferous material, and the crude idea is that gigantic meteors fell and plowed these deep holes, distributing diamonds in all directions as they passed. But the so-called pipes are really the vents of extinct volcanoes. Ignorant people do not realize that the chemical composition of the earth does not differ greatly from that of the bodies which surround it in space, so that the same process of manufacture under high temperature and at great pressure which creates a diamond in a meteor has equal powers here. In a word, what has happened in the outer universe has also happened at Kimberley. Iron acts as the solvent during the period of creation, so to speak. Then, in the lapse of ages, it oxidizes by the action of air or water, and the diamonds remain."

The magistrate nodded.

"There are particles of a mineral that looks like iron among these stones?" he said.

The question gave Isaacstein time to draw a fresh supply of breath. Sure of his audience now, he proceeded more slowly.

"That is a certain proof of a meteoric source. A striking confirmation of the fact is supplied by a district in Arizona. Here, on a plain five miles in diameter, are scattered thousands of masses of metallic iron, varying in weight from half a ton to a fraction of one ounce. An enormous meteoric shower fell there at some period, and near the center is a crater-like hole which suggests the impact of some very large body which buried itself in the earth. All mineralogists know the place as the Canyon Diabolo, or Devil's Gulch, and specimens of its ore are in every collection. Ordinary tools were spoiled, and even emery wheels worn by some hard ingredient in the iron, and analysis has revealed the presence therein of three distinct forms of diamond—the ordinary stone, like these now before you, both transparent and black graphite, and amorphous carbon; that is, carbon without crystallization."

"I gather that the diamantiferous material was present in the form of tiny particles and not in stones at all approaching these in size?" said Mr. Abingdon.

"Exactly. I have never either seen or heard of specimens like those. In 1886 a meteor fell in Russia, and contained one per cent. of diamond in a slightly metamorphosed state. In 1846 the Ava meteorite fell in

Hungary, and it held crystalline graphite in the bright as well as the dark form. But, again, the distribution was well diffused, and of slight commercial value. Sir William Crookes, or any eminent chemist, will bear me out in the assumption that the diamonds now before your eyes are absolutely matchless by the product of any recorded meteoric source."

Isaacstein, having delivered his little lecture, looked and felt important. The magistrate bent forward with a pleasant smile.

"I am very much obliged to you for the highly interesting information you have given," he said. "One more question—the inevitable corollary of your evidence is that the boy now in the dock has either found a meteor or a meteoric deposit. Can you say if it is a matter of recent occurrence?"

"Judging by the appearance of the accompanying scraps of iron ore, I should say that they have been quite recently in a state of flux from heat. The silicates seem to be almost eliminated."

The magistrate was unquestionably puzzled. Queer incidents happen in police courts daily, and the most unexpected scientific and technical points are elucidated in the effort to secure an accurate comprehension of matters in dispute. But never, during his long tenancy of the court, had he been called on to deal with a case of this nature. He smiled in his perplexity.

"We all remember the copy-book maxim: 'Let justice be done though the heavens fall,'" he said; "but here it is clearly shown that the ideal is not easily reached."

Of course, everyone laughed, and the reporters plied pen and pencil with renewed activity. Here was a sensation with a vengeance—worth all the display it demanded in the evening papers. Headlines would whoop through a quarter of a column, and Philip's meteor again run through space.

The boy himself was apparently the most disinterested person present. While listening to Isaacstein, he again experienced the odd sensation of aloofness, of lofty domination, amidst a commonplace and insignificant environment. The Jew was clever, of course, but his cleverness was that of the text-book, a dry record of fact which needed genius to illuminate the printed page. And these lawyers, reporters, policemen, with the vacuous background of loungers, the friends and bottle holders of thieves and drunkards—the magistrate, even, remote in his dignity and sense of power—what were they to him?—of no greater import than the paving stones of the streets to the pulsating life of London as it passed.

The magistrate glanced at Isaacstein and stroked his chin. The Jew gazed intently at the packet of diamonds and rubbed his simous nose. There was a deep silence in court, broken only by the occasional shuffle of feet among the audience at the back—a shuffle which stopped instantly when the steely glance of a policeman darted in that direction.

At last the magistrate seemed to make up his mind to a definite course of action.

"There is only one person present," he said, "who can throw light on this extraordinary case, and that is the boy himself."

He looked at Philip, and all eyes quickly turned toward the thin, ragged figure standing upright against the rail that shut him off from the well of the court. The professional people present noted that the magistrate did not allude to the strange-looking youth as "the prisoner."

What was going to happen? Was this destitute urchin going to leave the court with diamonds in his pocket worth fifty thousand pounds? Oddly enough, no one paid heed to Philip's boast that he owned far more than that amount. It was not he, but his packet of diamonds, that evoked wonder. And had not Isaacstein, the great merchant and expert, appraised them openly! Was it possible that those dirty-white pebbles could be endowed with such potentiality. Fifty thousand pounds! There were men in the room, and not confined to the unwashed, whose palates dried and tongues swelled at the notion.

Chapter VI

A Game of Hazard

Philip knew that a fresh ordeal was at hand. How could he preserve his secret—how hope to prevail against the majesty of British law as personified by the serene authority of the man whose penetrating glance now rested on him? His was a dour and stubborn nature, though hardly molded as yet in rigid lines. He threw back his head and tightened his lips. He would cling to his anonymity to the bitter end, no matter what the cost. But he would not lie. Never again would he condescend to adopt a subterfuge.

"Philip Morland," began the magistrate.

"My name is not Philip Morland," interrupted the boy.

"Then what is your name?"

"I will not tell you, sir. I mean no disrespect, but the fact that I am treated as a criminal merely because I wish to dispose of my property warns me of what I may expect if I state publicly who I am and where I live."

For the first time the magistrate heard the correct and well-modulated flow of Philip's speech. If anything, it made more dense the mist through which he was trying to grope his way.

"What do you mean?" he asked.

"I mean that if I state who I am, I will be robbed and swindled by all with whom I come in contact. I have starved, I have been beaten, for trying to earn a living. I was struck last night for saving a girl's life. I was arrested and dragged through the streets, handcuffed, this morning, because I went openly to a dealer to sell a portion—to sell some of my diamonds. I will take no more risks. You may imprison me, but you cannot force me to speak. If you are a fair man, you will give me back my diamonds and let me go free."

This outburst fairly electrified the court. Philip could not have adopted a more domineering tone were he the Governor of the Bank of England charged with passing a counterfeit half-crown. The magistrate was as surprised as any.

"I do not wish to argue with you," he said, quietly; "nor do I expect you to commit yourself in any way. But you must surely see that for a poverty-stricken boy to be found in possession of gems of great marketable value is a circumstance that demands inquiry, however honest and—er—well bred you may be."

"The only witness against me has said that the diamonds could not have been stolen," cried Philip, now thoroughly aroused, and ready for any war of wits.

"Quite true. The inference is that you have discovered a meteoric deposit of diamonds."

"I have. Some—not all—are before you."

A tremor shook the court. Isaacstein swallowed something, and his head sank more deeply below his shoulders.

"Then I take it that you will not inform me of the locality of this deposit?"

"Yes."

"And you think that by disclosing your name and address you will reveal that locality?"

Philip grew red.

"Is it fair," he said, with a curious iciness in his tone, "that a man of your age should use his position and knowledge to try and trip a boy who is brought before you on a false charge?"

It was the magistrate's turn to look slightly confused. There was some asperity in his reply.

"I am not endeavoring to trip you, but rather to help you to free yourself from a difficult position. However, do I understand that you refuse to answer any questions?"

"I do." The young voice rang through the building with an amazing fierceness.

Mr. Abingdon bent over the big book in front of him and scribbled something.

"Remanded for a week," he muttered.

"Downstairs," growled the court jailer, and Philip disappeared from sight. The magistrate was left gazing at the packet of diamonds, and he called Isaacstein, the clerk of the court, and two police inspectors into his private office for a consultation.

Meanwhile London was placarded with Philip's adventures that Saturday evening. Contents bills howled in their blackest and biggest type, newsvenders bawled themselves hoarse over this latest sensation, journalistic ferrets combined theory and imagination in the effort to spin out more "copy," Scotland Yard set its keenest detectives at work to reveal the secret of Philip's identity, while Isaacstein, acting on the magistrate's instructions, wrote to every possible source of information in the effort to obtain some clew as to recent meteoric showers.

No one thought of connecting the great storm with the "Diamond Mystery." Meteors usually fall from a clear sky, and are in no way affected by atmospheric disturbances, their normal habitat being far beyond the influence of the earth's envelope of air.

And so the "hunt for the meteor" commenced, and was kept up with zest for many days. "Have you found it?" became the stock question of the humorist, and might be addressed with impunity to any stranger, particularly if the stranger were a nice-looking girl. No one answered "What?" because of the weird replies that were forthcoming.

The police failed utterly in their efforts to discover Philip's identity or residence. Johnson's Mews, Mile End Road, might as well be in Timbuctoo for all the relation it bore to Ludgate Hill or Hatton Garden. An East End policeman might have recognized Philip had he seen him, but the official description of his clothing and personal appearance applied to thousands of hobbledehoys in every district of London.

Two persons among the six millions of the metropolis alone possessed the knowledge that would have led the inquirers along the right track. The doctor who attended Mrs. Anson in her last illness, had he read the newspaper comments on the boy's speech and mannerisms, might have seen the coincidence supplied by the Christian name, and thus been led to make some further investigation. But his hands were full of trouble on his own account. A dispenser mixed a prescription wrongly, and dosed a patient with half an ounce of arsenic instead of half an ounce of cream of tartar. The subsequent inquest gave the doctor enough to do, and the first paper he had leisure to peruse contained a bare reference to the "Diamond Mystery" as revealing no further developments. He passed the paragraph unread.

The remaining uncertain element centered in old O'Brien, the pensioner. Now it chanced that the treasury had discovered that by a clerical mistake in a warrant, the old man had been drawing twopence a day in excess of his rightful pension for thirty-three years. Some humorist in Whitehall thereupon sent him a demand for one hundred and three pounds and fifteen shillings, and the member of the Whitechapel Division was compelled to adopt stern tactics in the House before the matter was adjusted, and O'Brien was allowed to receive the reduced quarterly stipend then due. During that awful crisis the poor, old fellow hardly ate or slept. Even when it had ended, the notion remained firmly fixed in his mind that the "murdherin' government" had robbed him of a hundred gowlden sovereigns, an' more."

As for newspapers, the only item he read during many days was the question addressed by his "mimber" to the Chancellor of the Exchequer and the brief reply thereto, both of which were fixed beforehand by mutual arrangement.

In one instance the name given and afterward repudiated by the boy did attract some attention. On the Monday following the remand, a lady sat at breakfast in a select West End Hotel, and languidly perused the record of the case until her eye caught the words "Philip Morland." Then her air of delicate hauteur vanished, and she left her breakfast untouched until, with hawklike curving of neck and nervous clutching of hands, she had read every line of the police court romance. She was a tall, thin, aristocratic-looking woman, with eyes set too closely together, a curved nose, like the beak of a bird of prey, and hands covered with a leathery skin suggesting talons. Her attire and pose were elegant, but she did not seem to be a pleasant sort of person. Her lips parted in a vinegary smile as she read. She evidently did not believe one word of the newspaper report in so far as the diamonds were concerned.

"A vulgar swindle!" she murmured to herself. "How is it possible for a police magistrate to be taken in in such manner! I suppose the Jew person knows more about it than appears on the surface. But how came the boy to give that name? It is sufficiently uncommon to be remarkable. How stupid it was of Julie to mislay my dressing case. It would be really interesting to know what has become of those people, and now I may have to leave town before I can find out."

How much further her disjointed comments might have gone it is impossible to say, but at that moment a French maid entered the room and gazed inquiringly around the various small tables with which it was filled. At last she found the lady, who was breakfasting alone, and sped swiftly toward her.

"I am so glad, milady," she said, speaking in French. "The bag has found itself at the police station. The cabman brought it there, and, if you please, milady, as the value was given as eight pounds, he claimed a reward of one pound."

"Which you will pay yourself. You lost the bag," was the curt reply. "Where is it?"

The maid's voice was somewhat tearful as she answered:

"In milady's room. I paid the sovereign."

Her ladyship rose and glided gracefully toward the door, followed by the maid, who whispered to a French waiter—bowing most deferentially to the guest as he held the door open—that her mistress was a cat. He confided his own opinion that her ladyship was a holy pig, and the two passed along a corridor.

Lady Morland hastily tore open the recovered dressing case, and consulted an address book.

"Oh! here it is," she cried, triumphantly. "Number three, Johnson's Mews, Mile End Road, E. What a horrid-smelling place. However, Messrs. Sharpe & Smith will now be able to obtain some definite intelligence for me. Julie! My carriage in ten minutes."

Thus it happened that during the afternoon, a dapper little clerk descended from an omnibus in the neighborhood of Johnson's Mews, and began his inquiries, as all Londoners do, by consulting a policeman. Certain facts were forthcoming.

"A Mrs. Anson, a widow, who lived in Johnson's Mews? Yes, I think a woman of that name died a few weeks ago. I remember seeing a funeral leave the mews. I don't know anything about the boy. Sometimes, when I pass through there at night, I have seen a light in the house. However, here it is. Let's have a look at it."

The pair entered the mews and approached the deserted house. The solicitor's clerk knocked and then tried the door; it was locked. They both went to the window and looked in. Had Philip hanged himself, as he intended, they would have been somewhat surprised by the spectacle that would have met their eyes. As it was, they only saw a small room of utmost wretchedness, with a mattress lying on the floor in front of the fireplace. An empty tin and a bundle of old letters rested on a rickety chair, and a piece of sacking was thrust through two broken panes in the small window opposite.

"Not much there, eh?" laughed the policeman.

"Not much, indeed. The floor is all covered with dirt, and if it were not for the bed, one would imagine that the house was entirely deserted. Are you sure Mrs. Anson is dead?"

"Oh, quite sure. Hers was rather a hard case, some one told me. I remember now; it was the undertaker. He lives near here."

"And the boy. Has he gone away?"

"I don't know. I haven't seen him lately."

Each of these men had read all the reports concerning Philip and his diamonds. Large numbers of tiny, white pebbles were lying on the floor beneath their eyes, but the window was not clean, and the light was far from good, as the sky was clouded. Yet they were visible enough. The clerk noticed them at once, but neither he nor the policeman paid more heed to the treasures almost at their feet than was given by generations of men to the outcrop of the main reef at Johannesburg. At last they turned away. The clerk gave the policeman a cigar with the remark:

"I will just ask the undertaker to give me a letter, stating the facts about Mrs. Anson's death. I suppose the boy is in the workhouse?"

"Who knows! It often beats me to tell what becomes of the kids who are left alone in London. Poor, little devils, they mostly go to the bad. There should be some means of looking after them, I think."

Thus did Philip, bravely sustaining his heart in the solitude of a prison, escape the greatest danger that threatened the preservation of his secret, and all because a scheming woman was too clever to tell her solicitors the exact reason for her anxiety concerning the whereabouts of Mrs. Anson and her son.

The boy passed a dolorous Saturday night and Sunday. Nevertheless, the order, the cleanliness, the comparative comfort of a prison, were not wholly ungrateful to him. His meals, though crude, were wholesome, luxurious, even, compared with the privations he had endured during the previous fortnight. The enforced rest, too, did him good, and, being under remand, he had nothing to do but eat, take exercise, read a few books provided for him, and sleep.

With Monday came a remarkable change in his fare. A pint of first-rate cocoa and some excellent bread and butter for breakfast evoked no comment on his part, but a dinner of roast beef, potatoes, cabbage and rice pudding was so extremely unlike prison diet that he questioned the turnkey.

"It's all right, kid," came the brief answer. "It's paid for. Eat while you can, and ask no questions."

"But—"

The door slammed, and at the next meal Philip received in silence a cup of tea and a nice tea cake. This went on during three days. The good food and rest had already worked a marvelous change in his appearance. He entered the prison looking like a starved dog. When he rose on the Thursday morning and washed himself, no one would have recognized him as the same boy were it not for his clothes.

After dinner, he was tidying his cell and replacing the plates and the rest on a tin tray, when the door was suddenly flung open and a warder cried:

"Come along, Morland. You're wanted at the court."

"At the court!" he could not help saying. "This is only Thursday."

"What a boy you are for arguing. Pick up your hat and come. Your carriage waits, my lord. I hope you will like your quarters as well when you come back. A pretty stir you have made in the papers the last five days."

Philip glanced at the man, who seemed to be in a good humor.

"I will not come back," he said, quietly, "but I wish you would tell me who supplied me with food while I have been here."

They were passing along a lofty corridor, and there was no superior officer in sight. The warder laughed.

"I don't know, my lord," he said, "but the menoo came from the Royal Star Hotel, opposite."

Philip obtained no further news. He passed through an office, a voucher was signed for him, and he emerged into the prison yard, where the huge prison van awaited him. He was the only occupant, just as on the first memorable ride in that conveyance. When he came to the prison from the police court he had several companions in misery. But they were "stretched." His case was the only "remand."

During the long drive Philip endeavored to guess the cause of this unexpected demand for his presence. Naturally, he assumed that Johnson's Mews no longer held safe the secret of his meteor. Such few sensational romances as he had read credited detectives with superhuman sagacity. In his mind, Johnson's Mews was the center of the world. It enshrined the marvelous—how could it escape the thousands of prying eyes that passed daily through the great thoroughfare of the East End, but a few yards away? Judging from the remark dropped by the warder, all London was talking about him. A puzzling feature was the abundant supply of good food sent to him in the prison. Who was his unknown friend—and what explanation was attached to the incident?

Philip's emotions were no more capable of analysis than a display of rockets. Immured in this cage, rattling over the pavements, he seemed to be advancing through a tunnel into an unknown world.

At last the van stopped, and he was led forth into the yard of the police court. He followed the same route as on the previous Saturday, but when he ascended into the court itself he discovered a change. The magistrate, a couple of clerks, and some policemen alone were present. The general public and the representatives of the press were not visible.

He had scarcely faced the bench when the magistrate said:

"You are set at liberty. The police withdraw the charge against you."

Philip's eyes sparkled and his breast heaved tumultuously. For the life of him he could utter no word, but Mr. Abingdon helped him by quietly directing the usher to permit the lad to leave the dock and take a seat at the solicitors' table.

Then, speaking slowly and with some gravity, he said:

"Philip Morland—that is the only name by which I know you—the authorities have come to the conclusion that your story is right. You have unquestionably found a deposit of diamonds, and although this necessarily exists on some person's property, there is no evidence to show whose property it is. It may be your own. It may be situated beyond the confines of this kingdom. There are many hypotheses, each of which may be true; but, in any event, if others lay claim to this treasure trove—and I warn you that the Crown has a right in such a matter—the issue is a civil and not a criminal one. Therefore, you are discharged, and your property is now handed back to you intact."

A clerk placed before Philip his parcel of diamonds, his key, the rusty knife, the pieces of string, and the two buttons—truly a motley collection. The boy was pale, and his voice somewhat tremulous as he asked:

"May I go now, sir?"

Mr. Abingdon leaned back in his chair and passed his hand over his face to conceal a smile.

"I have something more to say to you," he answered. "It is an offense against the law to withhold your name and address. I admit the powerful motives which actuated you, so I make the very great concession that your earlier refusal will be overlooked if you privately tell me that which you were unwilling to state publicly."

Philip instantly decided that it would be foolish in the extreme to refuse this offer. He pocketed his diamonds, looked the magistrate straight in the face, and said:

"I will do that, sir. As the information is to be given to you alone, may I write it?"

The policemen and other officials sniggered at this display of caution, but the magistrate nodded, and Philip wrote his name and address on a sheet of foolscap, which he folded before handing it to the usher.

To his great surprise, Mr. Abingdon placed the paper in a pocketbook without opening it.

"I will make no use of this document unless the matter comes before me again officially. I wish to point out to you that I have brought you from prison at the earliest possible moment, and have spared you the publicity which your movements would attract were your case settled in open court. You are not aware, perhaps, that you figure largely in the eyes of the public at this moment. There are newspapers which would give a hundred pounds to get hold of you. There are thieves who would shadow your every movement, waiting for a chance to waylay and rob you—murder you, if necessary. I have taken precautions, therefore, to safeguard you, at least within the precincts of this court, but I cannot be responsible beyond its limits. May I ask what you intend to do?"

Philip, proud in the knowledge that he was cleared of all dishonor, was at no loss for words now.

"First, I wish to thank you, sir," he said. "You have acted most kindly toward me, and, when I am older, I hope to be permitted to acknowledge your thoughtfulness better than is possible to-day. I will endeavor to take care of myself. I am going now to see Mr. Isaacstein. I do not expect that he will send for a policeman again. If he does, I will bring him before you."

The magistrate himself laughed at this sally.

"You are a strange boy," he said. "I think you are acting wisely. But—er—you have no money—that is, in a sense. Hatton Garden is some distance from here. Let me—er—lend you a cab fare."

"Thank you, sir," said Philip, and Mr. Abingdon, unable to account for the interest he felt in the boy, quite apart from his inexplicable story, gave him five shillings and shook hands with him.

Chapter VII

A Business Transaction

Outside the police court, Philip drew as invigorating a breath of fresh air as the atmosphere of Clerkenwell permitted. He knew that an inspector of police and a couple of constables were gazing at him curiously through an office window, and the knowledge quickened his wits.

It was worth even more than his liberty to realize that, in all reasonable probability, his meteor was safe as yet. The police had failed in their quest; whom else had he to fear? The company had informed his mother that her tenancy of Johnson's Mews would not be disturbed before the thirty-first. Of course, her death was known to the firm, but their written promise to her was verbally confirmed to Philip by the manager. It was now the twenty-fifth. He had five clear days, perhaps six, in which to make all his arrangements. The forced seclusion of the prison had helped him in one way—it gave him a program, a detailed plan. Each step had been carefully thought out, and Isaacstein's office was the first stage in the campaign.

A prowling hansom passed. Philip whistled.

"Where's the fare?" demanded the cabman, angrily, looking up and down the street.

"Drive me to Holborn Viaduct, quick," said the boy, with his foot on the step.

Cabby eyed him with scorn.

"What's the gyme?" he growled. "D'yer tyke me for a mug, or what?"

"Oh, don't talk so much," cried Philip, impatiently. "Are you afraid I won't pay you? See! If you lose no more time, I will give you this," and he held up a two-shilling piece for the cabman's edification.

It is difficult to surprise your true Cockney whip. The man carefully folded the evening paper he had been reading, stuffed it under the strap which held his rug and cape, and chirruped to his horse:

"Kim up, lazy bones! We've got a millionaire crossin'-sweeper inside. What, ho! Any bloomin' perfession is better'n drivin' a keb."

The run was shorter than Philip anticipated, but, true to his promise, he proffered the two shillings.

The cabman looked at him. Something in the boy's face seemed to strike him as curious, and, notwithstanding Philip's rags, his skin was scrupulously clean.

"Gow on," he cried. "I'll make yer a present of that trip. 'Ope it'll giv yer a fresh stawt in the world. Kim up, will yer!" And the hansom swung away into the traffic, leaving the boy standing on the pavement on the north side of the viaduct. He made a mental note of the cab's number. It was easy to remember—three 8's and a 9—and walked on toward Hatton Garden.

Meanwhile the cabman, after varying luck, drove to his yard, changed horses, secured a fare to a theater, and joined the Haymarket rank while he took a meal in the cabmen's shelter.

"What's to-day's bettin' on the National?" he asked a friend.

The evening paper was passed and he cast an eye over its columns. Suddenly he rapped out a string of expressions that amazed his companions.

"What's the matter, Jimmie? Missed a twenty to one chance at Lincoln?"

"Great Scott! I thought he'd lift the roof off."

"Go easy, mate. There's lydies outside."

But the cabman still swore and gazed round-eyed at the sheet. And this is what he read:

"The boy, Philip Morland, whose possession of a collection of meteoric diamonds of great value has created so much sensation, was brought up on remand to-day at the Clerkenwell Police Court, and released. Mr. Abingdon thought fit to hear the case in camera, so this ragged urchin is wandering about London again with a pocketful of gems. He was last seen entering a cab in the neighborhood of the police court, and inquiry by our representative at the Hatton Garden offices of Mr. Isaacstein, the diamond merchant, whose name has figured in connection with the case, elicited the information that Morland called there about 3 P.M. Mr. Isaacstein positively refused to make any further statement for publication, but it is probable that developments in this peculiar and exciting affair will take place at any moment."

In a word, the journalistic world was exceedingly wroth with both Mr. Abingdon and the Jew for balking it of a very readable bit of news. No effort would be spared to defeat their obvious purpose. Philip must be discovered by hook or by crook, and badgered incessantly until he divulged the secret of the meteor.

At last the cabman became lucid.

"I'm done," he groaned. "My brains are a fuzzball. 'Ere! Some one drink my beer. I'm goin' in fer cow-cow. I 'ad this young spark in my keb to-d'y an' didn't know it. 'E offered me two bob, 'e did, an' I stood 'im a drive as a treat, 'e looked sich a scarecrow."

"Who's next?" cried a raucous voice at the door.

"I am," roared the disappointed one.

"Well, look sharp. There's a hold gent a-wavin' 'is humbreller like mad—"

"Keep 'im. Don't let 'im go. I'll be there in 'arf a tick. Who knows! P'raps it's Rothschild."

Meanwhile Philip did not hesitate an instant once he reached Isaacstein's office. A new note in his character was revealing itself. Always resolute, fearless and outspoken, now he was confident. He pushed open the swing door with the manner of one who expects his fellows to bow before him. Was he not rich—able to command the services of men—why should he falter? He forgot his rags, forgot the difficulties and dangers that might yet beset his path, for in very truth he had achieved but little actual progress since he first entered that office five days earlier.

But he had suffered much since then, and suffering had strengthened him. Moreover, he had taken the measure of Isaacstein. There was a score to be wiped off before that worthy and he entered into amicable business relations.

The instant the immature Jew behind the grille set eyes on Philip, he bounded back from the window and gazed at him with a frightened look. Had this young desperado broken out of prison and come to murder them all?

"Help! help!" he shouted. "Murder!"

Clerks came running from the inner office, among them the elderly man who interfered in Philip's behalf on the last occasion.

"Make that idiot shut up," said Philip, calmly, "and tell Mr. Isaacstein I am here."

The office boy was silenced, and the excitement calmed down. Yes, the diamond merchant was in. If Philip would walk upstairs to the waiting room, his presence would be announced.

"Thank you," he said; "but kindly see that this urchin does not let others know I am here. I don't want a crowd to be gathered in the street when I come out."

Such cool impudence from a ragamuffin was intolerable, or nearly so. But Isaacstein ruled his minions with a rod of iron, and they would fain wait the little man's pleasure ere they ventured their wrath on the boy. Besides, they were afraid of Philip. Like most people in London, they had read the newspaper reports of the police court proceedings, and they were awed by his strangely incomprehensible surroundings.

So he was silently ushered upstairs, and soon he caught the thick-voiced order of Isaacstein:

"Show him in."

The Jew, however, dived into his private sanctum before Philip entered the general office. The boy found him there, seated at his table.

The duel began with questions:

"How did you get out so soon? You were remanded for a week."

"Are you going to send for a policeman?"

"Don't be rude, boy, but answer me."

"I am not here to satisfy your curiosity, Mr. Isaacstein. I have called simply on a matter of business. It is sufficient for you to know that Mr.

Abingdon has set me at liberty and restored my property to me. Do you wish to deal with me or not?"

The diamond merchant tingled with anger. He was not accustomed to being browbeaten even by the representatives of the De Beers Company, yet here was a callow youngster addressing him in this outrageous fashion, betraying, too, an insufferable air of contempt in voice and manner. He glared at Philip in silent wrath for an instant.

The boy smiled. He took from his pocket the paper of diamonds and began to count them. The action said plainly:

"You know you cannot send me away. If I go to your trade rivals you will lose a magnificent opportunity. You are in my hands. No matter how rude I am to you, you must put up with it."

Nevertheless, the Jew made an effort to preserve his tottering dignity.

"Do you think," he said, "that you are behaving properly in treating a man of my position in such a way in his own office?"

In his own office—that was the sting of it.

The head of the firm of Isaacstein & Co., of London, Amsterdam and Kimberley, to be bearded in such fashion in his own particular shrine! Why, the thing was monstrous!

Philip looked him squarely in the eyes.

"Mr. Isaacstein," he said, calmly, "have you forgotten that you caused me to be arrested as a thief and dragged, handcuffed, through the open streets by a policeman? I have spent five days in jail because of you. At the moment when I was praising your honesty you were conveying secret signals to your clerks in the belief that I was something worse than a pickpocket. Was your treatment of me so free from blame at our first meeting as to serve as a model at the second?"

The chair was creaking now continuously; the Jew swung from side to side during this lecture. He strove hard to restrain himself, but the feverish excitement of Saturday returned with greater intensity than ever. He jumped up, and Philip imagined for a second that robbery with violence was imminent.

"Confound it all, boy!" yelled the merchant, "what was I to do when a ragged loafer like you came in and showed me a diamond worth a thousand pounds and told me he had dozens, hundreds, more like it? Did you expect me to risk standing in the dock by your side? Who could have given fairer evidence in your behalf than I did? Who proved that you could not have stolen the stones? Whom have you to thank for being at liberty now, but the expert who swore that no such diamonds had been seen before in this world?"

Philip waited until the man's passion had exhausted itself. Then he went on coolly:

"That is your point of view, I suppose. Mine is that you could have satisfied yourself concerning all those points without sending me to prison. However, this discussion is beside the present question. Will you buy my diamonds?"

Isaacstein recovered his seat. He wiped his face vigorously, but the trading instinct conquered his fury.

"Yes," he snapped. "How much do you want for them?"

"I notice that their value steadily increases. The first time you saw this diamond"—and he held up the stone originally exhibited to the Jew—"you said it was worth six or seven hundred pounds. To-day you name a thousand. However, I will take your own valuation for this unimportant collection, and accept fifty thousand pounds."

"Oh, you will, will you! And how will you have it, in notes or gold?"

He could not help this display of cheap sarcasm. The situation was losing its annoyance; the humor of it was beginning to dawn on him. When his glance rested more critically on Philip, the boy's age, the poverty of his circumstances, the whole fantastic incongruity of the affair, forced his recognition.

Not unprepared for such a retort, Philip gathered the stones together, and twisted the ends of the paper. Evidently the parcel was going back into his pocket. He glanced at a clock, too, which ticked solemnly over the office door.

"Here, what are you doing?" cried Isaacstein.

"Going to some one who will deal with me in a reasonable manner. It is not very late yet. I suppose there are plenty of firms like yours in Hatton Garden, or I can go back to Mr. Wilson—"

"Sit down. Sit down," growled the Jew, vainly striving to cloak his nervousness by a show of grim jocosity. "I never saw such a boy in my life. You are touchy as gunpowder. I was only joking."

"I am not joking, Mr. Isaacstein. Your price is my price—fifty thousand pounds."

"Do you think I carry that amount of money in my purse?" demanded Isaacstein, striving desperately to think out some means whereby he could get Philip into more amiable mood, when, perchance, the true story of the gems might be revealed.

"No," was the answer. "Even if you gave it to me I should not take it away. I want you to advance, say fifty pounds, to-day. I require clothes—and other things. Then, to-morrow, you can bring me to a bank, and pay a portion of the purchase price to my credit, giving me at the same time a written promise to pay the remainder within a week, or a month—any reasonable period, in fact."

The diamond merchant was quickly becoming serious, methodical, as he listened. This business-like proposal was the one thing needed to restore his bewildered faculties.

"Tell me, boy," he said, "who has been advising you?"

"No one."

"Do you mean to say you came here to-day to trade with me without consulting any other person?"

"I certainly told Mr. Abingdon I was coming, and I feel that I can always return to him for any advice if I am in a difficulty, but the offer I have just made is my own."

Watching Isaacstein's face was an interesting operation to Philip. Under ordinary conditions he might as well expect to find emotion depicted in a pound of butter as in that oily countenance, with its set expression molded by years of sharp dealings. But to-day the man was startled out of all the accustomed grooves of business. He was confronted with a problem so novel that his experience was not wide enough to embrace it.

So Philip caught a gleam of resentment at the introduction of the magistrate's name, and he instantly resolved to see Mr. Abingdon again at the earliest opportunity.

"Oh, he treated you kindly to-day, did he?" snarled Isaacstein.

"Yes, most kindly."

"You don't drink, I suppose?" broke in the other, abruptly.

"No. I am only a boy of fifteen, and do not need stimulants."

He was favored with a sharp glance at this remark, but he bent over his diamonds again and began to examine them, one by one. He knew that the action was tantalizing to his companion, and that is why he did it.

Isaacstein went to a sideboard and poured out a stiff glass of brandy. He swallowed it as an ordinary person takes an oyster.

"That's better," he said, returning to his desk. "Now we can get to close quarters. Hand over the stones."

Philip did nothing of the sort.

"Why?" he inquired, blandly. "You know all about them. You can hardly want to examine them so frequently."

"Confound it!" cried Isaacstein, growing red with renewed impatience, "what more can I do than agree to your terms?"

"I asked you for an advance of fifty pounds. I said nothing about leaving the diamonds in your charge. Please listen to me. I make no unreasonable demands. If you wish to keep the stones now you must first write me a letter stating the agreement between us. If it is right I will give you the diamonds. If it is not according to my ideas you must alter it."

"Do you think I mean to swindle you?"

"I have no views on that point. I am only telling you what my conditions are."

Isaacstein sat back in his chair and regarded Philip fixedly and with as much calmness as he could summon to his aid. A ray of sunshine illumined a bald patch on the top of his head, and the boy found himself idly speculating on developments in the Jew's future life. The man, on his part, was seeking to read the boy's inscrutable character, but the fixity of Philip's gaze at his denuded crown disconcerted him again.

"What are you looking at?" he demanded, suddenly.

"I was wondering how you will look when you go to heaven, Mr. Isaacstein," was the astounding reply.

For some reason it profoundly disturbed his hearer. He wobbled for a little while, and finally seemed to make up his mind, though he sighed perplexedly. The Jew was not a bad man. In business he was noted for exceeding shrewdness combined with strict commercial honesty. But the case that now presented itself contained all the elements of temptation. No matter how clever this boy might be, he was but a boy, and opportunities for cheating him must arrive. If not he, Isaacstein, there were others. The boy possessed a large store, possibly a very large store, of rough gems, and in dealing with them his agents could rob him with impunity. Yet, in answer to an unguarded question, this extraordinary youth admitted that Isaacstein might merit eternal bliss. Such an eventuality had not occurred to the Jew himself during unrecorded years. Now that it was suggested to him it disturbed him.

"You imagine then that I may deal fairly with you?" he said at last.

"Oh, yes. Why should you rob me? You can earn more money than you can ever need in this world by looking after my interests properly. If only you will believe this statement it will save you much future worry, I assure you."

"Were you in earnest when you said that you have an abundance of stones like those in your hands?"

"So many, Mr. Isaacstein, that you will have some trouble in disposing of them. I have diamonds as big, as big—let me see—as big as an egg."

The wonder is that the Jew did not faint.

"My God!" he gurgled, "do you know what you are saying? Where are they, boy? You will be robbed, murdered for their sake. Where are they? Let me put them in some safe place. I will deal honestly by you. I swear it, by all that I hold sacred. But you must have them taken care of."

"They are quite safe; be certain of that. Reveal my secret I will not. I have borne insult and imprisonment to preserve it, so it is not likely I will yield now to your appeals."

Philip's face lit up with a strange light as this protest left his lips. The meteor was his mother's bequest. She gave it to him, and she would safeguard it. Had she failed hitherto? Was not all London ringing with the news of his fortune, yet what man or woman had discovered the whereabouts of his treasure? In his pocket he felt the great iron key of No. 3, Johnson's Mews, and he was as certain now that his hiding place was unknown as that his mother's spirit was looking down on him from heaven, and directing his every movement.

The Jew, in spite of his own great lack of composure, saw the fleeting glimpse of spirituality in the boy's eyes. Puzzled and disturbed though he was, he made another violent effort to pull his shattered nerves into order.

"There is no need to talk all day," he said, doggedly. "Now I am going to tell you something you don't know. If your boast is justified—if you really own as many diamonds, and as good ones, as you say you own—there must be a great deal of discretion exercised in putting them on the market. Diamonds are valuable only because they are rare. There is a limit to their possible purchasers. If the diamond mines of the world were to pour all their resources forthwith into the lap of the public, there would be such a slump that prices would drop fifty, sixty, even eighty per cent. Do you follow me?"

"Yes," nodded Philip.

A week earlier he would have said, "Yes, sir," but his soul was bitter yet against Isaacstein.

"Very well. It may take me months, years, to realize your collection. To do it properly I must have some idea of its magnitude. If there are exceptionally large stones among it, they will be dealt with separately. They may rival or eclipse the few historical diamonds of the world, but their worth can only be measured by the readiness of some fool to pay hundreds of thousands for them. See?"

"Yes," nodded Philip again. His sententiousness brought the man to the point.

"Therefore you must take me into your confidence. What quantity of stones do you possess, and what are their sizes? I must know."

Isaacstein, cooler now, pursed his lips and pressed his thumbs together until they appeared to be in danger of dislocation. It was his favorite attitude when engaged in a deal. It signified that he had cornered his victim. Philip, appealed to in this strictly commercial way, could not fail to see it was to his own interest to tell his chosen expert the exact facts, and nothing but the facts.

The boy, singularly unflurried in tone and manner, hazarded an inquiry.

"What amount of ordinary diamonds, in their money value I mean, can you dispose of readily in the course of a year, Mr. Isaacstein?"

"Oh, two or three hundred thousand pounds' worth; it is a matter largely dependent on the condition of trade generally. But that may be regarded as a minimum."

"And the bigger stones, worth many thousands each?"

"It is impossible to say. Taking them in the lump, at values varying from a thousand each to fancy figures, perhaps fifty thousand pounds' worth."

"It would be safe to reckon on a quarter of a million a year, all told?"

"Quite safe."

"Then, Mr. Isaacstein, I will supply you with diamonds of that value every year for many years."

The Jew relaxed the pressure on his thumbs. Indeed he passed a tremulous hand across his forehead. He was beaten again, and he knew it—worsted by a gutter snipe in a war of wits.

The contest had one excellent effect. It stopped all further efforts on Isaacstein's part to wrest Philip's secret from him. Thenceforth he asked for, and obtained, such diamonds as he needed, and resolutely forbade himself the luxury of questioning or probing the extent of his juvenile patron's resources.

But there was a long pause before he found his tongue again. His voice had lost its aggressiveness when he said:

"In the police court I valued the diamonds you produced at fifty thousand pounds. It does not necessarily follow that I am prepared to give such a sum for them at this moment. I might do so as a speculation, but I take it you do not want me to figure in that capacity. It will be better for you, safer for me, if I become your agent. I will take your stones to Amsterdam, have them cut sufficiently to enable dealers to assess their true worth, and sell them to the best advantage. My charge will be ten per cent, and I pay all expenses. To-day I will give you fifty pounds. To-morrow I will take you to a bank and place five thousand to your credit. Meanwhile, I will give you a receipt for thirty stones, weighing, in the rough, so many carats, and you, or anyone you may appoint, can see the sale vouchers subsequently, when I will hand you the balance after deducting £5,050 and my ten per cent. The total price may exceed fifty thousand, or it may be less, but I do not think I will be far out in my estimate. Are you agreeable?"

Some inner monitor told Philip that the Jew was talking on sound business lines. There was a ring of sincerity in his voice. Apparently he had thrust temptation aside, and was firmly resolved to be content with his ten per cent.

And this might well be. Twenty-five thousand pounds a year earned by a few journeys to the Continent—a few haggling interviews in the Hatton Garden office! What a gold mine! Moreover, he would be the head man in the trade. He was that now, in some respects; but under the new conditions none could gainsay his place at the top. Even the magnates of Kimberley would be staggered by this new source of supply. What did it matter if the boy kept to his rags and amazed the world, so long as the diamonds were forthcoming? It was no silk-hatted gentleman who first stumbled across the diamond-laden earth of South Africa. Isaacstein had made up his mind. Fate had thrust this business into his lap. He would be a fool to lose it out of mere curiosity.

"Yes," said Philip. "I agree to that."

"Samuel!" yelled Isaacstein.

"Coming, sir," was the answering shout, and a flurried clerk appeared.

"Bring in the scales, Samuel."

The scales were brought, and a level space cleared for them on the desk. Philip, of course, had never before seen an instrument so delicately adjusted. A breath would serve to depress the balance.

The boy held forth his paper, and poured the contents into the tiny brass tray of the scales. Samuel's mouth opened and his eyes widened. It was his first sight of the diamonds.

"Four ounces, eight pennyweights, five grains—six hundred and twenty-nine carats in thirty stones. Oh, good gracious me!" murmured the clerk.

Isaacstein checked the record carefully.

"Right!" he said. "Put them in the safe."

Philip raised no protest this time. He knew that the Jew would keep his word. Indeed, Isaacstein told Samuel to bring him fifty sovereigns, and ere the man returned he began to write on a sheet of letter paper:

"Received from—Here! what's your name?" he broke in.

"Philip."

"Philip what?"

"That will do to-day, thank you. The next time I call I will give you my full name and address."

"Please yourself. I am no judge in this matter," and he wrote on:

"Received from Philip, a boy who refuses any other name, but the same whom I saw in this office on the twentieth inst., and again at the Clerkenwell Police Court on that date, thirty meteoric diamonds weighing in the gross six hundred and twenty-nine carats. I hereby agree to dispose of the same, and to render true account of sales to the said Philip or his agents. My commission to be ten per cent.; the expenses payable by me. I have to-day handed the said Philip fifty pounds in gold, and undertake to place five thousand pounds to his credit to-morrow with my bankers.

"Reuben Isaacstein."

After completing this acknowledgment he scribbled something else.

"There," he said, with a sigh of relief, "that is not a very formal document, but it will suffice. You can get it stamped to-morrow at Somerset House. Just sign this receipt for fifty pounds."

Philip took the two papers and read them carefully. Isaacstein's handwriting was a scrawl, but legible enough. The boy reached for a pen and signed his Christian name. He was on the point of adding his surname in an unguarded moment, but he felt the Jew's eye on him. So he simply wrote "Philip" across the stamp at the foot of the receipt.

Isaacstein fully appreciated the incident, and knew that his own eagerness defeated the chance, all the more powerful because it was involuntary, of ascertaining the name of this marvelous youth.

Philip gathered up his gold, not without counting the coins. They felt strangely heavy in his pocket, much heavier than the stones they replaced. Yet they formed but a thousandth part of the value of those flintlike pebbles. What a queer problem it was, this ratio of worth between a few stones and the bright, minted sovereigns.

"What time shall I call to-morrow?" he asked, standing, cap in hand, ready to take his departure.

"At eleven. But wait one moment. Have you no friends to look after you? See what trouble you may get into. Why, the mere possession of so much gold by a boy like you may—"

"I can take care of myself, Mr. Isaacstein. I will be here at eleven. Good-afternoon."

Chapter VIII

The Transition

It was four o'clock in the afternoon of a fine, but chilly March day when Philip regained Holborn with fifty pounds making a lump in his pocket, and Isaacstein's letter safely lodged in his coat. The mere weight of the gold suggested an unpleasant possibility. His clothes were so worn that the frail calico might give way and every golden coin rattle forth to the pavement.

So with one of Mr. Abingdon's shillings he made his first purchase, a capacious tobacco pouch with a snap mouth, for which he paid ninepence. Then he adjourned to an aërated bread shop and ordered some refreshments. While the waitress was bringing his cup of tea and piece of cake he contrived to slip all the sovereigns but one into the tobacco pouch.

He did this with his hand in the pocket itself, and more than once there was a pleasant clink as the coins fell into their novel receptacle.

A man sitting near caught the sound, and looked up suspiciously. Philip, whose senses were very much on the alert to-day, realized that his action was somewhat careless. Without even glancing at his neighbor, he took out his remaining couple of shillings and the three pennies, and affected to count them with a certain degree of astonishment, as if some were missing. The ruse was satisfactory. The man gave him no further heed, and soon quitted the restaurant.

Philip tendered the odd sovereign in payment of his bill. The girl cashier seemed to be surprised that such a ragged youth should own so large a sum.

"All silver, please," said Philip, when she began to count his change.

He would take no more risks if he could avoid them. Not a single policeman in London would have failed to arrest him at that moment were his store of gold revealed by any chance. Yet Philip was rich honestly, and there were men driving away from the city at that hour whose banking accounts were plethoric with stolen money. For their carriages the policemen would stop the traffic. In neither instance could the guardians of the peace be held blameworthy; such is the importance of mere appearances.

The boy, during his short and terribly sharp tussle with London life, had already grasped this essential fact, and with great skill and method he set about the task of altering his own shabby exterior.

In a side street leading out of Gray's Inn Road, he found a secondhand clothes shop. Here he purchased a worn, but decent, blue serge suit for eight shillings six pence, a pair of boots for five shillings, a cap for ninepence, a woolen shirt for two shillings, and a linen collar for threepence.

He haggled sufficiently over the bargain to suit the needs of a scanty purse.

"I've cut 'em dahn low enough," said the shopkeeper, mournfully. "Things isn't wot they was in the ole clo' line, let me tell yer. Not but what you do want a new rig-aht."

"Yes," said Philip. "I've got a job, and can't keep it unless I look decent."

For the life of him he could not burlesque the Cockney accent, and although he used the simplest phraseology, the man glanced at him sharply.

"Where are yer workin'?" he said.

"At Isaacstein's in Hatton Garden." The words had not left his lips ere he regretted them.

"Wot is 'e?"

"A Jew," and Philip laughed. This quip atoned for the error of the admission.

"Bli-me, you won't get a lot aht of 'im."

"No. It cost me some trouble to get an advance, I can assure you."

Philip rattled all his silver and coppers onto the counter. He counted out sixteen shillings sixpence.

"Not much left, is there?" he said.

"Well, look 'ere," said the man. "Gimme fifteen bob. You're a sharp lad. You'll myke yer w'y all right. Nex' time you want some duds come to me an' I'll treat you fair."

"Thank you very much," said Philip, considerably surprised by this generous act. "I certainly will not forget you."

"You can change in my little back room if you like. That lot you've got on ain't worth tykin' 'ome."

"I am obliged for your kindness, but I must be off now. It is late, and I have a long way to go."

"Where to? Holloway?"

"No, cityward."

The clothes and boots were made up in a parcel by this time. Philip hurried away, glad to escape further questioning.

"Queer sort o' kid, that," mused the shopkeeper. "My, but 'e must ha' bin 'ard up afore 'e took on wiv' a Jew. Wot did 'e s'y 'is nyme was? Isaacstein? I've seen that somewhere or other. Now where was it?"

He knew two hours later, for he, too, read the evening paper.

Philip sprang into a 'bus for the Bank. At the Royal Exchange he would catch a green 'bus for the Mile End Road.

It was almost dark when he reached the Bank. Thus far the

omnibuses going east were not crowded. Now the situation had changed.

The human eddy in that throbbing center of life was sending off its swirls to all points of the compass, and the eastbound vehicles were boarded by an eager crowd almost before the passengers arriving at the terminus could descend.

A poor woman, greatly hampered by a baby, was struggling with others to obtain a seat in the Mile End Road 'bus. Philip, coming late on the scene, saw her swept ruthlessly aside by a number of men and boys. The conductor jerked the bell-rope several times. There was no more room.

The woman, white-faced and disappointed, looked around with a woe-begone expression. Philip, who would have gladly paid for a cab to take her to her destination, dared do nothing of the sort. But he said:

"Keep close to me. I will get you a seat in the next 'bus."

"Oh, I wish you would," she said, with a wan smile. "I am so tired. I have walked here from Shepherd's Bush."

"That's a long way to carry a baby."

"What could I do? People won't take care of children without payment. I heard I could get work in a laundry there, so I went to look after it. There's nothing to be had down our way, is there?"

"Things turn up suddenly," said Philip.

"Not for the poor, my lad. I fear you know that without my telling you. But you are young, and will soon be a man."

Her wistful tone went to his heart.

"Didn't you succeed at the laundry?" he inquired.

"Yes; I ought to be thankful. I can earn nine shillings a week there. I start on Monday."

"Isn't your husband at work?"

"He is dead. Poor fellow, he caught cold last Christmas, and was buried in January. God only knows how I have lived since. If it wasn't for the kindness of neighbors, baby and I would have starved. I can ill afford this tuppence, but I can't walk any further."

"Well, look out now," he said, cheerily. "Here's our 'bus."

As the vehicle drew up he caught the brass rail with his left hand, and warded off assailants with the bundle under his right arm.

"Quick," he said to the woman, as soon as the people inside had descended. "Jump in."

She essayed to do so, but was rudely thrust aside by a young man who had paused on the roof to light a cigarette. Philip sprang onto the step and butted the young gentleman in the stomach with his parcel, causing the other to sit down heavily on the stairs. The boy caught the woman's arm with his disengaged hand and pulled her up. He dived in after her.

"You young—" roared the discomfited smoker.

"'Ere! Come orf of it," said the conductor. "Why didn't ye git dahn before? D'ye want a lift?"

Others hustled the protesting one out of the way.

"Confound the East End, I say," he growled, as he crossed to the Mansion House. "What the deuce Lady Louisa Morland wants to keep on sending me to that wretched mews for I can't imagine. Anyway, I can tell her this time that the place is empty, and will be pulled down next week."

And thus it was that Philip collided with Messrs. Sharpe & Smith's clerk, detailed by the anxious Lady Morland to discover his whereabouts. They met and bumped into each other in the whirlpool of London just as two ships might crash together by night in mid-Atlantic, and draw apart with ruffled feelings, or scraped paint, which is the same thing, without the slightest knowledge of each other's identity.

Within the omnibus the woman was volubly grateful. She had a kindly heart, and timidly essayed questions as to Philip's relatives, hoping that she might make their acquaintance.

"I'll be bound, now," she said, "that you have a good mother. You can always tell what the parents are like when you see the children."

"My mother was, indeed, dear to me," he replied sadly, again driven out of himself by the mournful recollections thus suddenly induced, "but she is dead, lost to me forever."

Some people in the 'bus ceased talking. They were attracted by the strong, clear voice of this unkempt boy, whose diction and choice of words were so outrageously opposed to his garments. Luckily, the silence warned him, or his new friend's sympathy might have brought about an embarrassing position.

"Poor thing! And is your father dead, too?"

"Yes. He died long ago."

"Where do you live now?"

"Oh," he said, "I have been staying in North London, but will leave there soon, and I have not settled anything definitely at present. Where is the laundry you spoke of? I will call some day, if I may, and learn how you are getting on."

"I will be so pleased. It is a little place in James Street—the only one there. Ask for Mrs. Wrigley."

"It is lucky you understand laundry work, or things might go hard with you."

She laughed pitifully.

"I don't! They asked me if I was a washer or an ironer. I thought washing required least experience, so I said I was a washer. I am quick to learn, and will watch the other women. If they find me out I may be discharged."

"Oh, cheer up," he said, pleasantly. "I don't suppose you'll find it very hard."

Her voice sank almost to a whisper.

"It is not the work I dread, but the surroundings. I was a school teacher before my marriage. My husband was an electrical engineer. We put all our savings into a little business, and then—the end came."

"Not quite the end. I am only a boy, but I've had ups and downs enough to know that the beginning of next week may be a very different affair to the end of this. Good-by."

They were passing the London Hospital, and he thought it prudent to alight at some distance from Johnson's Mews.

"Well, God bless you, anyhow," she said, earnestly.

"'E's got 'is 'ead screwed on tight, that lad," commented a man sitting next to her.

"Better than that, he has a good heart," said Mrs. Wrigley. Most fortunate Mrs. Wrigley—to have encountered Philip in that hour, which she deemed the blackest in her life.

He hastened through the familiar bustle of the busy thoroughfare with heightened expectancy, it is true, but devoid of the least fear that his meteor had been discovered. His mother would take good care of it. Why, the mere chance remark of the woman he had befriended showed that her gentle spirit watched over him wherever he went. Here was a stranger, a sad toiler among the millions, who went out of her way to praise the goodness of one she had never seen. He laughed joyously. Mrs. Wrigley should have further cause to bless his mother's memory.

He passed O'Brien's shop. He saw the old man seated behind the counter. Should he go in? No. Better keep wholly to himself at present. Yet he hesitated. Which was the more judicious course—to remain hidden, unknown, or to drop quietly into the groove where he was recognized? With rare perspicacity for one so young, he reflected that only five days had elapsed since he last saw the old pensioner. The period bulked largely in Philip's life; in O'Brien's it would be as naught.

Yielding to the second thought, he entered the shop.

"Glory be to God, Phil, but it's miself is glad to see ye," cried his old friend. "Where have ye bin to, at all at all? Have yez heard what the murtherin' War Office is afther doin' to me? I haven't had a sowl to sphake to about the throuble they've put on me in me owld age."

This was not strictly accurate. O'Brien had pestered the whole neighborhood with the story of his withheld pension and the preposterous claim made on him by some red-tape enthusiast in Pall Mall. But his plaint effectually stopped all further reference to Philip's disappearance. As to the "bit o' shtone," that was "naythur alum nor lime," he hadn't a word to say.

Philip borrowed a spade, a small sweeping brush and a strong sack without evoking the slightest comment from the pensioner, who discoursed incessantly on the iniquity of the "Govermint," and whose farewell remark dealt with the attempt to rob him of "a hundred gowlden sov'rins."

Decidedly the boy was in luck's way. He had secured some necessary implements without attracting any attention. Watching a favorable opportunity, he slipped unseen into the gloom of Johnson's Mews. He tried the door of No. 3. It was locked. He inserted the key and entered. The darkness within was that of utter blindness, but he dumped his impedimenta on the floor and locked the door behind him.

Then he groped his doubtful path to the mantelpiece where he had left a candle and a box of matches. His boots crunched, as he went, on what he knew to be mostly diamonds, and he stumbled over the mattress in front of the fireplace. Yes, the candle was there. Soon he had a light. The tiny gleam lifted the black curtain, and he surveyed his domain. A single glance showed him that all things remained exactly as he left them on Saturday morning. The packet of letters rested on the broken chair, the old sack was stuffed into the window, and the rope— that never-to-be-forgotten rope—dangled from the hook to which he had fastened it.

The sight brought a lump into his throat. He sank to his knees, pressed down, he felt, by some superior power.

"Mother!" he said, humbly, "forgive me, and ask God to forgive me, for what I would have done were you not watching over me."

In the spiritual exaltation of the moment he almost expected to find that sweet face peering at him benignantly from out the dim background. But he could not see her, and he rose, revivified by this spoken communion with her. He had no shadow of doubt as to her presence. God to him was the universe, and his mother the unquestionable means of communication with the Providence that governed his life. He would die rather than abandon that belief. Were it dispelled from his mind he was quite certain that his wealth would vanish with it. It was no haphazard accident which had sent the diamond-laden meteor headlong from the sky. He was despairing, dying; his mother appealed for him; and, behold! the very elements that control the world obeyed a mighty behest.

He began to work methodically. In the first place, he lit a fire, for the evening was chilly. Then he shook his mattress and swept the floor, gathering into a heap all the tiny particles with which it was littered. These he collected in a piece of newspaper, and folded them into a parcel, which again he inclosed in a stouter sheet of brown paper, finally tying the whole with a yard of string he carried in his pocket.

There were hundreds of tiny diamonds in that insignificant package, and not a few the size of small peas. As a matter of fact, he discovered subsequently that the net result of his sweeping brought him in over a thousand pounds.

Having examined every nook and crevice of the apartment by the aid of the candle, he satisfied himself that naught remained which would indicate to the most curious eye any event out of the common having occurred in that humble dwelling.

It was typical of Philip's implicit faith that he did not unlock the back door until his interior task was ended. He knew that his meteor was untouched.

There was no wind without. The candle, feeble as its rays were, illuminated the small yard sufficiently to reveal its débris of white stones and darker lumps of metal. Beginning at the doorway, he swept vigorously but with minutest care, until he had formed four good-sized piles on the flagstones.

He could not afford to differentiate between the débris of the damaged pavement and the fragments of the meteor. It was easy to distinguish the larger pieces of broken glass from the window inside the house—in the yard he had neither the time nor the light to select the bits of shattered stone. All must go together, to be sorted with leisured care subsequently.

He scrutinized the external window sills, the door posts, the chinks of the small coal-house door at the further end of the yard, even the rough surfaces of the walls, and removed every speck of loose material. More newspaper was requisitioned, but, after utilizing the twine on his parcel of clothing, he ran short of string.

He coolly went up the stairs, unfastened the rope with which he had intended to hang himself and loosened its stiff strands. Soon he had an abundance of strong cord, and four bulky packages were added to the first small one.

They were heavy, too, weighing several pounds each. In placing them side by side close to the wall beneath the front window, he suddenly realized an unforeseen difficulty.

If these shreds of matter—the mere husk, as it were, of the meteor— were so ponderous, what would be the weight of the meteor itself? How could he hope to lift it from the hole in which it lay—how convey it from Johnson's Mews to a new and safer habitation? He might as well endeavor to move an unwilling elephant.

The thought chilled him. For the first time since his parting interview with Mr. Abingdon, Philip experienced a dread of failure. With something of panic in his blood, he snatched the candle and ran hastily into the yard. He knelt and held the light low in the excavation. Then he cried aloud:

"What! Am I so ready to lose faith in mother?"

For the huge metallic mass—so big that it would not enter the bore of the largest cannon known to modern gunnery—was split asunder in all directions. Its fissures gaped widely as if to mock at him. The rain and steam had done their work well. It was even possible that he would not need the spade, but would be able to pick out each separate chunk with his hand.

Instantly he put the thought into execution, and succeeded in lifting several pieces to the yard level. He noted that they were gorged with the dull white pebbles, some being the size of pigeon's eggs. He could not help comparing them in his mind's eye with the collection now lodged in Isaacstein's safe. If those were worth fifty thousand pounds, these must be of fabulous value.

Any other person in the wide world might have been excused if he pinched himself, or winked furiously, or took out the gold-filled tobacco pouch for careful inspection, to assure himself that he was not dreaming. Not so, Philip. The only dominant feeling in his brain was one of annoyance that he should have doubted, for one single instant, that means would be given him to secure absolute and undisputed control of his treasure.

But there remained the problem of weight. His original idea was to wrap the actual body of the meteor in the stout sack he obtained from O'Brien, and then inclose all his valuables in a tin trunk which he would purchase next morning. Any ordinary trunk would certainly be spacious enough, but its phenomenal weight would unquestionably evoke more comment than he desired, and it would need two strong men to lift it.

This portion of his plan needed to be entirely remodeled, and he was now more than ever thankful that the Jew's fifty pounds, save one expended, reposed in his pocket. With money, all things, or nearly all things, were possible.

Owing to the cramped space in which the meteor lay it was no small task to bring it to the surface in sections. But he persevered. By strenuous endeavor he accumulated an astonishing pile of iron ore studded with diamonds, looking not unlike almonds in a brown cake, and the guttering candle held low down failed to reveal anything else in the hole. There was a good deal of débris at the bottom, and the depth was now over four feet. To reach to its full extent he was compelled to jam his head and shoulders into the excavation and feel blindly with one hand, so he rightly concluded that a final examination might be left until daylight.

By this time he was hot and covered with dirt. He stripped, washed himself in front of the fire, and changed into his new clothes.

He did not possess a looking-glass, but he felt sure that he presented a remarkably different appearance when attired in a neat serge suit, a clean shirt and reputable boots. His first impulse was to thrust his discarded garments into the fire, but sentiment prevailed, and he folded them into a parcel.

Then he extinguished his candle and went out. To his exceeding surprise he discovered that it was nearly nine o'clock—time had indeed flown.

The shops in the Mile End Road open early and close late. He entered a restaurant where he was unknown, passing, as a matter of policy, the coffee stall of his kindly helper of those former days now so remote in his crowded memories. After eating a hearty meal, for which he was thoroughly prepared, he tendered a sovereign in payment.

The proprietor barely glanced at him. Philip was now well dressed, according to local ideas, and his strong, erect figure, his resolute face, added two or three years to his age when contrasted with the puny standard of fifteen as set by the poverty-stricken East End.

He had forgotten to buy a necktie and a new pair of stockings. These omissions he now rectified, and he also purchased a warm, dark-gray traveling rug, several yards of drugget, a ball of twine and a pair of scissors. A couple of stout but worn leather portmanteaux caught his eye.

"Those are cheap," said the salesman, quickly, "only fifteen shillings each."

"I'm not sure I can afford so much," said Philip, hesitatingly, for the rug alone cost one pound six shillings.

"They're a rare bargain—real leather—they were never made under three pounds each."

"Oh, very well. I will take them."

He produced three pounds, got his change, and walked away with his goods without causing any wonderment. The shopman was only too glad to have such a customer at that late hour.

Philip now knew that he was fairly safe, but he decided that a billy-cock hat gave him a more mature appearance than a cap. This alteration being effected, he hurried off to Johnson's Mews and re-entered his domicile without incident worthy of note.

Very quickly, with the help of drugget, scissors and twine, the two small portmanteaux were packed with pieces of the meteor, and the paper-covered parcels already prepared. When each bag weighed about forty pounds he stuffed the remaining space with rolled-up newspapers, closed and locked them. He estimated that three larger leather bags—these being less noisy than tin—would hold the remainder of the meteor.

As the next morning would find him occupation enough, he decided to do as much as possible that night. Three times he sallied forth and returned with a good-sized valise. He paid prices varying from two pounds ten shillings to three pounds fifteen shillings, and always bought secondhand goods.

He had locked and strapped the fourth of his goodly array of traveling bags when he fancied he heard a footstep in the mews. Such an occurrence would have troubled him not a jot a week ago. To-night it was extremely disconcerting.

Notwithstanding the weight of the packed portmanteaux, especially the larger one, he lifted each bodily in his arms and ran with it into the tiny scullery. On the front window there was no blind, only a small, much-worn curtain covering the lower panes, and he did not want any stray loafer to gaze in at him and discover a large quantity of luggage in such a disreputable hovel.

When the fourth bag was disposed of in the dark recess of the scullery he paused for an instant to listen. There was not a sound. Through the window he could dimly discern the roof of the deserted stables opposite.

He bent again to the task of packing the fifth portmanteau, and was placing in it the last parcel of ore and diamonds when some of the heavy contents fell through one end where the drugget wrapping had been hastily folded.

Shaking the package on the floor as a grocer beats down the contents of a sugar bag, he picked up the fallen specimens and put them in, one by one. A large lump of ore had fallen apart when it dropped. Inside there was a huge kernel, a rough diamond quite as large as a hen's egg.

Philip smiled as he recalled his boast to Isaacstein. He examined the stone critically, and realized that if it were flawless it must be one of the marvels of creation. Without experiencing any positive motive he slipped this unique specimen into his pocket, and went on with the reconstruction of the damaged parcel.

At last he finished. The portmanteau was lying open on the floor, when the thought occurred to him that he might have avoided the flurry and trouble of carrying these heavy articles into the scullery if he had nailed a couple of yards of his drugget across the window.

It was not too late even now to rectify this defect. He glanced at the window to ascertain how much material he should cut off, and saw a face—an evil, brutal, suspicious face—peering at him over the top of the curtain.

Chapter IX

A Decisive Battle

It would be idle to deny that Philip was startled by the sight. No braver or more resolute boy breathed; but the silence, the mystery—the gloomy aloofness of Johnson's Mews—lent a sinister aspect to an apparition formidable enough under any circumstances, but absolutely threatening and full of danger to one situated as he at that moment.

He never remembered seeing the man before. Not that this repellent physiognomy was of a type to be soon forgotten. A bullet head with prominent, blood-shot eyes, a strong, cruel mouth, a huge nose badly broken—a certain strength of character in features debased by drink and criminality—these were the tokens writ legibly on the countenance glaring intently at the boy from without.

The two gazed at each other for an appreciable time. The man's face wandered from Philip's face to his costume, and then rested on the open portmanteau at the boy's feet. There was in his expression an air of astonishment—a certain gloating bewilderment—as of one who had stumbled unawares upon some object of such potential value that the finder could hardly believe it to be true. He was thinking, wondering, debating with himself. The goggle eyes seemed to see more than the brain was inclined to credit.

Philip, despite his alarm, felt that the right course was to resent this impertinent prying into his affairs.

"Hello, you!" he shouted. "What do you want?"

The man grinned. He seemed to be about to answer when he suddenly turned his head and looked down the yard toward the entry.

Instantly he swung round and vanished noiselessly, with the silent alertness of a cat, for the boy heard no sound. He simply disappeared in the darkness, and Philip, who knew every inch of the ground, realized that his most unpleasant-visaged spy had not only dived into the further obscurity of the mews—which formed a cul-de-sac—but also was either in his stocking feet or wore something over his boots to deaden any possible clatter on the paving stones.

Here was a nice thing—his habitat discovered by some tramp or criminal skulking in the untenanted building marked out for the housebreakers within a few days. It was too bad. He was sorely annoyed that he had not thought sooner of the potentialities of the window when the interior of the house was illumined by a candle and a ruddy fire. How long had the man stood there watching him? He had certainly seen some portion of the contents of the last portmanteau. Had he also witnessed the removal of the others to the pantry?

70

Philip's experience as a newspaper vender told him that all London was now familiar with his own personal appearance, as well as with the semblance and value of his meteoric diamonds. The white stones, the clumps of iron ore, had been described minutely by clever journalists, who supplemented Isaacstein's clear statement by facts gleaned from encyclopediæ and interviews with geologists.

Most probably this man had read long articles about him, for the story was such as to bring watery curses to the lips of every penniless vagrant in the kingdom. Indeed, the careful scrutiny bestowed on his face and clothes bore out this suspicion. Had he not changed his garments the stranger would have known his identity beyond all question. As it was, the man was puzzled, and disturbed at the very moment he was about to say something. What had happened to cause him to run away? What had he seen or heard? Above all, how much did he know of Philip and his affairs?

Well, the door was locked, and it would be folly to go out again that night. The house was absolutely unapproachable save by the front. Philip resolved to remain awake until daybreak. O'Brien's spade stood against the fireplace. It was a formidable weapon, and he would not hesitate to use it if forcible entry was attempted. He must sit quietly in the dark, listening for each sound, and threatening boldly when he heard anyone endeavoring to open door or window.

He sighed, for he was very tired, but the vigil was imperative.

He dropped the drugget and scissors and bent again over the portmanteau. The packing operations might as well be finished now, and, indeed, when the light was extinguished, it would be better to keep away from the window, through which a sudden thrust with an implement might do him an injury.

He took his discarded clothes and arranged them on top of the last parcels of ore and diamonds. Then he reached out for the small bundle of documents resting on the chair behind him, intending to place them in a little pocket in the flap which already covered one-half of the bag.

At that instant he again heard footsteps. Of course, a very few seconds had elapsed since he first caught sight of the living specter without. The ideas recorded at such length whirled through his active brain with lightning speed, just as the knowledge now came that the footsteps proceeded from the entrance to the mews and not from its extremity, while their firm regularity betokened the advent of some person who had no special reason to conceal his movements.

The boy listened breathlessly. The oncomer reached his door, passed it, stopped opposite the window, and then another face peered over the curtain.

This time it was a policeman.

For an instant their eyes met in mutual astonishment. Then the policeman came so close that his helmet rested against a pane of glass. He grinned affably, and cried:

"Here! I want to speak to you."

Intuitively grasping the essential fact that his best policy was one of ready acquiescence, Philip sprang toward the door and unlocked it. He stood on the step. The constable approached.

"I hope I didn't startle you," he began, "but I just looked in on the off chance—"

"I am very glad indeed, to see you," interrupted the boy. "I am leaving here to-morrow. Just now, while I was packing some of my belongings, a very nasty-looking man came and peeped in at me in the same way as you did."

He backed into the house. The policeman half followed him, his quick glance noting the open portmanteau and its array of old clothes.

"Just now?" he questioned. "Do you mean some time since?"

"No, no. Not half a minute—a few seconds ago."

"But where can he be? He hasn't left the mews, or I must have seen him. I crossed the road, and no one came out in so short a time."

"Well, he is somewhere in the place—he had a horrid appearance—a man with a broken nose. He made me jump, I can assure you."

"A man with a broken nose! By Jove, I'm looking for a party of that description. A rank wrong 'un. Robbery with violence and a few other little things. What sort of man was he? You saw his face only, I suppose?"

The constable stepped back into the paved court. A rapid twist of his hand sent a vivid beam of light dancing over ruined tenements, disheveled doorways and shattered windows.

"A tall man," said Philip, "taller than you, for I could see his chin over the string of the curtain. He had a big face, with eyes that stuck out boldly—"

"By the Lord, it's Jocky right enough!" cried the constable. "Now, where can he have got to? He's an ugly customer to tackle single-handed," he added, beneath his breath.

"Won't you wait a bit, until I get some help?" said Philip, anxiously.

The man appeared to debate the point. The nearest comrade was an acting sergeant, newly promoted. If he were summoned, the kudos of a smart capture would be his by right of seniority.

"No," announced the constable, stubbornly. "If he is here, I will handle him myself."

Again his lamp swept the small area of the mews and revealed no living object. He quickly unfastened his belt, took off his greatcoat, and readjusted belt and lamp again.

"Now I'm ready for him," he grinned. "Put my coat inside, boy, and stand at the door yourself with the candle in your hand. If you see anything, yell out to me."

Philip obeyed. These preparations for a deadly struggle appealed to his very soul, for your healthy-minded boy of fifteen has generally ceased to be a highwayman or a pirate in imagination, and aims rather at planting the Union Jack on a glacis bristling with hostile cannon.

The policeman, feeling for the loose strap of his truncheon, commenced a careful survey of the mews. He had not gone five yards when there was a loud crash of broken glass. The building at the other end of the yard possessed a couple of windows facing into another inclosure at the back. Obviously, the broken-nosed "Jocky," unseen himself, had observed the constable's movements.

Realizing that discovery was imminent, he was effecting a strategic movement to the rear.

The policeman instantly abandoned his cautious tactics. He ran toward the door of the house whence the sound came. It resisted somewhat, but yielded to his shoulder. He disappeared inside. Philip, after closing his own door, also ran to the new center of interest, shielding the candle with one hand lest it should blow out.

Quick as he was, he missed the first phase of a Homeric combat. The violent "Jocky," foiled by an unnoticed iron bar in his attempt to escape, turned like a madman on the policeman. There was no sort of parley between them. Cursing the luck that had revealed his hiding place, the man, an ex-convict, with the frame of a giant, sprang at his pursuer suddenly from an inner room.

The policeman had a second's warning. It was something, but not enough to give him an advantage. He got his truncheon out, but simultaneously his assailant was on him with the ferocity of a catamount. They closed in bone-breaking endeavor, and before they were locked together for ten fearful seconds the officer of the law bitterly regretted the professional pride which sent him single-handed into this unequal strife.

For he was physically outclassed, and he knew it, and there is no more unnerving knowledge can come to a man in such a supreme moment. Nevertheless, he was a brave man, and he fought with all the resolution that is born of the consciousness of justice and moral right. But Providence is on the side of big battalions, and "Jocky" was taller, heavier, very much more active. Moreover, liberty is as potent an incentive as law any day, and law was being steadily throttled when the pale gleam of Philip's candle lit up the confines of the ruinous hovel about which the two men stamped and lurched and wrestled.

At the precise moment of the boy's entrance the policeman's knees yielded and he fell, with his remorseless antagonist uppermost. Philip, gazing at them wide-eyed, almost fell too, for his left foot rolled on the constable's staff.

Being fashioned of the stuff which founds empires—on the principle that instant action is worth a century of diplomacy—he picked up the truncheon and brought it down on "Jocky's" hard skull with such emphasis that the convict emitted a queer sort of cough, and collapsed limply on top of his conquered adversary.

Then the boy was horrified. The two lay so still that he imagined both were dead. It is one thing to help the law, but quite another to kill a man. He did not want to be a murderer as well as a millionaire, not knowing then the qualities which go to form these varieties of the genus homo are strangely alike.

He gazed at them as in a trance, but relief came when he heard them breathing stertorously. At last, after a pause that apparently endured unnumbered minutes, the constable weakly rolled himself free from the bulky form of his would-be slayer, and sat up.

He inflated his lungs vigorously. Then he managed to gasp:

"Thank you! You've saved my life!"

He pressed his ribs with both hands and gingerly felt his throat. He stood up. His lamp was still alight, but a quantity of oil had run over his tunic and trousers.

"By Jove, boy, you are a brick," he said, and his voice was under control again.

Philip answered not a word; his eyes were glued on the prostrate form of Jocky. The policeman understood his fear, and laughed.

"Don't you worry about him. He'll do a stretch all right. I would have given him a harder one than that if I got a swing at him."

His words were quickly justified. The fallen man yowled unintelligibly and moved. With a rapidity born of much practice the officer handcuffed him. There must have been some sense of familiarity in the touch of the steel bracelets, for the recipient of this delicate attention stirred uneasily.

"You knocked him silly," grinned the policeman, "but he will get his wits back in a minute or two. Can you bring him a drink of water? It won't do me any harm, either."

Philip hurried away to comply with this request. His mind was relieved now, and with the backward swing of the mental pendulum came the reflection that the least said of his connection with the case the better.

He filled a small tin at the scullery tap and ran with it to the scene of the capture. The constable was gently shaking his prize and addressing him by name.

"Jocky! Jocky Mason! Pull yourself together. This way for the Old Bailey!"

"If you please," said Philip, "I would be very greatly obliged were my name not mentioned at all with reference to this affair."

The policeman, whose senses were normal again, was instantly impressed by the boy's grand manner. His accent was that of the men of the University Mission. And how many boys of his age would have struck so straight and truly at a critical moment?

"Well, don't you see, that will be rather difficult," was the answer. "It was you who told me where he was, and the man himself knows that without somebody's help I could not have arrested him. There is no need to mince matters. I have you to thank for not being laid here stiff."

Philip said no more. To press his request implied a powerful motive. The stars in their courses must have conspired that day to supply him with excitement.

Mason eagerly gulped the water held to his lips. Then he tried to raise his right hand to his head. Ah! He understood. A flood of oaths began to meander thickly from his mouth.

"That's better," said the constable, encouragingly. "Now, up you get! It's no use, Jocky. I won't let you kick me. You must either go quietly or I will drag you to the street over the stones, and that will hurt."

The man glared dully at his captor. With the apathy of his class he knew when he was beaten, and became submissive in demeanor. Philip, holding his candle aloft, marveled at his own temerity in hitting this giant, oxlike in size and strength.

Mason wobbled his head and craned his neck awkwardly.

"Oo gev me that crack on the nut?" he asked.

"The roof dropped," was the jocular reply.

"Not it. I 'ad yer dahn, Sailor. I was on yer afore ye could use yer stick. Ye was fairly bested until somebody ahted me wiv a welt on the skylight."

"Never mind, Jocky. It'll hurt you to think just now. Come on."

But the ex-convict became sensible of the unwonted light in the deserted house, and slowly turned his head until his glance rested on Philip.

"Why!" he roared, with an imprecation, "that's the bloomin' kid 'oo found the di-monds. I seed 'im a-countin' of 'em. White stones, the paper said, an' bits of iron, too. A trunk full of 'em. 'E 'as one in 'is pocket as big as an egg."

The policeman laughed. So did Philip, shrilly, with ready acceptance of the cue.

"Come along, Jocky, you're wool-gathering. I'll get you a pint of coffee at the station just to show there's no malice," said the constable.

"The water was too strong for him," put in Philip.

The ex-convict began to protest, but he wasted words in swearing. The "Sailor" grasped him by the arm and marched him down the yard, saying over his shoulder:

"Pull that door to. I'll come back for my coat in half an hour."

Philip followed, but in a sea of perplexity. He heard Mason's frantic

75

expostulations to the policeman—what was an extra stripe to the loss of untold wealth—that youngster was richer than Rothschild, the papers said—the small lot he showed in the police court were worth fifty thousand pounds—and he had tons more.

It was all of no avail. Certainly the constable had never heard such queer reasons advanced for stopping an arrest, but Mason was obviously dazed for the time—maundering about the story which everybody talked of. He would change his tune when he learned to whom he was indebted for his capture.

The boy walked behind them mechanically, shading the candle with his hand. He was so absorbed with his tumultuous thoughts that the first indication he received of anything bizarre in his appearance was the giggling of a girl who saw him standing in the arch of the mews carefully shielding the flickering wick.

He blew it out. A clock in the small jeweler's shop opposite showed the time—ten minutes past eleven. In that part of London, a busy hive of men and women of the working class, he had no chance of removing his belongings before the policeman returned.

What would happen if the friendly constable believed Jocky Mason's excited statements? True, Philip had no reason to fear the law. But with exposure might come other troubles. Would anyone advance a claim to his meteor? Mr. Abingdon hinted at such a thing. He paid no rent for his house; he might be turned out instantly—refused permission to remove anything except his few unsalable household goods.

Assuredly he was in an awkward predicament. Of course, there was a chance that the policeman would continue to laugh at the convict's folly. If he did not, there would certainly be complications. Could he avoid them by any means? Where was there a safe hiding place for his diamonds until next day? Would mother inspire him again as she had not failed to do during so many strange events? Would her spirit guide his footsteps across this new quicksand on whose verge he hesitated?

A few doors to the left was O'Brien's shop. The old man crept into sight, staggering under the weight of a shutter. Good gracious! Why had he not thought of this ally sooner? Some precious minutes were wasted already.

"Arrah, Phil, phwat in the worruld—"

"Wait just the least bit, Mr. O'Brien. I have some portmanteaux that I want to store for the night. Do let me put them at the back of your shop. My place is not very safe, you know."

"Sure, boy, that's a shmall thing to ax. Bring 'em, an' welcome."

With the speed of a deer Philip dived into the mews. He carried the two lesser bags without extraordinary difficulty, and deposited them behind O'Brien's counter. The third was almost too much for him, as the weight was all in one hand. But he got it there, breathless with the exertion.

He had to open the fourth and tear out the stuffing of paper. When filled with the packages taken from the fifth it was beyond his power to lift it. So he dragged it bodily along the mews and into the shop.

A passer-by offered to help him.

"No, thanks," he managed to say, though the effort to speak calmly took away his remaining breath. "I am only taking it to the shop there."

The man glanced at the shop—it was a marine store dealer's—a place where lead and iron and brass found ready sale. He passed on.

"Be the forchun uv war, Phil, where did ye get the iligant leather thrunks, an' phwat's in them?" inquired the astonished pensioner.

The boy bravely called a smile to his aid. "I have a big story to tell you one of these days, Mr. O'Brien, but I have no time to-night. These things will not be in your way until the morning?"

"The divil a bit. If things go on as they are, there'll soon be room enough in the poor ould shop. To think, afther all these years, that a murtherin' thief in the War Office—"

Philip was safe. He rapidly helped his friend to put up the shutters, and rushed back to No. 3. Even yet he was not quite prepared for eventualities. He ran upstairs and gathered a few articles belonging to his mother, articles he never endeavored to sell even when pinched by hunger.

The last dress she wore, her boots, a hat, an album with photographs, some toilet accessories from the tiny dressing table, the coverlet of the bed on which she died—these and kindred mementoes made a very credible bulk in the denuded portmanteau.

He gave one glance at the hole in the back yard as he went to the coal house for a fresh supply of coal. That must remain. It probably would not be seen. In any case it remained inexplicable.

He was stirring the fire when a tap sounded on the door and the policeman entered, followed by an inspector.

Chapter X

A Step Higher

"This is the boy, sir," said the policeman.

"Oh, is that him?" observed the inspector, sticking his thumbs into his belt and gazing at Philip with professional severity.

Philip met their scrutiny without flinching. He leaned against the wall with his hands in his pockets, one fist clinched over the pouchful of gold, the other guarding a diamond bigger than the Koh-i-Noor.

"I am sorry I have only one chair, gentlemen," he said, apologetically.

"That's all right, my lad," said the inspector. "The constable here tells me that you very pluckily helped him to capture a notorious burglar. The man was hiding in this mews, and it seems you first saw him looking in through your window. What were you doing at the time?"

"Packing my portmanteau."

"Oh, packing your portmanteau."

"Yes. That is it."

He stooped and nonchalantly threw it open. His clothes and boots, and some of the other contents, were exposed to view. The inspector laughed.

"Not many diamonds there, Bradley."

"No, sir. I told you Mason was talking rubbish."

"Did he say any more about me being the boy who found the meteor?" asked Philip, with a first-rate attempt at a grin.

"Wouldn't talk of anything else," volunteered P. C. Bradley.

"Judging by the way he dropped when I hit him, I expect he saw stars," said Philip.

"Are you leaving here?" asked the inspector.

"Yes, I must. The company which owns these premises intends to pull them down on the first of next month."

"What is your name?"

"Anson."

"Ah! I think I remember hearing something about your mother's death. Very nice woman, I was told. A lady, too."

"Yes, all that, and more."

"Of course, that accounts for your manners and appearance. Have you found some friends?"

The inspector's glance roved from the serviceable portmanteau to Philip's tidy garments, and it was his business to make rapid deductions.

"Yes, most fortunately."

"Anybody connected with Sharpe & Smith?" the constable put in.

"Sharpe & Smith! Who are they?"

"Don't you know? Their young man certainly didn't seem to know much about your movements. He has been here twice looking for you. The first time was, let me see, last Monday, about four o'clock. I was on duty in the main road, and he asked me for some information. We came and looked in, but your door was locked. The man on this beat this afternoon told me that the same clerk was making further inquiries to-day, so as soon as I came on night duty I strolled into the mews to find out if you were at home. That is how I happened to see you."

He turned toward the inspector.

"He was packing his bag at the moment, sir, and Mason had evidently been scared from the window by my footsteps in the arch."

The inspector pursed out his under lip.

"The whole thing is perfectly clear," he said. "Boy, have you got a watch?"

"No," said Philip, surprised by this odd question.

"Bradley, he hasn't got a watch," observed the inspector. He again addressed Philip.

"Where are you going to-morrow?"

"I am not quite sure, but my address will be known to Mrs. Wrigley, the James Street Laundry, Shepherd's Bush."

"Ah! The constable says you do not wish to be mixed up in the arrest of Mason. There is no need for you to appear in court, but—er—in such cases as yours, the—er—police like to show their—er—appreciation of your services. That is so, Bradley, isn't it?"

"Yes, sir. If it hadn't been for him, I shouldn't be here now. Jocky had me fairly cornered."

"You had no time to summon assistance?"

"I barely heard he was here, before the window was smashed, and I knew he was trying to get out the other way. You heard him, Anson?"

Philip looked the policeman squarely in the eyes.

"You had just taken off your greatcoat when the glass cracked," he said.

Police Constable Bradley stooped to pick up his coat. He did not wish this portion of the night's proceedings to be described too minutely. In moving the garment he disturbed the packet of letters. Instantly Philip recalled the names of the solicitors mentioned by the constable.

"You said that a clerk from Messrs. Sharpe & Smith called here twice?" he asked.

"Yes."

He picked out one of the letters, opened it, and made certain of his facts before he cried, angrily:

79

"Then I want to have nothing whatever to do with them. They treated my mother shamefully."

The inspector had sharp eyes.

"What is the date of that letter?" he inquired.

"January 18th of this year."

"And what are those—pawn tickets?"

"Yes, some of my mother's jewelry and dresses. Her wedding ring was the last to go. Most of them are out of date, but I intend to—I will try to save some of them, especially her wedding ring."

Jocky Mason's romance was now dissipated into thin air. The contents of the portmanteau, the squalid appearance of the house, the date of the solicitor's letter, the bundle of pawn tickets, offered conclusive evidence to the inspector's matter-of-fact mind that the ex-convict's story was the effect of a truncheon rapidly applied to a brain excited by the newspaper comments on a sensational yarn about some boy who had found a parcel of diamonds.

This youngster had not been favored by any such extraordinary piece of luck. Simple chance had led him to put the police on the track of a much-wanted scoundrel, and he had very bravely prevented a member of the force from being badly worsted in the ensuing encounter.

A subscription would be made among the officers and men of the division, and they would give him a silver watch, with a suitable inscription.

The inspector noted the address given by Philip. It was on the tip of his tongue to ask his Christian name, when the constable suggested that they should examine the stable in which Mason had hidden.

They went up the mews. Philip locked his door, extinguished the candle, and lay down on the mattress, fully dressed, with his newly bought rug for covering.

He was so utterly tired, so exhausted physically and mentally by the sturm und drang of this eventful day, that he was sound asleep when the two men returned.

They saw him through the window.

"He's a fine lad," said the inspector, thoughtfully. "I wonder what he is going to make of himself. We might have asked him who his friends were, but they are not badly off, or he couldn't have got that bag and his new clothes. What on earth caused Mason to connect him with that diamond story?"

"It's hard to say," observed the constable.

"I will look round and have a chat with him in the morning. Poor, little chap! He's sleeping like a top now."

The inspector called at No. 3, Johnson's Mews, soon after ten next morning, but the door was locked and the bird flown. He spoke to

Mason after that worthy was remanded for a week, but a night's painful seclusion had sealed the burglar's lips. He vowed, with fearful emphasis, to "get even" with the kid who "ahted" him, for the policeman's evidence had revealed the truth concerning the arrest. But not another word would Mason say about the diamonds, and for a little while the inspector placed his overnight revelations in the category of myths familiar to the police in their daily dealings with criminals.

Philip awoke shortly before seven.

He was cold and stiff. The weather was chilly, and there was no ardent meteor in the back yard to keep the temperature of the house at a grateful point during the night.

But his active, young frame quickly dissipated the effects of a deep sleep on a draughty floor. He washed his face and hands at the sink in the scullery, and his next thought was for breakfast, a proof, if proof were needed, that he arose refreshed in mind and body.

In the Mile End Road there are plenty of early morning restaurants. At one of them he made a substantial meal, and, on his return to the mews, he lost not a moment in carrying out a systematic search through all parts of the house and yard for any traces of the meteor which might have escaped his ken in the darkness.

Amidst the earth and broken stones of the excavation there were a few fragments of ore and some atomic specimens of the diamantiferous material—not sufficient, all told, to fill the palm of his hand. But he gathered them for obvious reasons, and then devoted five vigorous minutes with O'Brien's spade to the task of filling up the deep hole itself.

By lowering the flagstones and breaking the earth beneath, he soon gave the small yard an appearance of chaos which might certainly puzzle people, but which would afford no possible clew to the nature of the disturbing element.

At best they might imagine that the dread evidence of some weird crime lay in the broken area. If so, they could dig until they were tired. But, indeed, he was now guarding against a most unlikely hypothesis. The probability was that Johnson's Mews would soon cease to exist and become almost as fabulous as the Island of Atlantis.

Moreover, he had a project dimly outlined in his mind which might become definite if all went well with him that day. Then the ownership of No. 3, Johnson's Mews, would cease to trouble him, for Philip was quite sure the whole power of the law would be invoked to prevent him from dealing with his meteor if once the exact place where it fell became publicly known.

O'Brien's shop was scarcely open before Philip was there with his remaining portmanteau.

"Arrah, Phil, me bhoy, where in the name of goodness are ye gatherin' the bee-utiful, leather thrunks from?" asked the pensioner.

"This is the last one," laughed the boy. "I am off now to find a cab, and you won't see me again until Monday."

"Faix, he's a wonderful lad entirely," commented the old man. "What sort of plundher has he in the bags, at all at all?"

In idle curiosity he lifted the last addition to the pile. It was normal, even light in weight. Then he nodded knowingly.

"A lot of ould duds belongin' to Mrs. Anson, I'll be boun'. Ah, well, the Lord rest her sowl, 'tis she was the fine woman. I wish I had some one as cliver as her to write for me to that thafe of the worruld who thried—"

As there are no signs in the art of literature similar to those which serve the needs of musicians, whereby thoughts can be expressed da capo, like a musical phrase, without risk of wearying the reader, it must be understood that Philip had returned from far-away Fenchurch Street Station with a four-wheeler before O'Brien exhausted the first tirade of the day against the War Office.

With a cunning that amounted to genius, the boy placed the large, light portmanteau and the two small, heavy ones on the roof of the vehicle, where the driver did not notice the least peculiarity in their weight.

The two large, heavy bags he managed to lift into the interior, one of them needing all his resources to carry it from the shop door to the cab. Were he not fresh and untired, he could not have done it. As it was, the effort was a splendid success.

The cabman knew little, and O'Brien less, of the tremendous avoirdupois of this innocent-looking baggage. A long-suffering horse may have had his private views, but he did not express them.

Saying good-by to the pensioner in the shop, Philip took good care that none overheard his direction to the driver. In about three-quarters of an hour he lumbered into Charing Cross Station without a soul in the East End being aware of his destination.

"Where to, sir?" asked a porter who opened the door for him.

"I only want these bags to be taken to the luggage room," said Philip. "You had better get some one to help you with these two. They are very heavy. They contain specimens of iron ore."

The man took a pull at the solid one.

"By gum," he grinned. "You're right. That would surprise anybody who tried to pick it up and run away with it."

"Rather," agreed Philip. "I am glad to say it is not going very far— only to a laboratory for analysis."

He saw his belongings wheeled away on a barrow before he paid the cabman liberally. He only gave the porter sixpence. The man believed that Philip was a clerk in charge of the minerals; he was grateful for even so small a sum.

On leaving the station, with the receipt for his luggage in his pocket, Philip saw the four-wheeler turning into the Strand, on its way back to Fenchurch Street. He smiled. The tie between East and West was severed. No matter what else might happen to it, his meteor had left Johnson's Mews forever.

It was now a few minutes past nine, but he still had a good deal to do before he presented himself at Isaacstein's at eleven.

It was necessary to change his skin once more before the metamorphosis he contemplated was complete. He was acquainted with a large outfitting emporium in Ludgate Hill which exactly suited his requirements, so he rode thither on a 'bus.

Passing Somerset House, he recalled the Jew's remark about getting his letter "stamped." He did not know what stamping meant in a legal sense, but he guessed that it implied the affixing of a seal of some sort. There was no need to hurry over it, he thought.

At eleven o'clock Isaacstein would either keep his word about the five thousand pounds or endeavor to wriggle out of the compact. In either event, Philip had already determined to consult Mr. Abingdon.

He had now in his pocket about thirty-eight pounds. Half an hour later he was wearing a new tweed suit, new hat and new boots; he had acquired a stock of linen and underclothing, an umbrella and an overcoat. Some of these articles, together with his discarded clothes, were packed in two new, leather portmanteaux, on which his initials would be painted by noon, when he would call for them.

He paid twenty-six pounds for the lot, and the man who waited on him tried in vain to tempt him to spend more. Philip knew exactly what he wanted. He adhered to his program. He possessed sufficient genuine luggage and clothing to be presentable anywhere. He had enough money to maintain himself for weeks if necessary. For the rest, another couple of hours would place it beyond doubt whether he was a millionaire or not; for, if Isaacstein failed him, London was big enough and wealthy enough to quickly decide that point.

He entered the Hatton Garden office as the clocks struck the hour.

Some boys of his age might have experienced a malicious delight when the youthful Israelite on guard bounced up with a smirk and a ready:

"Yessir. Vat iss it, sir?"

Not so Philip. He simply asked for Mr. Isaacstein, but he certainly could not help smiling at the expression of utter amazement when his identity dawned on his hearer.

The "Yessir, vil you blease valk in," was very faint, though; the office boy ushered him upstairs as one in a dream, for he had been warned to expect Philip, a Philip in rags, not a smart, young gentleman like a bank clerk.

Isaacstein on this occasion looked and acted the sound man of business he really was.

He awaited Philip in his private office. He seemed to be pleased by the change effected in the boy's outward appearance. There was less of burlesque, less outrage to his feelings, in discussing big sums of money with a person properly attired than with one who wore the garments of a tramp.

"Good-morning," he said, pleasantly. "You are punctual, I am glad to see. Have you been to Somerset House?"

"No," said Philip.

"Why not? If you are going to control a big capital, you must learn business habits or you will lose it, no matter how large it may be."

"Would Somerset House compel you to pay me, Mr. Isaacstein?"

"Not exactly, but the stamping of important documents is a means toward an end, I assure you."

"I will see to it, but I wanted primarily to be certain of one of two things: First, will you pay the five thousand pounds as promised? Second, will you give me a fresh purchase note for my diamonds which will not indicate so definitely that I am the boy concerning whom there has been so much needless publicity during the last few days?"

It was of no avail for Isaacstein to bandy words with Philip. A boy of fifteen who casually introduced such a word as "primarily" into a sentence, and gave a shrewd thrust about "needless publicity" to the person responsible for it, was not to be browbeaten, even in business affairs.

The Jew whipped out a check book.

"Am I to make out a check for five thousand pounds to 'Philip'?" he asked.

"No; to Philip Anson, please."

"Thank you; and now, shall I put any address on the contract note which I will hand you?"

"The Pall Mall Hotel."

Isaacstein with difficulty choked back a comment. The Pall Mall Hotel was the most expensive establishment in London. He tossed the check and another document across the table.

"There you are," he said. "Come with me to my bank. You will excuse the hurry. I have a lot to do before I leave for Amsterdam to-night."

Philip saw that the acknowledgment of his diamonds appeared to be in proper form.

"There is no need at this moment to explain to the bank manager that I am the hero of the police court affair?" he said.

"None whatever. I am lending you the money, and will be paying you a good deal more very soon. That will be sufficient. He may draw his own conclusions, of course."

Philip was now looking at the check.

"Why do you put 'account payee' between these two strokes?" he said.

The Jew explained, and even found time to show him how to cross and indorse such important slips of paper.

Then they walked to the bank, a few doors away. The elderly manager was obviously surprised by the size of the check and the youth of the "payee."

"Oh, this is nothing—a mere flea bite," said Isaacstein. "In a few days he will have ten times the amount to his credit."

"Dear me. Are you realizing property on his behalf?"

"Yes."

"Well, Mr. Anson," said the manager, pleasantly, "I hope you will take care of your money."

"I want you to do that," smiled Philip, who was slightly nonplused by the prefix to his name, heard by him for the first time.

"Oh, if you leave it with me it will be quite safe."

"I cannot leave all, but certainly I will not spend five thousand pounds in a week. I mean to buy some property, though, and—can I have a hundred now?"

"By all means."

Philip wrote his first check and received twenty crisp five-pound notes. Isaacstein stood by, smiling grimly. He had not yet got over the farcical side of this extraordinary occurrence, and he was wondering what the bank manager would have said could he but see Philip as he, Isaacstein, saw him no later than the previous day.

"By the way," said Philip, whose heart was beating a little now, "suppose I wish to give a reference to anybody, will you two gentlemen answer for me?"

"The bank wall always say whether or not your check will be honored to a stated amount. In other respects, Mr. Isaacstein, who brought you here, will serve your purpose admirably—none better in the city of London," replied the banker.

Isaacstein placed both feet together and his head sank between his shoulders. He again reminded Philip of a top. The boy fancied that in a second or two he would begin to spin and purr. The bank manager's statement flattered the little man. It was the sort of thing he understood. Philip privately resolved to make this human top wobble when alone with him in the street again.

"One more question, and I have ended," he said. "Where is the best place to store some valuables?"

"It all depends on their nature. What are they? Plate, jewels, paper"

The Jew's ears were alert now, and the boy smiled faintly.

"Oh," he explained, "I have a very large quantity of rich ore which I wish to lodge in some place where it will be secure and yet easy of access."

"I would recommend you to rent a strong-room in the safe deposit across the street. There you have absolute security and quick access during business hours."

Philip expressed his thanks and quitted the bank with his agent.

In the middle of Holborn, in the midst of the jostling, hurrying occupants of one of the busiest thoroughfares in London, he pulled the giant diamond out of his pocket and suddenly held it under the Jew's nose.

"I told you I had them as big as hen's eggs," he cried. "What do you think of this one?"

Isaacstein glanced at it for one fascinated second. Then he looked around with the stealthy air of a man who fears lest he may be detected in the commission of a terrible crime.

"Are you mad?" he whispered.

"No, not mad," answered Philip, coolly, as he pocketed the gem. "I only wanted you to wobble."

"You wanted me to wobble!"

"Yes. You look so like a big top at times. When do we meet again, Mr. Isaacstein?"

"You are not going away by yourself with that stone in your pocket?"

"Why not! It attracted no special notice from the people as I came here. Nobody can smell it. It won't explode, nor burn a hole in my clothes. It is quite safe, I assure you."

"But let me take it to Amsterdam. Boy! boy! It must weigh four hundred carats!"

"Enough of business for to-day. I have a lot of things to attend to. Shall we say Tuesday?"

"No. Wednesday at eleven. One word. Let me put it in my safe."

"Good-by."

Philip hailed a hansom and drove off to Ludgate Hill, smiling graciously at Isaacstein as he whirled away.

The Jew swayed gently through the crowd until he reached the office, when he dropped limply into his chair. Then he shouted for his confidential clerk.

"Samuel," he murmured, "take charge, please. I'm going home. I want to rest before I start for Harwich. And, Samuel!"

"Yes, sir."

"While I am away you might order another scales. In future we will sell diamonds by the pound, like potatoes."

Chapter XI

In Clover

After picking up his belongings at the outfitter's, two smart Gladstone bags with "P. A." nicely painted on them, Philip stopped his cab at Somerset House. He experienced no difficulty in reaching the proper department for stamping documents, and thus giving them legal significance.

An official glanced at Isaacstein's contract note, and then looked at Philip, evidently regarding him as a relative or youthful secretary of the "Philip Anson, Esq., Pall Mall Hotel," whose name figured on the paper.

"I suppose you only want this to be indicated?" he said.

"Yes," agreed Philip, who had not the remotest idea what he meant.

"Sixpence," was the curt rejoinder.

Philip thought he would be called on to pay many pounds—some amount in the nature of a percentage of the sum named in the agreement. He produced the coin demanded, and made no comment. With stamp or without, he knew that Isaacstein would go straight in this preliminary undertaking. A single glimpse of the monster diamond in his pocket had made that quite certain.

For the rest, he was rapidly making out a plan which should secure his interests effectually. He hoped, before the day was out, to have set on foot arrangements which would free him from all anxiety.

From Somerset House he drove to the Pall Mall Hotel. A gigantic hall porter, looking like a youthful major-general in undress uniform, received him with much ceremony and ushered him to the office, where an urbane clerk instantly classed him as the avant courier of an American family.

"I want a sitting room and bedroom en suite," said Philip.

"One bedroom?" was the surprised query.

"Yes."

"How many of you are there, then?"

"I beg your pardon?"

"Are you alone?"

"Yes."

The clerk fumbled with the register. Precocious juveniles were not unknown to him, but a boy of Philip's type had not hitherto arisen over his horizon.

"A sitting room and a bedroom en suite?" he repeated.

"Exactly."

The clerk was disconcerted by Philip's steady gaze.

"On what floor?" he asked.

"Really," said Philip, "I don't know. Suppose you tell me what accommodation you have. Then I will decide at once."

The official, who was one of the most skilled hotel clerks in London, found it ridiculous to be put out of countenance by a mere boy, who could not be a day older than seventeen, and might be a good deal less. He cast a critical eye on Philip's clothing, and saw that, while it was good, it had not the gloss of Vere de Vere.

He would paralyze him at one fell blow, little dreaming that the other read his glance and knew the exact mental process of his reasoning.

"There is a good suite vacant on the first floor, but it contains a dressing room and bath room," he said, smiling the smile of a very knowing person.

"That sounds all right. I will take it."

"Ah, yes. It costs five pounds a day!"

Each of the six words in that portentous sentence contained a note of admiration that swelled out into a magnificent crescendo. It was a verbal avalanche, beneath which this queer youth should be crushed into the very dust.

"Five pounds a day!" observed Philip, calmly. "I suppose there would be a reduction if taken for a month?"

"Well—er—during the season it is not—er—usual to—"

"Oh, very well. I can easily arrange for a permanency later if I think fit. What number is the suite, please, and will you kindly have my luggage sent there at once?"

The clerk was demoralized, but he managed to say:

"Do you quite understand the terms—thirty-five pounds a week!"

"Yes," said Philip. "Shall I pay you a week in advance? I can give you notes, but it will oblige me if you take a check, as I may want the ready money in my possession."

Receiving a faint indication that, under the circumstances, a check would be esteemed a favor, Philip whipped out his check book, filled in a check to the hotel, and did not forget to cross it "ac. payee."

The clerk watched him with an amazement too acute for words. He produced the register and Philip signed his name. He was given a receipt for the payment on account, and then asked to be shown to his rooms.

A boy smaller, but not younger, than himself—a smart page, who listened to the foregoing with deep interest—asked timidly whether the guest would go by the stairs or use the elevator.

"I will walk," said Philip, who liked to ascertain his bearings.

The palatial nature of the apartments took him by surprise when he reached them. Although far from being the most expensive suite in the hotel, the surroundings were of a nature vastly removed from anything hitherto known to him.

Even the charming house he inhabited as a child in Dieppe contained no such luxury. His portmanteau followed quickly, and a valet entered. Philip's quick ears caught the accent of a Frenchman, and the boy spoke to the man in the language of his country, pure and undefiled by the barbarisms of John Bull.

They were chatting about the weather, which, by the way, ever since the nineteenth of March had been extraordinarily fine, when there was a knock at the door and the manager entered.

The clerk found the situation too much for him. He had appealed to a higher authority.

Even the suave and diplomatic Monsieur Foret could not conceal the astonishment that leaped to his eyes when he saw the occupant of Suite F.

"I think you will find these rooms very comfortable," he said, for lack of aught better. A commissionaire was already on his way to the bank to ask if the check was all right.

"Are you the manager?" asked Philip, who was washing his hands.

"Yes."

"I am glad you called. One of your clerks seemed to be taken aback because a youngster like me engaged an expensive suite. I suppose the proceeding is unusual, but there is no reason why it should create excitement. It need not be commented on, for instance?"

"No, no. Of course not."

"Thank you very much. I have a special reason for wishing to live at this hotel. Indeed, I have given this address for certain important documents. Will you kindly arrange that I may be treated like any ordinary person?"

"I hope the clerk was not rude to you?"

"Not in the least. I am only anxious to prevent special notice being taken of me. You see, if others get to know I am living here alone, I will be pointed out as a curiosity, and that will not be pleasant."

The request was eminently reasonable. The manager assured him that strict orders would be given on the point instantly, though he was quite certain, in his own mind, that inquiry would soon be made for this remarkable youth, perhaps by the police.

"You can leave us," said Philip to the valet in French.

Now the chance use of that language, no less than his perfect accent, went a long way toward removing the manager's suspicions. A boy who was so well educated must be quite out of the common. Perhaps some eccentric parent or guardian encouraged him to act independently thus early in life. He might be the son of a rich man coming to London for a special course of study. The name, Anson, was an aristocratic one. But his clothes—they were odd. Good enough, but not the right thing.

"Will you oblige me by recommending a good tailor?" said Philip. "I need a complete outfit of wearing apparel, and it will save me a lot of trouble if somebody will tell me exactly what to buy and where to buy it."

His uncanny trick of thought reading disconcerted the manager greatly. Undoubtedly the boy was a puzzle. Never had this experienced man of the world met anyone more self-possessed, more direct, and yet, with it all, exceedingly polite.

"I take it that you want the best?" he inquired, pleasantly.

"Yes."

"Are you lunching in the hotel?"

"I would like something sent here, if you please, and, there again, your advice will be most gratefully accepted."

The manager felt that a generation was growing up of which he knew nothing, but he simply answered:

"I will see to it. Do you—er—take wine?"

Philip laughed, that pleasant whole-souled laugh of his which instantly secured him friends.

"Not yet, Monsieur—"

"Foret is my name."

"Well, Monsieur Foret, I am far too young as yet for either wine or tobacco. I promised my mother I would touch neither until I am twenty-one, and I will keep my word. I think I would like some café au lait."

"I understand. Your déjeuner will be sent up in ten minutes. By the time you have finished, I will have people here from two or three establishments who will meet all your requirements in the shape of clothes and the rest."

An hour's talk and the payment of checks on account worked wonders. Before many days had passed, Philip was amply provided with raiment. His presence in the hotel, too, attracted no comment whatever. People who saw him coming or going, instantly assumed that he was staying with his people, while the manager took care that gossip among the employees was promptly stopped.

As for the ragged youth with the diamonds, he was forgotten, apparently. The newspapers dropped him, believing, indeed, that Isaacstein had worked some ingenious advertising dodge on his own account, and Messrs. Sharpe & Smith never dreamed of looking for the lost Philip Anson, the derelict from Johnson's Mews, in the Pall Mall Hotel, the most luxurious and expensive establishment in London.

That afternoon, Philip visited the Safe Deposit Company. He had little difficulty, of course, in securing a small strong-room. He encountered the wonted surprise at his youth, but the excellent argument of a banking account and the payment of a year's rent in advance soon cleared the air.

He transferred four of his portmanteaux to this secure environment—the fifth was sent to his hotel. When the light failed, he drove to the East End, and made a round of pawnbrokers' shops. Although some of the tickets were time-expired, he recovered nearly all his mother's belongings, excepting her watch.

The odd coincidence recalled the inspector's implied promise that he should receive one as a recognition of his gallantry.

How remote, how far removed from each other, the main events in his life seemed to be at this eventful epoch. As he went westward in a hansom, he could hardly bring himself to believe that barely twenty-four hours had elapsed since he traveled to the Mile End Road in company with Mrs. Wrigley.

And the curious thing was that he felt in no sense awed by the possession of thousands of pounds and the tenancy of palatial chambers in a great hotel. His career had been too checkered, its recent developments too stupendous, to cause him any undue emotion. Existence, for the hour, was a species of well-ordered dream, in which imagination was untrammeled save by the need to exercise his wits in order to keep the phantasy within the bounds, not of his own brain, but of other men's.

At the hotel he found the French valet setting forth a shirt. The man explained that he required a spare set of studs and links.

This reminded Philip that there was still a good deal of shopping to be done. He was about to leave the room for the purpose, when the valet said:

"Another portmanteau has arrived for monsieur. Will you be pleased to unlock it?"

"No," said Philip. "It must remain untouched." He smiled at the thought of the sensation his tattered rags and worn boots would make in that place. Yet, just a week ago, he passed through the street outside, bound in the pitiless rain for Johnson's Mews, and bent on suicide.

He walked into Regent Street and made a number of purchases, not forgetting some books. A double silver-mounted photograph stand caught his eye. It would hold the two best pictures he possessed of his father and mother, so he bought it. He also acquired a dispatch box in which he could store his valuables, both jewelry and documents, for he had quite a number of receipts, letters and other things to safeguard now, and he did not wish servants' prying eyes to examine everything belonging to him.

When alone in his room, he secured the album and locked that special portmanteau again, after stowing therein the letters found beneath Mrs. Anson's pillow. Soon his mother's dear face smiled at him from a beautiful border of filigree silver. The sight was pleasant to him, soothing to his full mind. In her eyes was a message of faith, of trust, of absolute confidence in the future.

It was strange that he thought so little of his father at this time, but the truth was that his childhood was passed so much in his mother's company, and they were so inseparable during the last two years, that memories of his father were shadowy.

Yet the physiognomist would have seen that the boy owed a great deal of his strength of character and well-knit frame to the handsome, stalwart man whose name he bore.

Philip loved his mother on the compensating principle that persons of opposite natures often have an overpowering affinity for each other. He resembled her neither in features nor in the more subtle traits of character.

After a dinner the excellence of which was in nowise diminished by lack of appreciation on his part, he undertook a pilgrimage of curiosity to which he had previously determined to devote the evening.

He wondered unceasingly to whom he was indebted for the good meals he had enjoyed in prison. Now he would endeavor to find out.

A hansom took him to Holloway, but the first efforts of the driver failed to discover the whereabouts of the "Royal Star Hotel."

At last Philip recollected the warder's added direction—"opposite."

He dismissed the cab and walked to the prison entrance. Directly in front he saw a small restaurant called the "Star." Its titular embellishments were due to the warder's gift of humor.

He entered. A woman was knitting at a cash desk.

"Until yesterday," he said, "you sent food regularly to a boy named Anson, who was confined in the prison—"

"Yes," interrupted the lady. "I on'y heard this mornin' that he was let out."

"Would you mind telling me who paid the bill? I suppose it was paid?"

"Well, as a matter of fact, it was overpaid," was the reply. "You see, the pore lad was remanded for a week, an' Mr. Judd, a man 'oo lives in the Farringdon Road, kem 'ere an' arranged for 'is week's board. Hav' ye heard wot 'appened to 'im?"

Philip's heart was in his mouth, but he managed to answer that the boy was all right; there was no charge against him. Then he escaped into the street. The one man he had forgotten was his greengrocer friend, who had indeed acted the part of the Good Samaritan.

There was some excuse for this, but the boy's abounding good nature would admit of none. He hastened to Farringdon Road with the utmost speed, and found his fat friend putting up the shutters of his shop.

The restaurant next door was open. Philip approached quietly.

"Good-evening, Mr. Judd," he said, holding out his hand.

"Good-evenin', sir," said the greengrocer, his eyes revealing not the remotest idea of the identity of the smart, young gentleman who addressed him so familiarly.

"Don't you know me, Mr. Judd?"

"Well, sir, I can't exactly bring to min'—"

"I suppose the good fare you provided for me at Holloway has so altered my appearance that you fail to recognize me again?"

"Wot! Ye don't mean to s'y—'Ere, Eliza, this young gent is the lad I was a-tellin' you of. Remanded till Saturday, you was. I saw in the piper last night. Well, there, I'm done!"

By this time Philip was inside the shop, and the stout greengrocer and his equally stout spouse were gazing open-mouthed at this well-dressed youth who had supplanted the thin tatterdemalion so much discussed by them and their neighbors.

Judd and the restaurant keeper were the only men in the locality who could claim actual acquaintance with the boy whose strange proceedings as reported by the newspapers made London gape. Indeed, both men had been interviewed by police and reporters many times. They were living links with the marvelous, a pedestal of common stone for an aërial phantasy.

And now, here he was, back again, dressed like a young gentleman, and hailing Judd as a valued friend. No wonder the greengrocer lost his breath and his power of speech.

But Philip was smiling at him and talking.

"You were the one man out of many, Mr. Judd, who believed in me, and even stuck up for me when you saw me led through the street by a policeman to be imprisoned on a false charge. I did not know until an hour ago that I was indebted to you for an abundance of excellent food while I was remanded in prison. I will not offer to refund you the money you spent. My gratitude will take another form, which you will learn in a few days. But I do want to pay you the ninepence I borrowed. Would you mind asking the proprietor of the restaurant to step in here for a moment? Don't say I am present. I wish to avoid a crowd, you know."

Judd had time to collect his scattered ideas during this long speech.

"Blow the ninepence!" he cried. "Wot's ninepence for the treat I've 'ad? People I never set eyes on in my life afore kem 'ere an' bought cabbiges, or taters, or mebbe a few plums, an' then they'd stawt: 'Mr. Judd, wasn't it you as stood a dinner to the Boy King of Diamonds?' That's wot they christened yer, sir. Or it's: 'Mr. Judd, cahn't yer tell us w'ere that young Morland lives? Sure-ly yer know summat abaht 'im or yer wouldn't hev paid 'is bill.' Oh, it 'as bin a beano. Hasn't it, Eliza?"

"But we never let on a word," put in Mrs. Judd. "We was close as wax. We told none of 'em as how Mr. Judd went to 'Olloway that night, did we, Willyum?"

"Not us. Ye see, I took a fancy to ye. If ahr little Johnnie 'ad lived 'e'd ha' bin just your ige. Fifteen, aren't ye?"

At last Philip got him persuaded to summon his neighbor. Judd did so with an air of mystery that caused the bald-headed restaurateur to believe that a burglar was bottled up in the greengrocer's cellar.

Once inside the shop, however, Mr. Judd's manner changed.

"Wot did I tell yer, Tomkins?" he cried, elatedly. "Wot price me as a judge of karak-ter! 'Ere's Mr. Morland come back to p'y me that ninepence. Eh, Tomkins! 'Oo's right now, old cock?"

Philip solemnly counted out the money, which he handed to his delighted backer.

"There was a bet, too," he said.

"Ra-ther!" roared Judd. "Two bob, w'ich I've pide. Out wi' four bob, Tomkins. Lord lumme, I'll stand treat at the George for this!"

"There's something funny in the kise," growled Tomkins, as he unwillingly produced a couple of florins.

"I was sure you would see the joke at once," said Philip. "Good-by, Mr. Judd. Good-by, ma'am. You will hear from me without fail within a fortnight."

He was gone before they realized his intention. They saw him skip rapidly up the steps leading into Holborn, and London had swallowed him forever so far as they were concerned.

Ten days later a firm of solicitors wrote to the greengrocer to inform him that a client of theirs had acquired the freehold of his house and shop, which property, during the life of either himself or his wife, would be tenantable free of rent, rates or taxes.

So Mr. Judd's investment of ninepence, plus the amount expended on eatables at the Royal Star Hotel, secured to him and his wife an annual revenue of one hundred and seventy-five pounds.

And Tomkins never heard the last of it.

Chapter XII

The Close of One Epoch

Before retiring to rest, Philip ascertained Mr. Abingdon's London address, and wrote asking for an appointment the following evening.

He also interviewed the manager.

"I want the help of a thoroughly reliable solicitor," he said. "I wish to purchase some property—not valuable property, but of importance to me. Can you give me the address of some one known to you?"

M. Foret named a reputable firm in the locality.

"They may refer to you," added Philip. "Of course, I do not ask you to say more than that I am staying here, but the point is, I do not wish you to mention my age."

"Will you not see them, then?"

"No. I will endeavor to conduct the whole business by post."

The manager laughed.

"You certainly are the coolest young gentleman I ever met. However, Mr. Anson, it may please you to know that your bank gave you the best of recommendations. I will say so to anybody."

So Philip first drafted and then copied the following letter:

"Dear Sirs: M. Foret, of this hotel, has given me your names as a firm likely to transact certain negotiations for me. I want to purchase a small property in the Mile End Road, known as Johnson's Mews; also a shop near the entrance to the mews, tenanted by a marine-store dealer named O'Brien. The mews is owned by the Cardiff and Havre Coal Company, Ltd. I do not know who owns the shop. I wish to acquire these properties for a philanthropic purpose, but I am most desirous that my name should not figure in the transaction. I propose, therefore, when you have ascertained the price, which should be at the earliest possible moment, to pay to your credit the requisite amount. You can have the properties transferred to any nominee you choose, and again transferred to me. Kindly add your costs, etc., to the purchase price. My movements are somewhat uncertain, so please send all communications by letter. It will be an obligation, and lead to future business, if you attend to this matter to-morrow morning. Yours faithfully,

"Philip Anson."

He did not compose this letter without considerable trouble. The "philanthropic purpose" he had already decided upon, but he thought it was rather clever to refer to the possibilities of "future business."

95

As for the double transfer, he distinctly remembered copying letters dealing with several such transactions at the time of the coal company's conversion into a limited liability concern.

He was early to bed, and his rest was not disturbed by dreams. He rose long before the ordinary residents. Deferring his breakfast, he walked to Fleet Street and purchased copies of morning and evening papers for the whole of the week.

He could thus enjoy the rare luxury of seeing himself as others saw him. He read the perfervid descriptions of the scene in court, and found himself variously described as "pert," "masterful," "imperious," "highly intelligent," "endowed with a thin veneer of education," and "affected."

Philip could afford to laugh at the unfavorable epithets. Up to the age of thirteen, he had been trained in a first-rate lycée, and his work was supervised by his mother, a woman of very great culture. He spoke French as well as English, and spoke both admirably. He knew some Greek and Latin, was well advanced in arithmetic, and had a special penchant for history and geography.

It was in the glowing articles which appeared during his imprisonment that he took the keenest interest. Oddly enough, one ingenious correspondent blundered onto a clew. Gifted with an analytical mind, he had reasoned that the diamond-laden meteor fell during the extraordinary storm of the nineteenth, and the Meteorological Department in Victoria Street helped him by describing the center of the disturbance as situated somewhat to the east of the London Hospital.

This writer had actually interviewed a member of the staff of that institution who amused himself by noting barometrical vagaries. His instrument recorded an extraordinary increase of pressure soon after ten o'clock on the night of the storm.

"Alas!" added the scribe, "it did not indicate where the meteor fell, and not a policeman, 'bus driver or railway official can be found who observed anything beyond a phenomenal electrical display and a violent downpour of rain."

That was too close to be pleasant, and Philip was glad to hear from M. Foret that the solicitors, after telephoning to ask for some particulars concerning Mr. Anson, were giving prompt attention to his instructions.

"What did you tell them?" asked Philip.

"I said that you impressed me as the kind of young gentleman who would pay well for services given unsparingly."

"Did that satisfy them?"

"Perfectly. Such clients do not abound in these hard times."

Three hours later, a letter came for "Philip Anson, Esq.," by hand. It was from the solicitors, and read:

"We are in receipt of your esteemed instructions. Although Saturday is a day on which it is difficult to do business, we lost no time in inspecting the premises in the Mile End Road, accompanied by a surveyor. We found that the mews stand approximately on an area of three thousand two hundred superficial feet, while the shop tenanted by O'Brien has a frontage on the main road of eighteen feet, with a probable depth of thirty or thirty-five feet. The owner of this shop is a resident in the neighborhood, and he will accept four hundred and fifty pounds for the freehold.

"We were fortunate in finding the managing director of the Cardiff and Havre Coal Company, Ltd., at his office. Although the company require the mews for the purpose of a depot, they are not unwilling to sell, with a stipulation that the premises shall not be used by any competing company during a period of twenty years from the date of transfer. We stated that the site was required for a philanthropic purpose, but the latter stipulation is insisted on. The price asked is two thousand two hundred pounds, which we consider excessive, there being a very inadequate approach. Moreover, we wish to point out that O'Brien's shop does not adjoin the mews, and it would be necessary to purchase two other houses to make the entire property a compact one.

"However, adhering to the letter of your instructions, we have pleasure in informing you that the two properties can be acquired with very little delay, for two thousand six hundred and fifty pounds. The legal and other charges will not exceed one hundred and fifty pounds. We trust, etc."

Philip immediately wrote:

"I am greatly obliged by your promptitude in the matter of Johnson's Mews and the shop. I inclose check herewith for two thousand eight hundred pounds. The purchase of the other houses can stand over for a few days."

This he dispatched by special messenger, and in a few minutes he held a formal receipt.

A telegram came for him. It was from Mr. Abingdon.

"Can see you after six at my house."

Then Philip enjoyed his first real breathing space during hours of daylight. He went by train to the cemetery in which his mother was buried, carrying with him a beautiful wreath.

It was a remarkable fact that this was the first visit he had paid to her grave. During the days of misery and partial madness which followed her death he never lost the delusion that her spirit abided with him in the poor dwelling they called "home."

Hence, the narrow resting place beneath the green turf in no way

97

appealed to him. But now, that a succession of extraordinary external events had restored the balance of his mind, he realized that she was really dead and buried; that what he revered as her spirit was in truth a fragrant memory; that he would be nearest to her mortal remains when standing in the remote corner of the burial ground allotted to the poorest of the poor—those removed by one degree from pauperdom and a parish grave.

It happened, by mere chance, that since Mrs. Anson's funeral no one had been interred on one side of the small space purchased for her. There were three vacant plots here, and a surprised official told Philip there would be no difficulty in acquiring these for the purpose of erecting a suitable monument.

The boy filled in the necessary forms there and then. It was some consolation to know that he could perpetuate her memory in this way, though he had formulated another project which should keep her name revered through the ages.

On the site of Johnson's Mews should arise the Mary Anson Home for Destitute Boys. He would build a place where those who were willing to work and learn would be given a chance, and not driven, starving and desperate, to pick up an existence in the gutter.

He was too young to devise all the details of such a splendid institution, but he had got the idea and would possess the money. He would leave the practical part of the undertaking to older heads.

The one essential feature was that generations yet unborn should learn to love and honor the name of Mary Anson. Provided that were achieved, he knew the work would be successful.

Soon after leaving the cemetery he came face to face with Bradley, the policeman, who was in plain clothes, and walking with a lady, obviously Mrs. Bradley, judging by the matronly manner in which she wheeled a perambulator containing a chubby infant.

"Well, I'm blowed!" cried the policeman, "who would have thought of meeting you! I looked in at the mews last night, but you had gone. Some one is looking after you pretty well; eh?"

He cast a patronizing eye over Philip's garments, which were, of course, considerably smarter in appearance than those in which the constable had seen him on Thursday evening.

"Yes," said Philip. "I am in good hands now."

"They haven't given you a watch?" This anxiously.

"No. I am watchless."

"That's right. You'll have one soon. The inspector has your address. By the way, he wants to know your Christian name."

"Philip."

"Thanks. I won't forget."

Philip raised his hat and took the quickest route westward. He did not count on being recognized so easily.

Mr. Abingdon received him with some degree of reserve. The

magistrate could not understand the receipt of a letter bearing the address of the Pall Mall Hotel, a place where he had been entertained at dinner occasionally by one of his wealthy friends, but which was far removed from the limit imposed on the pocket of any man whose resources depended on the exercise of an ordinary profession.

But Philip still figured in his mind as a ragged urchin. Not even the skilled police magistrate could picture him as the actual owner of millions of pounds worth of portable property. Hence, the boy's appearance now told in his favor. Cursory impressions soon yielded to positive bewilderment when Philip began to relate his story faithfully from beginning to end, neither exaggerating nor suppressing any salient detail save the actual locality where his astounding adventures found their center and genesis.

Mr. Abingdon did not doubt for one moment that the boy was telling the truth. The romance of his narrative was far beyond fiction.

Philip himself grew enthusiastic as he went on. His brown eyes blazed again with the memory of his wrath and shame at the arrest. He told the magistrate exactly how the proceedings in court had affected him, and gave a vivid picture of his bargaining with Isaacstein, the packing of the diamonds, the fight between the policeman and a burglar, his interviews with all sorts and conditions of men, and the ruses he had adopted to preserve his secret.

At last he came to the transaction which secured for him the ownership of the mews itself. He read copies of his letters to the solicitors, and their replies, and then, of course, the magistrate knew where the meteor had fallen.

"That is a very clever move on your part," he said, smiling. "It invests you with all the rights and usages of that particular piece of earth, and effectually stops anyone from disputing your possession of the meteor. How did you come to think of it?"

"You put the idea into my mind, sir," said Philip, modestly.

"I? In what manner?"

"You hinted, at our last meeting, that some one might lay claim to my diamonds on the ground that they had fallen on their property. I do not intend that anyone living, except yourself, shall ever know the history of my meteor, but I thought it best to buy the place outright in the first instance, and then devote it to a charity which I intend to found in memory of my mother."

Mr. Abingdon smiled again.

"Your confidence is very flattering," he said. "I suppose you took up your quarters at the Pall Mall Hotel in order to impress people with your importance and secure instant compliance with your wishes?"

"That was my motive, sir."

"Then, my young millionaire, in what way do you wish me to serve you? Of course, you have not sought this interview and told me your story so unreservedly without an ulterior object in view? You see, I am beginning to understand you already a little better than when we first met."

Philip did not reply immediately. He did not want to risk a refusal, and he was not yet quite sure that the magistrate fully comprehended the extent of the fortune which had been showered on him from nature's own mint.

"When Mr. Isaacstein returns from Amsterdam he will pay me something like forty thousand pounds," he said.

"Yes. It would seem so from the receipt you have shown me."

"That will be determined on Wednesday next at the latest."

"Yes."

"If the money is forthcoming it will be proof positive that my diamonds are of good quality, and, as I picked up these dirty stones quite promiscuously, it follows that the others are of the same standard?"

"Undoubtedly."

"Well, Mr. Abingdon, I can form no estimate of their collective value, but they must be worth many millions. According to Mr. Isaacstein's views, I will be able to command a revenue of between a quarter and half a million sterling per annum."

"It is marvelous, perfectly appalling in some senses," cried the perturbed lawyer, throwing up his hands in the extremity of his amazement.

"You are right, sir. I am only a boy, and the thing is beyond my powers. I can see quite clearly that while I ought to be at college obtaining a proper education, I will be worrying about the care of great sums of money. I do not know anything about investments. How should I? Isaacstein is a Jew, and he will probably endeavor very soon to get the better of me in the necessary business transactions. How can I stop him? I have no older relatives, no friends whom I can trust. For some reason, I do feel that I can have faith in you. Will you take charge of my affairs, advise me during the next few years, tell me how to act as my mother would have told me—in a word, become my guardian?"

For a little while Mr. Abingdon was silent. When words came he could only gasp:

"You certainly are the most extraordinary boy I have ever encountered."

Then Philip laughed merrily.

"I don't think, sir, that I am so much an extraordinary boy as a boy who has been pitchforked into an extraordinary position. I hope most sincerely that you will do what I ask. If I may say so without presumption, it will be a good thing for you. I suppose a man who looks after millions of money is entitled to a vastly bigger income than one who sits hours in a police court dealing with offenses against the law."

"Such has certainly been my experience," said the magistrate, who appreciated the nice manner in which Philip hinted at a good, fat salary for controlling the estate of the King of Diamonds.

"Then you agree," cried Philip, joyously.

"Not so fast, my youthful friend. Even a police magistrate must bow to his wife. Mrs. Abingdon would never forgive me if I took such an important step without consulting her. Will you remain to dinner?"

Then Philip knew that he had gained his point. Nothing was said before the servants, but when they were cozily ensconced in the library before a pleasant fire, he was asked to relate again his entrancing history for Mrs. Abingdon's benefit.

That good lady was overwhelmed. She, like everybody else, had read the newspapers, and, of course, had the additional benefit of her husband's views on the subject of the unkempt boy with his small parcel of valuable gems.

But the presence of Philip under their roof, the glamour of the tale as it fell from his lips, cast a spell over her. She was a kindly soul, too, and tears gathered in her eyes at some portions of the recital.

"What a pity it is that your mother died," she murmured, when he had ended.

The words endeared her to Philip instantly. A worldly, grasping woman would have thought of nothing save the vista of wealth opened up for her husband and herself. Not so Mrs. Abingdon. If anything, she was somewhat afraid of the responsibilities proposed to be undertaken by her spouse, to whom she was devoted.

The magistrate did not promise definitely that night to accept the position offered to him. He would think over the matter. He could retire on a pension at any time. This he would now do without delay, and Philip could certainly count on his friendship and advice, while his house would always be open to him.

Meanwhile, he would give one word of advice—intrust no human being with the power to sign any binding document without his— Philip's—consent. Then it would be difficult for anyone to deal unscrupulously with him.

The boy went away at a late hour. He left behind him an exceedingly perplexed couple, but he felt that when Mr. Abingdon had time to assimilate the facts, and realize the great scope of the work before him, there was little doubt he would gladly associate himself with it.

At the hotel a telegram awaited him:

"Have realized for fifty-two thousand. Returning Monday. Isaacstein."

Here was the final proof, if proof were wanting. Philip was a millionaire many times over.

Chapter XIII

After Long Years

A tall, strongly built man, aged about forty-five, but looking older, by reason of his grizzled hair and a face seamed with hardship—a man whose prominent eyes imparted an air of alert intelligence to an otherwise heavy and brutal countenance, disfigured by a broken nose, stood on the north side of the Mile End Road and looked fixedly across the street at a fine building which dwarfed the mean houses on either hand.

He had no need to ask what it was. Carved in stone over the handsome arch which led to an interior covered court was its title— "The Mary Anson Home for Destitute Boys." A date followed, a date ten years old.

The observer was puzzled. He gazed up and down the wide thoroughfare with the manner of one who asked himself:

"Now, why was that built there?"

A policeman strolled leisurely along the pavement, but to him the man addressed no question. Apparently unconscious of the constable's observant glance, he still continued to scrutinize the great pile of brick and stone which thrust its splendid campanile into the warm sunshine of an April day.

Beneath the name was an inscription:

"These are they which passed through great tribulation."

A queer smile did not improve the man's expression as he read the text.

"Tribulation! That's it," he continued. "I've had ten years of it. And it started somewhere about the end of that fine entrance, too. I wonder where Sailor is, and that boy. He's a man now, mebbe twenty-six or so, if he's alive. Oh, I hope he's alive! I hope he's rich and healthy and engaged or married to a nice, young woman. If I've managed to live in hell for ten long years, a youngster like him should be able to pull through with youth and strength and a bag full of diamonds."

Without turning his head, he became aware that the policeman had halted at some little distance.

"Of course, I've got the mark on me," said the man, savagely, to himself. "He's spotted me, all right. Well, I'll let him see I don't care for him or any of his breed. I never did care, and it's too late to begin now."

He crossed the road, passed between two fine, iron gates standing hospitably open, and paused at the door of the porter's lodge, where a stalwart commissionaire met him.

"Have you called to see one of the boys?" said the official, cheerfully.

"No. I'm a stranger. It's a good many years since I was in these parts before. In those days there used to be a mews here, and some warehouses at the back, with a few old shops—"

"Oh, I expect so, but that is long before my time. The Mary Anson Home was founded ten years ago, and it took two years to build. It's one of the finest charities in London. Would you like to look round?"

"Is that allowed?"

"Certainly. Everybody is welcome. If you go in by that side door, there, you'll find an old man who has nothing else to do but take visitors to the chief departments. Bless your heart, we lose half our boarders that way. People come here, see the excellences of the training we give, and offer situations to boys who are old enough."

The man appeared to be surprised by the commissionaire's affability. He did not know that civility and kindness were essential there if any employee would retain an excellent post.

He passed on, measuring the tessellated court with a backward sweep of the eye. In the sunlit street beyond the arch stood the policeman. The visitor grinned again, an unamiable and sulky grin, and vanished.

The policeman crossed over.

"What is that chap after?" he inquired.

"Nothing special," was the answer. "Last time he was here the place was a mews, he said."

"Unless I am greatly mistaken, he has a ticket in his pocket."

"You don't say! Do you know him?"

"No. I'll look him up in the album in the station when I go off duty."

"Well, he can't do any harm here. O'Brien takes visitors over a regular round, and, in any case, the man seemed to be honest enough in his curiosity."

"You never can tell. They're up to all sorts of dodges."

"Thanks very much. I'll ring for O'Brien's relief and tell him to keep an eye on them, as the old man is blind as a bat."

Meanwhile the stranger was being conducted up a wide staircase by a somewhat tottering guide, who wore on the breast of his uniform the Crimean and Indian Mutiny medals.

As he hobbled in front, he told, with a strong, Irish brogue, the familiar story of the Mary Anson Home—how it fed, lodged and clothed six hundred boys of British parentage born in the Whitechapel district; how it taught them trades and followed their careers with fostering care; how it never refused a meal or a warm sleeping place to any boy, no matter where he came from or what his nationality, provided he satisfied the superintendent that he was really destitute or needed his small capital for trading purposes next day.

103

The great central hall where the six hundred regular inmates ate their meals, the dormitories, the playgrounds, the drill shed and gymnasium, the workshops, the library, the theater, were all pointed out, but the big man with the staring eyes was not interested one jot in any of these things.

"Who was Mary Anson?" he asked, when the well-worn tale was ended, "and how did she come to build such a fine place here?"

"Ah, ye may well ax that," said old O'Brien. "Sure, she didn't build it at all at all. She was a poor widdy livin' alone-st wid one son, Mr. Philip that is now. She was a born lady, but she kem down in the worruld and died, forlorn an' forgotten, in a little shanty in Johnson's Mews, as it was called in those days."

"I remember it well."

"Ye do, eh? Mebbe ye know my ould shop, the marine store near the entrance to the court?"

"Yes."

"Arrah, ye don't tell me so. Me eyes are gettin' wake, an' I can't make out yer face. What's yer name?"

"Oh, I'm afraid we didn't know one another. I can't recall your name, though I recollect the shop well enough. But, if Mrs. Anson died so poor, how was her son able to set this great house on its legs? It must have cost a mint of money."

"Faix, ye're right. Quarter of a million wint afore there was a boy under its roof. And they say it costs fifty thousand pounds a year to keep it goin'. But Mr. Philip would find that and more to delight the sowl of the mother that's dead. Sure it's aisy for him, in a way. Isn't he the Diamond King!"

"The Diamond King! Why is he called that?"

"D'ye mane to say you nivver—Man alive, what part of creation did ye live in that ye didn't hear tell of Mr. Philip Anson, the boy who discovered an extra spishul diamond mine of his own, no one knows where. Sure, now, what's wrong wid ye?"

For the visitor was softly using words which to O'Brien's dull ears sounded very like a string of curses.

"I'm sorry," growled the other, with an effort. "I've been to Africa, an' I get such a spasm now an' then in my liver that I can hardly stand."

"That's no way to cure yourself—profanin' the name of th' Almighty," cried O'Brien.

"No. I'm sorry, I tell you. But about this boy—"

"There's no more to see now, if ye plaze. That's the way out."

O'Brien was deeply offended by the language used beneath a roof hallowed by the name of Mary Anson. The sightseer had to go, and quickly. Another commissionaire, who was observing them from a distance, came up and asked O'Brien what the stranger was talking about.

"Ye nivver heard sich a blaggard," said the old man, indignantly. "I was in the middle of tellin' him about Mr. Philip, when he began to curse like Ould Nick himself."

In the Mile End Road the rawboned person who betrayed such excitement found the policeman awaiting him. He sprang onto a 'bus, and purposely glared at the officer in a manner to attract his attention. When at a safe distance he put his fingers to his nose. The constable smiled.

"I knew I was right," he said. "I don't need to look twice at that sort of customer."

And he entered the Mary Anson Home again to ask the porter what had taken place.

It was an easy matter for Jocky Mason, released from Portland Prison on ticket-of-leave, after serving the major portion of a sentence of fourteen years' penal servitude—the man he assaulted had died, and the ex-convict narrowly escaped being hanged—to ascertain the salient facts of Philip Anson's later career.

It was known to most men. He was biographed briefly in Who's Who and had often supplied material for a column of gossip in the newspapers. Every free library held books containing references to him.

It was quite impossible that the source of his great wealth should remain hidden for all time. In one way and another it leaked out, and he became identified with the ragged youth who created a sensation in the dock of the Clerkenwell Police Station.

But this was years later, and the clever manipulation of Mr. Abingdon, as his estate agent, and of Mr. Isaacstein, as his representative in the diamond trade, completely frustrated all attempts to measure the true extent of the meteor's value.

For now Philip owned a real diamond mine in South Africa; he had a fine estate in Sussex, a house in Park Lane, a superb sea-going yacht, a colliery in Yorkshire, and vast sums invested in land and railways. The latent value of his gems had been converted into money-earning capital.

Mr. Abingdon proved himself to be a very able business man. When the administration of Philip's revenue became too heavy a task for his unaided shoulders, he organized a capital estate office, with well-trained lawyers, engineers and accountants to conduct its various departments, while he kept up an active supervision of the whole until Philip quitted his university, and was old enough to begin to bear some portion of the burden.

They agreed to differ on this important question. Philip was fond of travel and adventure. With great difficulty his "guardian" kept him out of the army, but compromised the matter by allowing the young millionaire to roam about the odd corners of the world in his yacht for eight months of the year, provided he spent four months of the season in London and Sussex attending to affairs.

In this month of April he was living in his town house. In July he would go to Fairfax Hall, in August to Scotland, and a month later would joyfully fly to the Forth, where the Sea Maiden awaited him.

This lady, whose waist measured eighteen feet across and whose length was seventy feet, with a fine spread of canvas and auxiliary steam, was the only siren able to charm him.

He was tall now, and strongly built, with something of the naval officer in his handsome, resolute face and well set-up figure. As a hobby, he had taken out a master mariner's certificate, and he could navigate his own ship in the teeth of an Atlantic gale. He loved to surround himself with friends, mostly Oxford men of his year, but he seldom entertained ladies, either on board the Sea Maiden or in either of his two fine mansions.

He avoided society in its general acceptance, refused all overtures to mix in politics, took a keen delight in using his great wealth to alleviate distress anonymously, and earned a deserved reputation as a "bear" among the few match-making mammas who managed to make his acquaintance.

In other respects, as the boy was so was the man—the same downright character, the same steadfast devotion to his mother's memory, the same relentless adherence to a course already decided on, and the same whole-hearted reciprocity of friendship.

As he stood in his drawing room before dinner on the evening of the day Jocky Mason re-visited the locality, if not the surroundings, of his capture, Philip's strong face wore an unwonted expression of annoyance. He walked to and fro from end to end of the beautiful room, pausing each time he reached the window to gaze out over the park.

A servant, who entered for the purpose of turning on the electric lights and lowering the blinds, was bidden, almost impatiently, to wait until Philip and his guests were at dinner.

A telegram came. Anson opened it and read:

"Was dressing to come to your place when Grainger telegraphed for me to act as substitute Lincoln Quarter Sessions. Must go down at once.

"Fox."

"No answer," he said, adding, to himself:
"That's better. Fox's caustic humor would have worried me to-night. I wish Abingdon would come. I am eager to tell him what has happened."

106

Now, punctuality was one of Mr. Abingdon's many virtues. At half-past seven to the tick his brougham deposited him at the door.

The two met with a cordial greeting that showed the close ties of mutual good fellowship and respect which bound them together.

"Fox won't be here," said Philip. "Grainger has broken down—ill health, I suppose—and wired for him to go to Lincoln."

"Ah, that's a lift for Fox. He is a clever fellow, and if he manages to tell the jury a joke or two he will influence a verdict as unfairly as any man I know."

"Does it not seem to you to be rather an anomaly that justice, which in the abstract is impeccable, too often depends on other issues which have no possible bearing on the merits of the dispute itself?"

"My dear boy, that defect will continue until the crack of doom. Pascal laid it bare in an epigram—'Plaisante justice! qu'une rivière ou une montaigne borne! Vérité au deçà du Pyrénées, erreur au delà!' It all depends on which side the Pyrenees Fox happens to be."

"Unfortunately, I am straddling the water shed at this moment. I have made a very unpleasant discovery, Abingdon, and I am glad we are alone to-night—we can speak freely. Some people named Sharpe & Smith wrote to me yesterday."

"I know them—an old-established firm of solicitors."

"Well, they urged me to give them an appointment on a private matter, and I did so. They began by trying to cross-examine me, but that was an abject failure. Seeing that whatever they had to say must stand on its own legs, they told me an extraordinary story. It appears that at a place called The Hall, Beltham, Devon, lives an elderly baronet, named Sir Philip Morland."

"Morland! Philip Morland!"

"Ah, you remember the name! It was given to a young derelict who once figured in the dock before you on a charge of being in unlawful possession—"

"The matter is not serious, then?"

"It is very serious. The real Philip Morland is my uncle."

"Do you mean to say that you learned this fact for the first time to-day from Sharpe & Smith?"

Philip laughed. By this time they were seated at the table, and their talk depended to a certain extent on the comings and goings of servants. At a dinner en famille, the presence of a ponderous butler and solemn lackeys was dispensed with.

"Oh, you lawyers!" he cried. "That's a nice sort of leading question. But, marvelous as it may seem to you, I must answer 'Yes.' My mother's maiden name was Morland. Her brother was much older than she, and it appears the dear woman married to please herself, thereby mortally offending the baronet."

"Why the 'offense'?"

107

"Because my father's social position was not equal to that of the aristocratic Morlands. Moreover, her brother had an accident in his youth which rendered him irritable and morose. From being a pleasant sort of man; which, indeed, he must have been did he share aught of my mother's nature—he grew into a misanthrope, and gave his life to the classification of Exmoor beetles. He treated my mother very badly, so vilely that even she, dear soul, during her married life held no further communication with him, and never mentioned him to me by name. Now, one day on Exmoor he found a lady who also was devoted to beetles. At least, she knew all that the Encyclopædia Britannica could teach her. She was a poor but handsome widow."

"Ah!"

"It is delightful to talk with you, Abingdon. Your monosyllables help the narrative along. Sir Philip married the widow. She brought him a son, aged five. There were no children born of my uncle's marriage."

"Oh!"

"When poverty overtook my dear one, she so far obliterated a cruel memory as to appeal, not once, but many times, to the human coleopterus of Exmoor, but she was invariably frozen off either by Lady Louisa Morland or by Messrs. Sharpe & Smith."

"Did they admit this?"

"By no means. I am telling you the facts. I am still on top of the Pyrenees."

"Then how did you ascertain the facts?"

"I have in my possession ever since my mother's death the letters they wrote to her. They were fresh in my memory when you and I first met in the Clerkenwell Police Court. That is why the name of Philip Morland was glib on my tongue."

"So I have only heard historical events, events prior to the last ten years?"

"Exactly. My uncle is now sixty years of age. Lady Louisa Morland's son is twenty-four. Her ladyship's whole aim in life has been to secure him as the baronet's heir. The title, of course, he cannot obtain. But, most unfortunately, he has no penchant for beetles. Indeed, Lady Louisa's researches have long since diminished in ardor. Her son's interests are divided between the Sports Club and the coryphées of the latest musical comedy—moths are more in his line, apparently. My uncle, who is preparing a monograph on the fleas which patronize Exmoor wild ponies, came to town last week to visit the British Museum. Unhappily, he heard something about his stepson which disturbed his researches. There was a row."

"Why do you say 'unhappily'?"

"Because I am dragged into the wretched business on account of it. After a lapse of more than twenty-five years, he remembered his sister, went to his solicitors, made a fearful hubbub when he heard of letters received from her and answered without his knowledge, and ascertained that she was dead, and had a son living. At any cost, they must find that son. They have guessed at my identity for some time. Now they want to make sure of it."

"And what did you say?"

"I told them I would think over the situation and communicate with them further."

"Were they satisfied?"

"By no means. They are exceedingly anxious to placate the old man. They probably control a good deal of his money."

"Um!"

"Of course! You see the delicacy of their position. After playing into the hands of Lady Louisa for nearly a quarter of a century, they suddenly find the whole situation changed by the baronet's belated discovery that he once had a sister."

"You have not told me all this without a purpose. Do you want my advice?"

Philip's face was clouded, his eyes downcast.

"You understand," he said, after a long pause, "that some one, either the man or the woman—the woman, I think—is morally responsible for my mother's death. She was poor—wretchedly, horribly poor—the poverty of thin clothing and insufficient food. She was ill, confined to a miserable hovel for weary months, and was so utterly unprovided with the barest necessaries that the parish doctor was on the point of compelling her to go to the workhouse infirmary when death came. Am I to be the instrument of God's vengeance on this woman?"

Mr. Abingdon, who had risen to light a cigar, placed a kindly hand on the young man's shoulder.

"Philip," he said, with some emotion, "I have never yet heard you utter a hasty judgment. You have prudence far beyond your years. It seems to me, speaking with all the reverence of man in face of the decrees of Providence, that God has already provided a terrible punishment for Lady Louisa Morland. What is the name of her son?"

"I do not know. I forgot to ask."

"I have a wide experience of the jeunesse dorée of London. Hardly a week passed during many years of my life that one of his type did not appear before me in the dock. What is he—a roué, a gambler, probably a drunkard?"

"All these, I gathered from the solicitors."

"And if your mother were living, what would she say to Lady Morland?"

"She would pity her from the depths of her heart. Yes, Abingdon, you are right. My uncle's wife has chosen her own path. She must follow it, let it lead where it will. I will write to Messrs. Sharpe & Smith now. But step into my dressing room with me for a moment, will you?"

In a corner of the spacious apartment to which he led his guest stood a large safe. Philip opened it. Within were a number of books and documents, but in a large compartment at the bottom stood a peculiar object for such a repository—an ordinary, leather portmanteau. He lifted it onto a couch and took a key from a drawer in the safe.

"This is one of my treasures which you have never seen," he said, with a sorrowful smile. "It has not been in the light for many years."

He revealed to his friend's wondering eyes the tattered suit, the slipshod boots, the ragged shirt and cap, the rusty doorkey, associated with that wonderful month of March of a decade earlier. He reverently unfolded some of his mother's garments, and his eyes were misty as he surveyed them.

But from the pocket of the portmanteau he produced a packet of soiled letters. One by one he read them aloud, though he winced at the remembrance of the agony his mother must have endured as she experienced each rebuff from Lady Morland and her husband's solicitors.

Yet he persevered to the end.

"I wanted a model for a brief communication to Messrs. Sharpe & Smith," he said, bitterly. "I think the general purport of their correspondence will serve my needs admirably."

As he closed the Gladstone bag his stern mood vanished.

"Do you know," he said, "that this odd-looking portmanteau, always locked and always reposing in a safe, has puzzled my valets considerably? One man got it out and tried to open it. I caught him in the act. I honestly believe both he and the others were under the impression that I kept my diamonds in it."

"By the way, that reminds me of a request from Isaacstein. As all the smaller diamonds have now been disposed of, and there remain only the large stones, he thinks that some of them might be cut into sections. They are unmarketable at present."

"Very well. Let us appoint a day next week and overhaul the entire collection. I intend to keep the big ones to form the center ornaments of a tiara, a necklace, and gewgaws of that sort."

"I am glad to hear it."

"My dear fellow, I suppose there will be a Mrs. Anson some day, but I have not found her yet."

> "'Who'er she be,
> That not impossible she,
> That shall command my heart and me.'"

And a ripple of laughter chased away the last shadows from his face.

Chapter XIV

An Adventure

Mr. Abingdon took his departure at an early hour; his excellent wife was indisposed, and her age rendered him anxious.

Philip wrote a curt letter to Sharpe & Smith. He had given thought to their statements, he said, and wished to hold no further communication with either Sir Philip Morland or his representatives.

Then he ordered his private hansom, intending to visit the Universities' Club.

It was a fine evening, one of those rare nights when blasé London abandons herself for an hour to the delights of spring. The tops of omnibuses passing through Park Lane were enlivened by muslin dresses and flower-covered hats. Men who passed in hansoms wore evening dress without an overcoat. Old earth was growing again, and if weather-wise folk predicted that such an unusually high temperature meant thunderstorms and showers it would indeed be a poor heart that did not rejoice in the influences of the moment.

Two powdered and noiseless footmen threw open the door as Philip appeared in the hall. He stood for a little while in the entrance buttoning his gloves. A strong electric light—he loved light—fell on him and revealed his firm face and splendidly proportioned frame.

He cast a critical eye on a sleek horse in the shafts, and smiled pleasantly at the driver.

"Good gracious, Wale," he said, "your cattle are becoming as fat as yourself."

"All your fault, sir," was the cheerful reply. "You don't use 'em 'arf enough."

"I can't pass my time in being driven about town to reduce the weight of my coachman and horses. Wale, if you don't do something desperate, there will be an 'h' after the 'w' in your name."

He sprang into the vehicle. With a lively "Kim up!" Wale got his stout steed into a remarkably fast trot.

A tall man, who had been loitering and smoking beneath the trees across the road for a long time, sauntered toward a tradesman's cart which was standing near the area gate of the next house, while the man in charge gossiped with a kitchenmaid.

"Beg pardon," he said to the couple, "is that Mr. Philip Anson's place?" with an indicatory jerk of his thumb.

"Yes," said the man.

"An' was that Mr. Anson himself who drove away in a private cab?"

"Yes," said the girl.

"Thanks. It does one good to see a young chap like him so jolly and

111

comfortable, and provided with everything he can want in the world; eh?"

"I wish I 'ad a bit of 'is little lot," sighed the greengrocer's assistant, with a side glance at the maid.

The stranger laughed harshly.

"It's hard to say when ye're well off," he growled. "Up one day and down the other. You never know your luck."

Away he went, southward. His long vigil on the pavement near the railings seemed to have ended. In Piccadilly he took an omnibus to the Circus, and there changed to another for the Elephant and Castle.

He walked rapidly through the congeries of mean streets which lie to the east of that bustling center, and paused at last before a house which was occupied by respectable people, judging by the cleanly curtains and general air of tidiness.

He knocked. A woman appeared. Did Mrs. Mason live there? No. She knew nothing of her. Had only been in the place eighteen months.

The man evidently appreciated the migratory habits of the poor too well to dream of prosecuting further inquiries among the neighbors. He strolled about, reading the names over the small shops, the corner public house, the dressmakers' semiprivate residences.

At last he paused before a somewhat grim establishment, an undertaker's office. He entered. A youth was whistling the latest music hall song.

"Do you know anything of a Mrs. Mason, who used to live in this locality about ten years ago?" he asked.

"Mrs. Mason? There may be forty Mrs. Masons. What was her Christian name an' address?"

"Mrs. Hannah Mason, 14 Frederick Street."

The youth skillfully tilted back his stool until he reached a ledger from a shelf behind him. He ran his eye down an index, found a number, and pulled out another book.

"We buried her on the twentieth of November, nine years since," he said, coolly, rattling both tomes back into their places.

"You did, eh? Is there anybody here who remembers her?"

Something in the husky voice of this stark, ill-favored man caused the boy to become less pert.

"Father's in," he said. "I'll ring for him."

Father came. He had a vague memory of the woman, a widow with two children—boys, he thought. Somebody helped her in her last days, and paid for the funeral—paid cash, according to the ledger. He did not know who the friend was, nor had he any knowledge of the children's fate. Workhouse, most probably. What workhouse? Parish of Southwark. Easy to find. Just turn so-and-so, and so-and-so.

With a grunt of acknowledgment the inquirer passed into the street. He gave an eye to the public house, but resolutely quickened his pace. At the workhouse he succeeded, with some difficulty, in interviewing the master. It was after office hours, but as he had journeyed a long way an exception would be made in his case.

Books were consulted to ascertain the fate of two boys, John and William Mason, who would now be aged twenty and eighteen respectively. Youthful Masons had certainly been in the schools—one was there at the moment, in fact—but none of them answered to the descriptions supplied. The workhouse master was sorry; the records gave no clew.

Again the man sought the dark seclusion of the street. He wandered slowly toward a main thoroughfare, and entered the first public house he encountered. He ordered six pennyworth of brandy, and drank it at a gulp. Then he lit a pipe and went forth again.

"That was an ugly-lookin' customer," said an habitué to the barman.

"'E 'ad a fice like a fifth act at the Surrey," agreed the other.

If they knew the toast that Jocky Mason had pledged so readily, they would have better grasped the truth of this unfavorable diagnosis of his character.

"Ten years' penal servitude, four years' police supervision, my wife dead, and my children lost, all through a smack on the head given me by Philip Anson," he communed. "Here's to getting even with him!"

It was a strange outcome of his long imprisonment that the man should have acquired a fair degree of culture. He was compelled to learn in jail, to a certain extent, and reading soon became a pleasure to him. Moreover, he picked up an acquaintance with a smooth-spoken mate of the swell mobsman and long firm order—a dandy who strove to be elegant even in convict garb. Mason's great strength and indomitable courage appealed to the more artistic if more effeminate rogue; once the big man saved his comrade's life when they were at work in the quarries.

The influence was mutual. They vowed lasting friendship. Victor Grenier was released six months before Mason, and the latter now crossed the river again to go to an address where he would probably receive some news of his professed ally's whereabouts.

Grenier's name was imparted under inviolable confidence as that which he would adopt after his release. His real name, by which he was convicted, was something far less aristocratic.

Philip's driver, being of the peculiar type of Londoner which seems to be created to occupy the dicky of a hansom, did not take his master down Park Lane, along Piccadilly, and so to Pall Mall. He loved corners. Give him the remotest chance of following a zigzag course, and he would follow it in preference to a route with all the directness of a Roman road.

Thus it happened, as he spun round Carlos Place into Berkeley Square, he nearly collided with another vehicle which dashed into the square from Davies Street.

Both horses pulled up with a jerk, there was a sharp fusillade of what cabmen call "langwidge," and the other hansom drove on, having the best of the strategical position by a stolen yard.

Philip lifted the trapdoor.

"Has he a fare, Wale?"

"Yes, sir, a lydy."

"Oh. Leave him alone, then. Otherwise, I would have liked to see you ride him off at the corner of Bruton Street."

Wale, who was choleric, replied with such force that Philip tried to say, sternly:

"Stop that swearing, Wale."

"Beg pawdon, sir, I'm sure, but I wouldn't ha' minded if it wasn't my own old keb. Didn't you spot it?"

"You don't tell me so. How odd!"

"And to think of a brewer's drayman like that gettin' 'old of it. Well—"

Wale put the lid on in case his employer might hear any more of his sentiments.

Philip, leaning back to laugh, for Wale's vocabulary was amusing, if not fit for publication, suddenly realized the queer trick that even the events in the life of an individual have of repeating themselves.

In one day, after an interval of many years, he had been suddenly confronted by personages connected with the period of his sufferings, with the very garments he wore at that time, with the cab in which he drove from Clerkenwell to Hatton Garden. Abingdon had dined with him; Isaacstein had sent him a message; his driver, even, was the cabman who made him a present of two shillings, a most fortunate transaction for Wale, as it led to his selection to look after Philip's London stable.

All who had befriended the forlorn boy in those early days had benefited to an extraordinary degree. The coffee-stall keeper who gave him coffee grounds and crusts, the old clothes man who cut down the price of his first outfit, Mrs. Wrigley, going hopelessly to her toil in a Shepherd's Bush laundry; Mr. Wilson, of Grant & Sons, the kindly jeweler of Ludgate Hill, were each sought out, and either placed in a good business or bounteously rewarded for the services they had rendered. O'Brien, of course, was found a sinecure office at the Mary Anson Home.

As for the doctor, he owed his Harley Street practice to the millionaire's help and patronage.

It is worthy of note that Philip never wore a watch other than that presented to him by the police of the Whitechapel Division.

It was an ordinary English silver lever, and he carried it attached to a knotted bootlace.

Did he but know how far the historical parallel had gone that day—how Jocky Mason had waited for hours outside his residence in the hope of seeing him and becoming acquainted with his appearance—he might have been surprised, but he would never have guessed the evil that this man would accomplish, and, in some measure, accomplish unconsciously.

He was not in his club five minutes when a friend tackled him for a concert subscription.

"Anson, you are fond of music. Here is a new violinist, a Hungarian, who wants a start. I heard him in Budapest last autumn. He is a good chap. Take some stalls."

Philip glanced at the program.

"Eckstein at the piano. I see! He must be a star. Who is the soprano? I have never heard her name before."

"Miss Evelyn Atherley," read his friend over his shoulder. "I don't know her myself. Dine with me here to-morrow night. We will go and hear the performance afterward."

"Can you distribute stalls among your acquaintances?"

"My dear fellow, I will be delighted. Sorry I can't help Jowkacsy a bit myself."

"You are helping him very well. I will take a dozen; two for you and me; ten elsewhere, for the claque."

"You are a good chap. Hello! There's Jones. Jones is good for a couple. Don't forget to-morrow night."

And the good-natured enthusiast, who was a terror to many of his friends, ran off to secure another victim.

Philip had sent his hansom home. Shortly before eleven he quitted the club, intending to walk to Park Lane by a circuitous route, long enough to consume a big cigar.

He chanced to pass the hall in which the concert was to take place. A few people were hurrying from the stage door. Evidently a rehearsal had just taken place. A short man, with a huge cluster of flowing locks, that offered abundant proof of his musical genius, ran out with a violin case in his hand.

He was about to enter a hansom waiting near the curb, but the driver said:

"Engaged, sir."

The man did not seem to understand, so the cabby barred his way with the whip and shook his head. Then the stranger rushed to a neighboring cab rank—evidently an excitable gentleman, with the high-strung temperament of art.

A lady quitted the hall a few seconds later.

"Are you engaged?" Philip heard her ask the cabman.

"No, miss."

"Take me to No. 44, Maida Crescent, Regent's Park," she said. After arranging her skirts daintily, she entered the vehicle.

"That is odd," thought Philip, who had witnessed both incidents in the course of a six yards' walk. He glanced at the cabman, and fancied the man gave a peculiar look of intelligence toward a couple of fashionably dressed loungers who stood in the shadow of the closed public entrance.

The two men, without exchanging a word to Philip's hearing, went to a brougham standing at some little distance. They entered. The coachman, who received no instructions, drove off in the same direction as the hansom, and, as if to make sure he was being followed, the cab driver turned to look behind him.

Once, in Naples, Philip saw a man stealthily following a woman down an unlighted alley. Without a moment's hesitation he went after the pair, and was just in time to prevent the would-be assassin from plunging an uplifted stiletto into the woman's back. The recollection of that little drama flashed into his mind now; there was a suggestion of the Neapolitan bravo's air in the manner in which these men stalked a girl who was quite unaware of their movements.

He asked himself why a cabman should refuse one fare and pick up another in the same spot. The affair was certainly odd. He would see further into it before he dismissed it from his thoughts. The distance to Maida Crescent was not great.

While thinking he was acting. He sprang into the nearest hansom.

"A brougham is following a hansom up Langham Place," he said to the driver. "Keep behind them. If they separate, follow the brougham. When it stops, pull up at the best place to avoid notice."

The man nodded. Nothing surprises a London cabman. Soon the three vehicles were spinning along the Outer Circle.

It was not a very dark night, the sky being cloudless and starlit. Away in front, at a point where the two lines of lamps curved sharply to the right and vanished amidst the trees, a row of little, red lights showed that the road was up.

The leading hansom drove steadily on. There was nothing remarkable in this. When the driver reached the obstruction, he would turn out of the park by the nearer gate—that was all.

But he did nothing of the kind. There was a sudden crash of wood, a woman's scream, and the horse was struggling wildly amidst a pile of loose, wooden blocks, while one wheel of the cab dropped heavily into a shallow trench.

Simultaneously the brougham pulled up and its two occupants rushed to the scene of the accident.

Philip's driver, of course, obeyed instructions, but he shouted to his fare as he jumped into the road:

"That feller's either drunk or 'e did it a-puppuss."

Philip was of the same opinion. He reached the overthrown barricade almost as soon as the two hurrying men in front, both of whom were in evening dress.

One of them held the horse's head and steadied him; the other was just in time to help the young lady to leave her dangerous conveyance.

"I hope you have received no injury, madam," he said, politely.

"Oh, not at all. I was frightened for an instant. How could it have happened? I saw the lamps quite plainly. The man seemed to pull his horse deliberately into the barrier."

The voice was singularly sweet and well modulated. A neighboring arc lamp illuminated the girl's face with its white, unpitying radiance. It revealed features beautifully modeled, and large, startled eyes that looked wonderingly from the man who came so promptly to her rescue to the driver who had caused the mishap. Philip, behind the hansom, was unseen. He remained a critical observer.

"I fear he is intoxicated," was the reply. "Here, you! How came you to make such a blunder?"

"Blind as an owl," came the gurgling answer. "I saw some red spots dancin' abaht, but I thort it must be that larst gill o' beer."

Nevertheless the cabman extricated his horse and vehicle from their predicament with singular ease for a half-drunken man.

"Goin' on, miss?" he grinned. "There's nothin' extry for the steeplechise."

"No, no," cried the lady. "I will walk. I will pay you now."

"Take my advice and pay him not a cent," protested the man by her side. "Leave him to me. My friend here will take his number. If you will accept a seat in my brougham—"

The cabman began to swear and threaten them all with personal violence. The lady, clearly unwilling to avail herself of the accommodating offer made to her, tried to edge away. The driver of the hansom whipped his horse on to the pavement. By this time he had turned his back to the road-menders' barrier.

The girl, angered and alarmed, shrank toward the gentleman, who seemed to give her some measure of protection from the infuriated cause of all the trouble.

"Do step into my brougham," he said, civilly. "Victor, just grab the gee-gee's head again, and keep that idiot quiet until we get away. Now, madam, take my advice. You will be quite safe instantly."

Even yet she hesitated. There was, perchance, a timbre in the quiet, cultured tone of the speaker that did not ring truly. The note of a bell cannot be perfect if there is a flaw in the metal, and the human voice often betrays a warped nature when to all outward seeming there is a fair exterior.

The man who addressed her was youthful, not much older than herself. He was evidently a gentleman, with the polish and easy repose of society. His words, his attitude, were in the best of taste. Yet—

A loud altercation broke out between the cabman and "Victor." The latter did not appear to be so ready to lay hands on the reins again, and the whip fell viciously on the horse's flank, causing him to plunge forward in dangerous proximity to the couple on the sidewalk. He came close, but not too close. Philip was now quite certain that he was witnessing the dexterous display of a skilled driver.

"Really, I am at a loss for words to persuade you that your only course is to use my carriage. Otherwise there will be a confounded row."

The stranger's voice was a trifle petulant She was such an unreasonable young lady. She turned to him irresolutely—to find Philip at her side—thrusting himself in front of her would-be rescuer.

"You have been the victim of a plot, madam," he said. "Your driver is not drunk. He caused the accident purposely. These two scoundrels are in league with him. If—"

"What the devil—" cried the other, fiercely, but Philip swung him bodily against the iron railings.

"If you care to take my cab, alone, it is at your service. I will look after these cads."

His quick eyes caught a signal from Victor to the cabman. He was sorry for the horse, but this comedy must be stopped. He instantly caught the bridle, and backed the cab violently toward the excavation. The cabman lashed at him in vain, and swore, too, with remarkable fluency for one so drunk. Both wheels crunched on top of the stout barrier, and became locked there.

Then Anson ran back toward the girl, whose arm was held by the owner of the brougham.

"Take your hands off that lady, or I will hurt you," said Philip, and there was that in his emphatic order which brooked no delay.

The stranger dropped his restraining hand, but shouted furiously:

"By what right do you interfere? I am only offering the lady some assistance?"

Philip ignored him.

"What do you say, madam?" he inquired, somewhat sternly, for she seemed loath to trust any of them. "Will you occupy my cab? It is there. Rest assured that neither of these men shall follow you."

She stood her ground, came nearer to him.

"I believe you," she murmured. "I thank you from my heart. It is inexplicable that such wretches can exist as these two seeming gentlemen, who stooped to such artifice against a helpless woman."

"Most fortunately I saw you leaving the Regent's Hall," he replied. "This cab was waiting for you, and you only. The man refused at least one fare to my presence. The others followed in a brougham. Do you know them?"

"No. I have never, to my knowledge, seen either of them before in my life. How came you—"

"I happened to hear your address. I will write to you and explain. Go now," he quickly interrupted, for Victor and his friend were approaching them after a hasty conference.

"Leave you to deal with these assassins alone! Not I! I can defend myself. I can help you. I will scream for assistance. There are too many of them for you to resist them single-handed."

118

Philip vowed afterward that fire flashed in her eyes. There was a splendid passion in the gesture with which she pointed to the enraged hansom driver, who had climbed from his perch, and was running to join his employers.

This was a new experience for Philip, and the blood leaped in his veins at the girl's courageous words. But he laughed, in his pleasant, musical way.

"Men who would attack a defenseless woman," he said, "are poor creatures where a man's heart is needed. Now just watch me, and don't be alarmed."

He strode to meet the advancing trio. They halted.

"I give you a last warning," he cried. "Drive off in your carriage, and you," to the cabman, "go back and help your horse. You must go now, this instant, or take the consequences."

There was the silence of indecision. This strong-faced man, with the figure of an athlete, meant what he said.

Victor caught his friend's arm.

"Come away," he whispered. "She does not know you. You have failed this time."

Without another word the pair crossed the road to their waiting brougham. The cabman, who became remarkably sober, began to whine:

"It's on'y a lark, guv'nor. The lydy would ha' took no 'arm. I didn't mean—"

Philip was strongly tempted to kick him, but refrained. He grasped the man's shoulder and lifted his badge to the light.

"I will spare you for the lady's sake," he said, grimly, "but I want your number, in case you try any more such tricks."

"My Gawd, it's Mr. Anson!"

For the first time the driver saw Philip's face clearly.

"Ah, you know me then? Who were those blackguards who employed you?"

"S'elp me, sir, I on'y know one of 'em. 'E's a Mr. Victor Grenier. I offen pick 'im up at the Gardenia. 'E said 'is pal was sweet on the young lydy an' wanted a put-up job ter 'elp 'er. That's all, guv'nor, on me life."

"You ought to be ashamed of yourself," was Philip's only comment.

He rejoined the girl, who was watching the retreating brougham.

"Now," he cried, pleasantly, "you can go home."

"Please drive me there. I will not deprive you of your cab."

So they drove away together, and the driver of the hansom, striving to free his vehicle from the broken trestles, paused to scratch his head.

"'E fairly bested the crowd," he growled, "an' got the girl as well. My eye, but she's a beauty."

Chapter XV

A Face From the Past

Maida Crescent was little more than half a mile beyond the park.

Philip thought it due to the lady he had beguiled that she should know exactly how he came to interfere in her behalf. She listened in silence, and when she spoke, there was a suggestion of shy nervousness oddly at variance with her spirited action of a few minutes earlier.

"I cannot understand it at all," she said. "I am seldom out so late. My professional engagements are few and far between, I am sorry to say."

"Were you attending a rehearsal at the Regent's Hall?"

"Yes."

"A rehearsal for Monsieur Jowkacsy's concert?"

"Yes."

She volunteered no further information, but Philip was a persistent person.

"I do not remember another day in my life previously," he said, "when so many fortuitous events grouped themselves together in such a curious relationship. Even this adventure is a sequel to a prior incident. Just before I joined in the chase after you I had purchased some tickets for Jowkacsy's musicale. The strangest item of all is that I was practically walking away from the direction in which I live when my attention was drawn to the cabman's behavior."

"Good gracious!" she protested, "am I taking you out of your way? I thought you merely happened to be driving after us through the park."

She invited no confidences. She adhered strictly to the affair of the moment, and he had no option but to follow her cue.

"I do not think I have ever been in Regent's Park before."

"What an amazing circumstance—that you should gallop off in such fashion to the rescue of an unknown woman, I mean."

"That, again, is original, or nearly so."

"Are you a Londoner?"

"To some extent—a little while each year. I live mostly on the sea."

"Oh, that accounts for your gallantry. You are a sailor."

"A yachtsman," corrected Philip.

"How delightful. I have not even seen the sea for ages. One has to work so hard nowadays to obtain recognition. I do not object to the work, for I love music, but the bread-and-butter aspect is disagreeable, and—and—you have learned to-night how even the small amount of publicity I have achieved brings with it the risk of insult."

"By the way," he said, quietly, striving not to add to the excitement under which she was certainly laboring, "one of those men is named Victor Grenier. You ought to know."

"Thank you. How did you ascertain it?"

"The cabman told me. He knew me."

"The cabman knew you?"

"Yes. I fly about town in hansoms. I am too lazy to walk."

He regretted the slip. He was known to the tribe of Jehus on account of his generosity to their charities; moreover, was not one of the order his horse-master?

The girl laughed, with a delightful merriment that relieved the tension.

"You acted like an indolent person," she cried. "Do you know, I felt that you would have banged the heads of those men together in another instant."

Their vehicle slackened pace, and curved toward the pavement in a quiet street.

"Here I am at home," she said, and Philip assisted her to alight.

"Oh, my music!" she wailed, suddenly. "I left it in that horrid cab."

Philip repressed a smile.

"Tell me your name," he said, "and I will recover it for you early in the morning."

"Are you sure? Oh, what a trouble I have been. How good you are."

"It is not the least trouble. I took the cabman's number."

"Indeed, indeed, I am grateful to you. My name is Evelyn Atherley. I would ask you to call some day and see my mother, but—but—"

"You do not wish her to hear of your adventure to-night? It would frighten her."

"She would be terrified each time I went out alone. Believe me, I can ill afford a hansom, but I take one late at night to please her, as the walk from the nearest 'bus route is lonely."

"You are singing at the Regent's Hall. I will be there. By the way, my name is Philip Anson."

The girl's big eyes—he fancied they were blue, but in the dim light he could not be sure—looked into his. There was a sparkle of merriment in them, he thought—a quick perception of a hint delicately conveyed. But she said, quite pleasantly:

"My last song is at ten-fifteen. I will leave the hall at ten-thirty. I hope my mother will be with me. I will be most pleased to see you there, and thank you more coherently than is possible now, especially if you recover my music."

The quick trot of a fast-driven horse came round the corner.

Philip was assuring her that they would certainly meet next evening, when a hansom pulled up behind the waiting vehicle, and the driver said:

"Beg pawdon, miss, you left this," and he held forth the lost portfolio. The cabman was anxious to atone for his share in the night's proceedings.

Philip tipped him in a manner that caused the man to murmur his renewed regret, but he was sternly told to go. Philip's own reward from Miss Atherley was a warm handshake, and a grateful smile.

He drove homeward, wondering how he could best help her in her career.

And she, after kissing her mother "Good-night," went to her room to wonder also, but her wonderment was mixed with regret. For such a nice young man as Philip Anson must have troops of friends, he must be rich, he must be far removed from the orbit of a girl who, whatever her birth and breeding, was driven in the flower of her youth to earn her living on the concert platform.

Jowkacsy won his laurels with superb ease. Philip, listening to the Polish genius, found himself hoping that the fair English girl might achieve some measure of the rapturous applause bestowed on the long-haired enthusiast. He murmured the thought, in guarded commonplace, to his musical friend.

"Impossible, my dear fellow," was the instant verdict. "She is mediocre; just an average singer, and no more. Music is divine, but its exploiters suffer from the petty jealousies of housemaids. Jowkacsy can have no rivals to-night. Eckstein is a master, of course, but a necessary evil as an accompanist. The other artists are mere fill-ups—good, or they would not be here, but not in the front rank. Listen. I am connected with a choral society in my county, and we once engaged a leading tenor and a second-rate baritone. The tenor had a name with fourteen letters, and the baritone only owned four. The unfortunate local printer selected his type to fill the lines on the bills by size and not by merit. The moment the tenor saw the four-letter man looming large across the poster he absolutely refused to sing a note unless fresh bills were printed with his fourteen letters in larger type. And we were compelled to humor him. That is music from the agent's point of view."

When Miss Evelyn Atherley advanced to the front of the platform Philip thought he had never seen a woman so beautiful. She had the grace of a perfect figure and the style of an aristocrat. She was dressed in light blue chiffon, with a spray of forget-me-nots, the color of her eyes, arranged across the front of her bodice. Anson experienced a thrill of pleasure when he saw that the bouquet he caused to be forwarded to her contained flowers of a kindred hue. The skill of the florist had correctly interpreted his description, which, indeed, was largely guesswork on his part.

A high forehead and a mouth and chin of patrician mold gave an air of caste to an otherwise sweetly pretty face.

"By Jove!" whispered the critic, "if she sings as well as she looks I may be mistaken."

Her first song was Goring Thomas' "A Summer Night." Instantly it was perceptible that her voice was true, the outpouring of a soul. In volume it was in no way remarkable, but its melodious cadence was fresh, innocent, virginal. The notes were those of a joyous bird.

Anson, biassed by other sentiments, thought he had never heard her equal, but his friend, after joining in his vigorous applause, gave him a douche of accurate judgment.

"The old story," he growled; "a fine artist retarded, perhaps spoiled, by the need to make too early an appearance. She wants a year in Milan, another year with Randegger or Leoni, and she might, if all went well, be a star."

His hearer chafed inwardly, but only hazarded the opinion that she was already a singer of rare intensity, while, as for appearance—

"Ah, there you are right," was the ready rejoinder. "The Gaiety is her right place. She would be admirable in light opera."

The conversation languished. The suggestion that Miss Atherley was best fitted for the stage was displeasing to Philip, he scarce knew why.

The girl was given a hearty encore, and her next song was a simple, humorous little ballad about a miller and a maid. It was charmingly sung and acted. The critic leaned back in his chair, and smiled at Philip with the indulgent air of the man who says:

"I told you so."

Soon Philip rose to go.

"Good heavens, man, you do not intend to leave before Jowkacsy plays the suite in F minor?" queried his amazed acquaintance.

"Sorry. I have an engagement."

He quitted the hall, his tall figure riveting a good many eyes as he made his way toward an exit. One man, watching from the gallery, smiled cynically, and rose at the same time.

Philip found the foyer to be practically deserted. He asked a policeman on duty to call Mr. Anson's carriage from the ranks, and a footman came, quickly running lest he had incurred a reprimand for not being on the lookout for his master at the entrance.

In a very little time Miss Atherley appeared, and with her a handsome, elderly lady, who was quite obviously her mother. The girl was radiant. She never expected a cordial reception from a high-class audience, such as gathered to worship the violinist.

"Mother dear," she cried, "this is Mr. Anson, who very kindly came to my assistance when a cabman gave me some trouble last night."

Mrs. Atherley gave him a pleasant greeting, but turned to her daughter.

"Why didn't you tell me of any dispute when you returned home? You know how nervous I am when you are out at night."

The girl laughed merrily.

"You have answered your own question, carissima. That is precisely why I did not tell you."

"Miss Atherley was good enough to permit me to meet you here after the concert," put in Philip, "so that I might add my assurances to her own that the affair was of no consequence. It is early yet. Will you come with me for some supper, and thus give me a chance of telling you how much I enjoyed your daughter's singing?"

Wise Philip, to pay court to the mother.

Mrs. Atherley, in no way deceived, yet gratified by the deference shown to her, gave the girl a questioning glance.

"Oh, do let us go, mamma! I am famished, I candidly admit it. Mr. Anson, I have subsisted since luncheon without a morsel."

"We will be delighted—" began the older lady, but her attention was attracted by the footman holding open the door of the carriage.

"Is that carriage yours?" she said to Philip.

"Yes."

"Where do we sup?"

"At the Savoy."

She flushed slightly.

"Not the Savoy," she faltered.

"Why not, mother?" cried the girl, spiritedly. "Mr. Anson, my mother does not care to meet associates of—of other days. I tell her she thinks far too much of these considerations. Why should she fear to face them simply because we are poor?"

"I think, Mrs. Atherley," he said, quietly, "that you are very rich, far richer than many a mère de famille we shall meet at the restaurant."

This neat compliment turned the scale of the mother's hesitation. Indeed, she might well be proud of her beautiful daughter.

The two ladies seated themselves in the luxurious landau with an ease that showed familiarity, but Mrs. Atherley, being a woman, could not help being troubled in the matter of dress.

"The Savoy!" she murmured, as the rubber-tired vehicle glided away noiselessly. "I have not been there for years. And people at supper are always attired so fashionably. Could we not—"

The girl put her arm around her waist.

"Just for once, mamma, you shall not care a little bit, and none may be the wiser. Here is Mr. Anson—quite an élégant himself—he would never guess that our gowns were homemade."

"The women, dear one. They will know."

"Oh, you deceiver! You said my toilet was perfect, and I am quite sure yours is."

This logic was incontrovertible. Mrs. Atherley sighed, and asked what took place the previous night.

Philip imagined that the girl hung back, so he boldly undertook an explanation. By describing the cabman as apparently intoxicated, and certainly impudent, he covered a good deal of ground, and the rest was easy.

When they reached the Savoy, the anxious mother had relegated the incident to the limbo of unimportant things. Only one other matter troubled her—the somewhat unconventional origin of her daughter's acquaintance with this pleasant-mannered young gentleman.

She was far too tactful to hint at such a point just then. It should be reserved for home discussion.

Meanwhile, they were early arrivals. The head waiter marshaled them to a window table. Mrs. Atherley smiled; she knew her London.

"You were sure we would accompany you?" she cried.

"Not at all sure; only hopeful," said Philip.

"Ah, well. It is good occasionally to revisit the old scenes. No, Elf, I will sit here; I will not be en face to that row of tables. Half a dozen people would certainly recognize me, and I do not wish it."

Elf! The name drove Philip's thoughts backward with a bound—back to a torrential night in a London square, and the tearing open of a carriage door in time to save a sweet little girl all robed in white, who, but for him, would have fallen with an overturned vehicle.

Elf! It was an unusual pet name. The child of ten years ago would be about the age of the lively and spirituelle girl by his side. The child had faced her enraged uncle on that memorable night; the woman had refused to leave him when she thought danger threatened in the park.

Could it be possible! He was startled, bewildered, utterly dumfounded by even the remote possibility that another figure from the past should come before him in such wise.

"Mr. Anson! What have you found in the menu to perplex you so terribly? Does danger lurk in the agneau du printemps? Is there a secret horror in the salmi?"

Evelyn's raillery restored his scattered wits.

"May I say something personal?" he inquired.

"About the lamb?"

"About you? Mrs. Atherley called you 'Elf' just now."

"Yes. I regret that I earned the title in ages past. The habits have ceased, but the name remains."

"I once met a little girl named Elf. It was ten years ago, on a March evening, in a West End square. There had been a carriage accident. A pair of horses were frightened by a terrific thunderstorm. The girl was accompanied by a somewhat selfish gentleman. He jumped out and left her to her own devices; indeed, slammed the door in her face. A ragged boy—"

"A boy with newspapers—a boy who spoke quite nicely—saved her by running into the road. The carriage overturned in front of Lord Vanstone's house. I was the girl!"

Both ladies were amazed at the expression on Philip's face. He betrayed such eagerness, such intense longing, such keen anxiety to establish her identity with the child who figured in an accident of no very remarkable nature, that they could not help being vastly surprised.

Their astonishment was not lessened when Philip exclaimed:

"And I was the boy!"

"But I said 'a boy with newspapers.'"

"Yes, a very urchin, a waif of the streets."

"My uncle struck you."

"And you defended me, saved me from being locked up, in fact."

"Oh, this is too marvelous. Mother, you must remember—"

"My dear one, I remember the event as if it had taken place yesterday. Your uncle would not have cared were you killed that night. All he wanted was your money. Now he has that, and mine. He was, indeed, a wicked man."

"Mother dear, he is unhappy. Are we? But, Mr. Anson, what wonderful change in your fortunes has taken place since our first meeting? Is the newspaper trade so thriving that a carriage and pair, a supper at the Savoy, stalls at the Regent's Hall, and a bouquet from Rosalind's, are mere trimmings, so to speak, to a busy day?"

"Evelyn!" protested Mrs. Atherley.

But the girl was too buoyant, too utterly oblivious of all that this meeting meant to Philip, to cease from chaffing him.

"Please, Mr. Anson, do tell us the secret. I will sell any paper you name. I get five guineas for singing two songs, I admit, but I may only sing them once a month. I have loads of time to run about crying, 'Extrey speshul! 'Orrible disawster.' Or does the magic spring from writing those thrilling stories one sees placarded on the hoardings? I believe I could do it. I once won a prize in a lady's magazine for a set of verses, the genuine and unaided production of a girl aged under fourteen."

Philip compelled himself to respond to her mood. He promised to reveal his specific for money-making at some future period, when she was sufficiently dazzled to accept his words as those of a prophet.

With the tact of a woman of the world, Mrs. Atherley led the conversation back to less personal channels. The great restaurant was rapidly filling now. The occupants of neighboring tables cast occasional glances at the merry trio which discussed the foibles of the musical world, the ways of agents, the little meannesses and petty spites of the greatest artists, and, incidentally, did ample justice to an excellent meal.

Philip thought he had never before met such a delightful girl. Evelyn was quite certain that some unknown good fairy had given her this pleasant acquaintance, and Mrs. Atherley, after a silent spasm of regret that her daughter should be denied the position in the greater world for which she was so admirably fitted, abandoned herself to the infectious gayety of the younger people.

Both she and Evelyn confessed to a feeling of renewed surprise when Philip happened to mention his London address.

Whatever faults the denizens of Park Lane may possess, that of being unknown cannot be reckoned among them, and Mrs. Atherley, in a period not very remote, knew the occupants of every house in that remarkable thoroughfare. She could not, however, recall the name of Anson.

At last a most enjoyable meal came to an end. Philip, supported most ably by a skilled head waiter, spun it out to the utmost possible limit, but the inexorable clock would not be denied.

He thought the two ladies might prefer to drive home alone, so he sent them away in his carriage, and made an excuse that he had an appointment at his club. In truth, he wished to be free to walk far and fast, while his excited brain demanded a solution of the strange congeries of events which had so crowded into his life during forty-eight hours.

About the time that Philip's coachman safely deposited Evelyn and her mother at their residence, Victor Grenier, again attired in evening dress and accompanied by Jocky Mason, whose huge frame was encased in a suit of gray tweed, entered a fashionable West End bar, and found an elegant young person leaning against the marble-topped counter, engaged in a war of wits with a barmaid.

The arrival of the two men, however, put a quick stop to the badinage. The youth quitted the counter with a careless discourtesy that annoyed the girl to whom he was talking.

"Well," he demanded from Grenier, "did anything happen?"

"Jimmie," was the cool reply, "I told you that your stupid ruse last night would result in failure. Far worse, it has supplied you with a rival against whom you may as well give up the game at once."

"Rot!" cried the other, fiercely, with an oath. "Don't irritate me. Tell me plainly what has gone wrong now."

"She was there, and sang delightfully. 'Pon my honor, she is a pretty girl. But the man was there, too, and he managed to improve so well on the opportunity you were kind enough to provide for him, Jimmie, that after her show was over she and her mother met him at the main entrance, and they drove off together to the Savoy in a carriage and pair."

"Then who the deuce is he?" demanded the angry youth.

"I tell you, Jimmie, you have no earthly chance. Last night's intruder was none other than Mr. Philip Anson, the millionaire."

"Philip Anson. Great Scott! He—of all men in the world."

The younger man became very pale, and his eyes rolled in a species of delirious agitation. But Jocky Mason had caught the name, though he did not comprehend the exact subject of their discourse.

"Philip Anson!" he said. "If there's anything on foot where Philip Anson is concerned, count me as his enemy. Curse him! Curse him to all eternity!"

And he struck a table with his great fist until other men began to stare, and Grenier was forced earnestly to counsel his associates to control themselves in such a public place.

Chapter XVI

The Master Fiend

"Come to my chambers," muttered the youngest of the trio. "We are fools to discuss such things here. It is your fault, Grenier. Why did you drop this bombshell on me so unexpectedly? You confounded actors are always looking out for a curtain. You should not try the experiment on your chums in a crowded bar."

"Now, my dear Langdon, do be reasonable. How could I tell that the mere name of Philip Anson would create a scene? You look as sick as a man who has just been sentenced to be hanged, and my old pal Hunter seems to have suddenly gone mad."

Indeed, his words were justified. Mr. James Crichton Langdon was corpselike in pallor, and Mason, alias Hunter, though his tongue was stilled, bore every indication of a man enraged almost beyond control.

"Come away, then," said Langdon, with a horrible attempt to smile indifferently.

"No, no. There are too many eyes here that we should leave with the air of a set of stage murderers. Sit down. Let us have a nip of brandy. Talk about racing, women, anything, for a little while, and then go out quietly."

Grenier was right. A detective had already nudged an acquaintance and whispered:

"The pigeon seems to be upset. And one of the hawks is in a rare temper, too. I'll keep an eye on that collection."

He watched them through a mirror. He saw Grenier exert himself to put his companions in a better humor. When they went out he followed, and ascertained from the commissionaire at the door that they had gone toward Shaftesbury Avenue.

By walking rapidly he sighted them again, and saw them turn into a doorway.

"Grenier's chambers!" he said. "What a splendid nerve that fellow has. Reports himself coolly at Scotland Yard every month, and lives in style not half a mile away. How does he manage it? I must make some inquiry about the others."

Certainly the methods of the superior scoundrels of London are peculiar. Grenier knew that he was a marked man in the eyes of the police. He knew that the particular saloon bar he affected was the rendezvous not only of others like himself, but of the smartest detective officers of the metropolitan force. Yet this was his favorite hunting ground. Where the carcass is there are the jackals; he would never dream of honest endeavor in a new land to begin life anew. The feast was spread before his eyes, and he could not resist it.

But Grenier was a careful rogue. After a boyhood of good training and education, he drifted into a bad set at the beginning of his adult career. Once, indeed, he endeavored to put his great natural abilities to some reasonable use by going on the stage. The industrious hardship of the early years of an actor's striving were not to his liking, however. No sooner had he attained a position of trust as manager of a touring company than he tampered with moneys intrusted to his care.

He was not actually found out, but suspected and dismissed. Then the regular gradations of crime came naturally to him. Gambling, card-sharping, company frauds, even successful forgery, succeeded each other in their recognized sequence, until, at last, came detection and a heavy sentence, for the authorities had long waited for him to drop into the net.

Now that he was free, he did not intend to revisit any of His Majesty's convict settlements if he could help it.

His wits were sharpened, his cool intellect developed, by prison life and associations. He personally would keep clear of the law and make others support him.

He would depend on two classes of contributories—fools, like Langdon, and slow-witted criminals, like Mason. Being a really clever man, it would be strange if his own middle path were not kept clear of fetters.

In the mystery surrounding Philip Anson's influence over these two he scented interesting developments. Beginning with a young rake's attempt to ensnare a beautiful girl, he suddenly discovered a situation pregnant with the potentiality of gain to himself. It did not matter to him who paid him, whether Anson or Langdon. He would betray one or the other, or both impartially.

Mason he liked. The man's rugged strength of character, his sledge-hammer villainy, his dogged acceptance of the leadership of a more skilled rascal, appealed to him. Mason was a tool, and a hard-hitting one. He would use him, safeguard him if he could, but use him anyhow.

In the seclusion of Grenier's small flat Langdon poured out his spleen.

Anson was the bane of his life. His stepfather was Anson's uncle, and the old idiot recently found out certain facts concerning the life led by his stepson that caused a family rupture. His mother endeavored to patch matters with ill success, and the baronet was intent on finding his sister's son, and atoning to him for years of neglect by making him his heir.

Lady Louisa concealed nothing of this from her scapegrace son. She hoped to frighten him by the threatened loss of supplies. But neither fright nor hatred could bring him to leave London, and settle down to a quiet life in Devonshire, when, perhaps, the elderly naturalist's fit of indignation might gradually wear itself out.

At this crisis came his discovery of Evelyn Atherley, and a mad desire to win her affections. He even dreamed of persuading her to marry him, and by this means succeed in rehabilitating himself with Sir Philip Morland.

The girl was well-born. Mrs. Atherley was Lord Vanstone's half-sister, and, although his lordship had ruined himself and his relations by his extravagance, the match was in every other respect suitable.

He was not content with the slow formula of seeking an acquaintance in the ordinary way. Accustomed to speedier conquests, he confided his wishes to Grenier, and resented the latter's condemnation of his suggestion of a mock accident, in which Langdon should figure as the gentlemanly rescuer, as a ready means of winning the girl's grateful regard.

The result was worse than failure. He was wild with himself, wild with Grenier, and reached a higher pitch of fury when Mason surlily refused to say what grievance he harbored against Anson.

"A nice muddle I've made of everything," cried the disappointed youth, "and a precious lot of friends I've discovered. I tell you everything, place myself unreservedly in your power, and you not only let me drift into a stupid blunder, but decline to share your confidences with me."

He rose to go, but Grenier firmly pushed him back into a chair.

"Don't be a bigger fool than you are, Jimmie, and leave those who will help you. I told you the cab adventure was a mistake. It might go wrong in twenty ways and right only in one. And you must admit that I never heard of Anson from you until to-night."

"I may be to blame," was the sulky admission, "but who is your friend Hunter, and why does he not be as outspoken as I?"

"There are reasons. Hunter was cleaned out in Africa on account of Anson's manipulation of a diamond mine. He wants to get even with him. That should be enough for you."

Mason smiled sourly at his leader's ready explanation, and Langdon saw only the venom in the man's face.

"He ought to have said so," he muttered. "I am in no mood to be denied the confidence of those who act with me in this matter. In any case, what can we do?"

Grenier procured a decanter of brandy and passed his cigarette case.

"We can accomplish nothing without money."

"Money! What avail is money against a millionaire?"

"None, directly. You would be swamped instantly. But we must know more about Anson. He has servants. They can be made to talk.

He has susceptible cooks and housemaids in Park Lane, and at whatever place he owns in the country. I am great with cooks and housemaids. There is a mystery, an unfathomable mystery, about his supply of diamonds. It must be probed—"

"No mystery at all," snarled Jocky Mason. "He found a meteor in a slum called Johnson's Mews. It was cram full of diamonds. I saw some of 'em."

"You saw them!"

His hearers allowed all other emotions to yield to the interest of this astounding statement.

"Yes. I don't say much. I act. You'll get no more out of me. I want none of your girls or property. I want Philip Anson's life, and I'll have it if I swing for it!"

"My dear Hunter, you are talking wildly. Have another drink?"

Grenier, cool as an icicle, saw unexpected vistas opening before him. He must be wary and collected. Here was the man who would pay, and the man who would dare all things.

Mason's truculent determination gave hope even to Langdon. He, too, gifted with a certain power of vicious reasoning, saw that this new ally might prove useful. But he was afraid of such bold utterances, and hoped to achieve his purposes without binding himself even tacitly to the commission of a crime, for Mason not only looked, but talked murder.

"I think I had better go," he said, suddenly. "Your brandy is too strong for my head, Grenier. Call and see me in the morning."

The astute rogue whom he addressed raised no objection to his departure. He instantly embraced Langdon's attitude in his wider horizon.

"Yes," he agreed, "let us sleep on it. We will all be better able to discuss matters more clearly to-morrow."

Thenceforth the flat in Shaftesbury Avenue became a spider's web into which the flies that buzzed around Philip's life were drawn one by one, squeezed dry of their store of information, and cast forth again unconscious of the plot being woven against their master.

Within a month, Grenier knew Anson's habits, his comings and goings, his bankers, his brokers, many of his investments, the names of his chief employees, the members of his yacht's crew, the topography of his Sussex estate. Nothing was too trivial, no detail too unimportant, to escape a note undecipherable to others and a niche in a retentive memory.

He made a friend of one of Philip's footmen by standing treat and listening reverently to his views on the next day's racing. He persuaded one kitchen maid in Park Lane and another at Fairfax Hall that he had waited all his life to discover a woman he could love devotedly. It was a most important discovery when he unearthed in a dingy hotel the man whom Philip had dismissed for tampering with the locked portmanteau. From this worthy he first heard of the quaint adjunct to the belongings of the young millionaire, and judicious inquiry soon revealed that there was hardly a servant in Philip's employ who did not credit the Gladstone bag with being the repository of the millionaire's fortunes.

Ordinary people will credit any nonsense where diamonds are concerned. Even an educated criminal like Victor Grenier believed there might be some foundation for the absurd theory which found ready credence among the domestics.

He never made the error of planning a burglary or adroit robbery whereby the bag might come into his possession. If it did contain diamonds, and especially if it contained unique specimens, it was absolutely useless to him. But his vitals yearned for Anson's gold, and the question he asked himself in every unoccupied moment was how he might succeed in getting some portion of it into his own pocket.

One day a quaint notion entered his mind, and the more he thought of it the more it dominated him. He was tall and well-made, if slim in figure, and his face had never lost the plasticity given it by his stage experience.

He had only heard Philip's voice once, but his features and general appearance were now quite familiar to him, and he undertook a series of experiments with clothing and make-up to ascertain if he could personate Anson sufficiently well to deceive anyone who was not an intimate acquaintance. Soon the idea became a mania, and the mania absorbed the man's intellect. To be Philip Anson for a day, a week! What would he not give for the power!

One evening, when Jocky Mason entered Grenier's apartments he started back with an oath, as a stranger approached him in the dim light and said:

"Well, Mason, and what do you want?"

The ex-burglar and man-slayer seemed to be so ready to commit instant murder that Grenier himself was alarmed.

"Hold hard, old chap," he said, in his natural voice. "I am only trying an experiment on you."

"What tomfoolery is this?" shouted the other, gazing at him with the suspicious side glance of a discomfited dog which has been startled by some person familiar to it in ordinary guise but masquerading in outré garments.

"A mere pleasantry, I assure you. Good heavens, man, how you must hate this fellow, Anson, if you are so ready to slay him at sight. From your own story, he only acted as ninety-nine people out of a hundred would have done in helping the cop."

"What I want to know is, why you are playing tricks on me. I won't stand it. I'm not built that way."

"Now, Mason, be reasonable. Can I ask anybody else if I resemble Philip Anson when made up to represent him?"

"Perhaps not, but you ought to have warned me. Besides, I am worried to-day."

"What has happened now?"

"I went to report myself at Southwark Police Station. Who should I find there but Bradley, the chap we used to call 'Sailor.' He is an inspector now, and, of course, he knew me at once."

"What of that?"

"He pretended to take an interest in me, and tried to lead me on to talk about you."

"The devil he did!"

"Oh, I know their ways. They can't do anything to me as long as I show up regularly and keep a clean slate."

"But what about me?"

"I said you had been a good friend—there was no use in denying that I was here pretty often—and that we both thought of emigrating."

"Good. We will."

"Not me. I have a score to settle—"

"Patience, my worthy friend. Your score shall be settled in full. I cannot prevent it, even if I would. Do you think I have been idle, or that I spend Langdon's money on a wild-goose chase? Not me. Langdon has taken my advice at last. He has met this charmer with whom he is so infatuated. She almost recognized him, but he pretended such complete ignorance of her, and even of London, that her suspicions were quieted."

"What good is that to us?"

"Little, but it gave him the opportunity to try and ingratiate himself. He failed most completely, and why?"

"How do I know? He is an ass, anyway."

"Exactly. More than that, the young lady is in love with Philip Anson."

"I'm not."

"But he is in love with her. At first, both Mrs. Atherley and the girl kept him at arm's length. She was too poor, he too rich. That difficulty was smoothed over quite recently, and they meet now nearly every day. Langdon hasn't a dog's chance, and if all goes well, the happy pair will soon be off to Norway or Switzerland for their honeymoon."

"Oh, indeed. Then where does all your clever scheming come in? Why have you held me back? He went to Sussex. You wouldn't let me follow him. He was out late several nights on his motor car along the North Road. I would have met him and smashed his face in with a life-preserver, but you held me back. What are you driving at? What's the game?"

"You shall see."

Grenier went to a cupboard and took out a small box. From this he produced a single check, and several slips of paper on which were written names and signatures.

"That is an old check signed by Philip Anson," he said, coolly. "Here is his signature repeated several times for amusement. It only needs a man of action like you, an accomplished actor like myself, to possess the necessary nerve—the nerve that risks all on a supreme coup—and we will be not only rolling in money, but able to enjoy life pleasantly in any part of the world we select—even in London when the wind changes a little."

"You must talk plainly if you want me to understand you," said Mason, doggedly.

"Very well. You think I am somewhat like Philip Anson at this moment?"

"His image, confound him!"

"No, not his image. I would not humbug his friends. I might puzzle them for a moment, at a distance, but let them speak with me and I am done. It is sufficient that I resemble him. But the handwriting, that is good?"

"First-class."

"There I agree with you. My skill in that direction has been admitted by three bank clerks and an Old Bailey judge. And now for the coup. If you intend to kill this young gentleman you may as well kill him to our mutual advantage. There is no gain in being hanged for him unnecessarily, eh?"

Mason glared at him in silence.

"I see I must keep to the point. We must, by some means, inveigle him to a place where you can work your sweet pleasure on him. Ah, that interests you. It must be known that he is going to that place. It must be quite certain that he leaves it."

"Leaves it!"

"Yes, I, Philip Anson the second, will leave it. I will lay my plans quite surely. I will even telegraph my movements to his fiancée and to his agent, Abingdon, who used to be stipendiary magistrate at Clerkenwell. Now, don't interrupt. You spoil my train of thought. Philip Anson will live again for days after you have—er—disposed of him. By that time you will have established such an alibi that an archangel's testimony would not shake it. Then Philip Anson will disappear, vanish into thin air, and with him a hundred thousand or more of his own money, some in gold, but mostly in notes, which will have been changed so often as to defy anyone to trace them. As a precautionary measure, he will go out of his way to annoy or insult the young lady whom he intends to make his wife, and that alone will supply an explanation, of a sort, for his wish to conceal his movements. With proper management, Philip Anson should leave the map without exciting comment for weeks after he is dead, and when the weeks grow into months, people will class his disappearance with the other queer mysteries familiar to everyone who reads the newspapers. Neat, isn't it?"

"Too neat. You can't do it."

"Have you or I evolved the idea? Who runs the greatest risk, the man who strikes one blow, and hides a disfigured corpse, or he who calmly faces hundreds of men, and says he is Philip Anson?"

"I don't care about risk, but if it comes to that, I suppose you are the more likely to be found out."

"Thank you. You see my way at last. In any event, you are safe. Even suppose I am discovered, will I split on you? Will I add a charge of murder to one of forgery? Not much! I tell you the scheme is workable, not by timid bunglers, but by clever men. I admit I haven't the nerve to kill anybody, nor would I care to suggest this present arrangement to an accomplice merely to make money. But if you are resolved to end Philip Anson's earthly pilgrimage, I can't prevent you, and I fail to see any reason why I shouldn't profit by the transaction."

"What about me when the thing is done?"

"Oh, you are beginning to appreciate the other side of events. Now, we will assume that Philip Anson has been dead a couple of months, and Victor Grenier has amassed a fortune by a sheer run of luck on the turf, it is fairly evident that Victor Grenier must divvy with Jocky Mason, or the latter can make the world too hot to hold him, even if an old friend were unkind enough to refuse to disgorge unless under pressure."

Mason's brows wrinkled in thought. The project sounded plausible enough. Determined as he was to wreak his vengeance on Philip, Grenier's ingenious idea not only offered him a reliable means of escape, but promised a rich harvest of wealth. Certainly it was worth trying. Not once but many times during the preceding month, Grenier had withheld the murderer's willing hand. When it did fall, what keener satisfaction could he have than the knowledge that he would be enriched by the deed?

"I can't see ahead like you," said Mason, at last. "But I will obey orders. You tell me where and when; I will be there."

Grenier shifted his feet uneasily.

"I don't quite mean that," he said. "I will acquaint you with certain facts on which you may rely absolutely. I will forthwith act myself on the assumption that the real Philip Anson won't interfere with me. That is all."

The other man guffawed most unpleasantly. This sophistry did not appeal to him.

"Put it any way you like," he said. "You can depend on me for my part of the bargain."

"And you can be quite certain that in a very little while we need not trouble our active wits any further as to the wherewithal to enjoy life. I have thought this idea out in all its bearings. It simply can't fail. Come, let us drink to a glorious future."

He reached for a decanter, but a sudden knock at the door jarred the nerves of both men considerably.

"See who is there," whispered Grenier, whose face showed white through the paint and grease it bore.

"What about you in that rigout?" growled the stronger ruffian.

"I will slip into my bedroom. Quick! See who it is."

Langdon entered.

"Where's Victor?" he said, eagerly.

"In his room; he will be here in a moment. What's the matter? You look pretty glum."

"I've had a piece of wretched luck. I was at Mrs. Atherley's 'At Home' to-day, when Anson turned up. I met him without winking, but he knew me at once. He called me outside and treated me like a dog."

"He did, eh?"

"Yes. It was no good trying to bluff him. Only on the guarantee that I would never meet Miss Atherley again would he consent not to expose me. I'm done. My last chance is gone. I have wasted my money on Grenier's mad notions, and was fool enough to think you meant what you said when you swore to have Anson's life."

Grenier, who had heard every word, reappeared.

"Does Philip Anson know that Mr. James Crichton Langdon is Sir Philip Morland's stepson?" he asked.

"I can't tell. What does it matter, anyhow?"

"Think, man, think! Does he even know your name?"

"He can easily find it out."

"Not he. This young spark has a fine sense of honor. You promised to keep away from the lady in future. He will never even mention you. And your money is not lost. It has been well spent, every farthing. Take care Miss Evelyn does not see you until she is heartbroken about Philip Anson. She will be; you can be quite sure of it. Then your opportunity will come."

Chapter XVII

The Inmates of the Grange House

Philip walked on roses during those glorious days. He had found his mate. His life was complete. How bright the world, and how fair the future.

The only disagreeable incident marring the utter joy of existence, and that only for an instant, was his encounter with Langdon at Mrs. Atherley's pretty flat in Mount Street.

Grenier, endowed by nature with an occasional retrospective glimpse of a nobler character, read him correctly, when he said that Anson would never condescend to name the intruder in the presence of the woman he loved.

But he did ask a servant who it was with whom he had just been conversing in the entrance hall, and the girl said the gentleman was a Mr. Langdon. No; Mrs. Atherley did not know him well. He was brought to her "At Home" on a previous Wednesday by a friend.

Obviously Evelyn could not have more than a passing acquaintance with the man, or she would have recognized him herself. Her agitation that night in the park, the terror of a difficult situation, was enough to account for her failure in this respect, nor was Philip then aware that at her previous meeting with Lady Morland's son she entertained a curious suspicion, instantly dispelled by his glib manner, that Langdon was the man who sought to thrust his unwelcome attentions upon her.

Mount Street—how came Mrs. Atherley and her daughter to return to the precincts of Mayfair? That was a little secret between Philip and Lord Vanstone.

When Evelyn slyly endeavored to make her new admirer understand that there could be no intimacy between a millionaire and a young lady who was embarking on a professional career—she thought so, be it recorded; this is no canon of art—he seemingly disregarded the hint, but interviewed Lord Vanstone next morning.

The conversation was stormy on one side and emphatic on the other. Philip had heard sufficient of Mrs. Atherley's history by judicious inquiry to enable him to place some unpleasant facts before his lordship.

When the facts had been thrust down the aristocratic gorge, Anson turned to pleasanter topics. He informed Lord Vanstone, who bore the title as the third son of a marquis, that his niece's future was more important than his lordship's dignity. He must eat mud for her sake, and willingly withal.

Various firms of solicitors set to work, and, marvelous to relate, Lord Vanstone was able to write and inform his half-sister that certain speculations in which he had invested her fortune were turning out well. A cash payment of two thousand pounds would be made to her at once, and she possessed an assured income of at least one thousand five hundred pounds per annum during the remainder of her life.

The poor lady had heard these fairy tales before; indeed, some such story of more gorgeous proportions had converted her consols into waste paper.

But a lawyer, not Lord Vanstone's, sent her a check for the larger amount, and, at a subsequent interview, affirmed the statements made by her unreliable relative.

So she went back to her caste, and her caste welcomed her with open arms, and the dear woman thanked Providence for the decree that her daughter might now accept the attentions of any man, no matter how rich he might be, for she saw the drift of Philip's wishes, and, if Evelyn were married to him, surely all their previous trials might be deemed fortunate.

She little dreamed that imperious Philip had ordered matters his own way.

It was not to his thinking that his bride should come to him from the genteel obscurity of Maida Crescent. He would give her a great position, worthy of the highest in the land, and it was better for her that he should woo and win her from the ranks of her order.

It should not be imagined that he was hasty in his decision. To his mind, Evelyn and he were known to each other since they were children. It was not by the wayward caprice of chance that he met her on the night of the meteor's fall, nor again, that he came to her assistance a second time after the lapse of years.

It was his mother's work. He was faithful to her memory—she to her trust. Never did his confidence waver. On the day that Evelyn consented to marry him he showed her his mother's photograph, and told her his belief.

The girl's happy tears bedewed the picture.

"A good son makes a good husband," she murmured. "Mamma says I have been a good daughter, and I will try to be a good wife, Philip."

Apparently these young people had attained the very pinnacle of earthly happiness. There was no cloud, no obstacle. All that was best in the world was at their feet.

Some such thought flitted through Philip's active brain once when Evelyn and he were discussing the future.

"Of course we will be busy," he said, laughing. "You are such an industrious little woman—what? Well—such an industrious tall woman—that the days won't be long enough for all you will find to do. As for me, I suppose I must try and earn a peerage, just to give you your proper place in society, and then we will grow old gracefully."

"Oh, Philip," she cried, placing her hands on his shoulders. "We met once as children for a few minutes. Fate ordained that we should meet again under strange circumstances. We were separated for years. Can fate play us any uncanny trick that will separate us again?"

"Well, sweetheart, fate, in the shape of Wale, is coming for me at six. Unless you wish me to send for my man and dress here—"

"Sometimes I cannot quite credit my good fortune," she said, softly. "Tell me, dearest, how did you manage to live until you were twenty-five without falling in love with some other girl?"

"That is ridiculously easy. Tell me how you managed to escape matrimony until you were twenty-two and you are answered."

"Philip, I—I liked you that night I saw you in the square. You were a woe-begone little boy, but you were so brave, and gave me your hand to help me from the carriage with the air of a young lord."

"And I have cherished your face in my waking dreams ever since. You looked like a fairy. And how you stuck up for me against your uncle!"

"Tell me, what did you think of me when you saw me standing disconsolate in the park?"

Tell, tell, tell—it was nothing but sweet questions and sweet assurances that this pair of turtle doves had been seeking each other through all eternity.

Their wedding was fixed for the middle of July. Sharp work, it may be said, but what need was there to wait? Mr. Abingdon was greatly pleased with Philip's choice, and urged him to settle down at the earliest possible date.

Mrs. Atherley, too, raised no protest. The sooner her beloved daughter was married, the more rapidly would life resume its normal aspect; they would not be long parted from each other.

The young people had no housekeeping cares. Philip's mansions were replete with all that could be desired by the most fastidious taste. His yacht was brought to the Solent, so that they could run over to Portsmouth on a motor car to inspect her, and Evelyn instantly determined that their honeymoon in Etretat should be curtailed to permit them to go for a three-weeks' cruise around the British coast.

This suggestion, of course, appealed to Philip. Nothing could be more delightful. He whispered in Evelyn's ear that he would hug her for the idea at the first available opportunity.

One morning, a day of June rain, a letter reached Philip. It bore the printed superscription, "The Hall, Beltham, Devon," but this was struck out and another address substituted. It was written in a scrawling, wavering hand, the caligraphy of a man old and very ill. It read:

"My Dear Philip: I am lying at the point of death, so I use no labored words to explain why I address you in such manner. I want to tell you how bitterly I regret the injustice I showed to your dear mother and my sister. If, of your charity, you will come to my bedside, and assure a feeble old man of your forgiveness, I

139

can meet the coming ordeal strong in the certainty that Mary Anson will not refuse what you have given in her behalf.

> "Your sorrowing uncle,
> "Philip Morland"

With this piteous epistle was inclosed another.

> "Dear Mr. Anson: I join my earnest supplication to my husband's that you will console his last hours with a visit. He blames himself for what has happened in the past. Yet the fault was more mine than his—far more. For his sake I willingly admit it. And I have been punished for my sin. Ruined in fortune, with my husband at death's door, I am indeed a sorrowing woman.
>
> "Yours faithfully,
> "Louisa Morland"

The angular Italian handwriting of the second letter recalled a faded script in his safe at that moment. The address in each case was a village on the Yorkshire coast, a remote and inaccessible place according to Philip's unaided recollection of the map. "Grange House" might be a farm or a broken-down manor, and Lady Morland's admission of reduced circumstances indicated that they had chosen the locality for economy's sake.

These appeals brought a frown of indecision to Anson's brow. His uncle, and his uncle's wife, had unquestionably been the means of shortening and embittering his mother's life. The man might have acted in ignorance; the woman did not.

Yet what could he do? Refuse a dying relative's last request! They, or one of them, refused his mother's pitiful demand for a little pecuniary help at a time when they were rich.

And what dire mischance could have sunk them into poverty. Little more than two months had passed since Sir Philip Morland was inquiring for his—Philip's—whereabouts through Messrs. Sharpe & Smith with a view toward making him his heir.

Was the inquiry Lady Morland's last ruse to save an encumbered estate? Why was all pretense of doubt as to his relationship swept aside so completely?

He glanced again at the address on the letter, and asked a servant to bring him a railway guide. Then he ascertained that if he would reach Scarsdale that day he must leave London not later than noon. There was a journey of nearly seven hours by rail; no chance of returning the same night.

He went to the library and rang up Sharpe & Smith on the telephone.

A clerk assured him that Mr. Sharpe, who attended to Sir Philip Morland's affairs, had been summoned to Devonshire the previous day.

"To Devonshire!" cried Philip. "I have just received letters from Sir Philip and Lady Morland from Yorkshire."

"Mr. Sharpe himself is puzzled about the matter, sir. Lady Morland wrote from Yorkshire, but told him to proceed to Devonshire without delay."

"Has there been some unexpected development affecting the estate?"

"I am sorry, sir, but you will see I can hardly answer any further questions."

Of course the clerk was right. Philip had hardly quitted the telephone when a note reached him by hand from Evelyn: "Please come at once. Must see you."

He was at Mount Street in three minutes.

Evelyn looked serious and began by holding out a letter to him. He recognized Lady Morland's writing.

"Philip—those people—who behaved so badly to your mother—"

"Have they dared to trouble you?"

"Oh, it is so sad. Your uncle is dying. They are wretchedly poor; an unforeseen collapse. See." And she read:

> "Of your pity, Miss Atherley, ask your affianced husband to come to us, and to help us. I want nothing for myself, but the mere sight of a few checks to pay tradespeople, doctor and the rest will soothe Sir Philip's last hours. He is a proud man, and I know he is heartbroken to think he is dying a pauper among strangers."

So it ended as might be expected. Philip wired to Grange House, Scarsdale, to announce his coming. Accompanied by his valet, he left King's Cross at twelve o'clock, but his parting words to Evelyn were:

"See Mr. Abingdon after luncheon, dear, and tell him what I am doing. I will return to-morrow; meanwhile, I will keep you informed by telegraph of my movements."

After leaving the main line at York there was a tiresome crawl to the coast, broken by changes at junctions—wearying intervals spent in pacing monotonous platforms.

At last the train reached Scarsdale at twenty minutes to seven. A few passengers alighted. The place was evidently a small village not given over to the incursions of summer visitors.

A tall man, with "doctor" writ large on his silk hat and frock coat, approached Philip.

"Mr. Anson?"

"Yes."

"I am Dr. Williams. I have brought you a letter from Lady Morland. Perhaps you will read it now. I expect it explains my errand."

"Sir Philip is still living?"

"Yes, but sinking fast."

Anson tore open the note. It was brief.

"Thank you for your prompt kindness. Dr. Williams will drive you to the house. If you have brought a servant he might take your luggage to the Fox and Hounds Inn, where Dr. Williams has secured rooms for you. I regret exceedingly we have no accommodation here, but, in any event, you will be more comfortable at the inn."

He looked at the doctor. In a vague way, his voice recalled accents he seemed to recognize.

"Is there a telegraph office here?"

"Yes. We pass it. It closes at eight."

"I will not be back from the Grange House before then?"

"Hardly. It is a half-hour's drive."

"Thank you. You will stop a moment at the telegraph office?"

The doctor hesitated.

"There is so little time. Is it of great importance? Of course—"

"Oh, I know what to do. Green—take my traps to the Fox and Hounds Inn. Then go to the telegraph office and send a message in my name to Miss Atherley, saying: 'Arrived. Sir Philip worse.' That is all."

Anson's valet saluted and left them. Dr. Williams said cheerfully:

"That disposes of a difficulty. Are you ready, Mr. Anson?"

They entered a ramshackle dogcart, for which the doctor apologized.

"These hills knock one's conveyances to pieces. I am having a new cart built, but it will be done for in a couple of years. Out in all weathers, you see. To carry you I had to leave my man at home."

The doctor himself seemed to be young and smart-looking. Evidently Scarsdale agreed with him, if not with his vehicles. The horse, too, was a good one, and they moved through a scattered village at a quick trot.

They met a number of people, but Dr. Williams was talking so eagerly to his companion that he did not nod to any of them.

As the road began to climb toward a bleak moorland he became less voluble, more desirous to get Anson to speak. Philip thought that the doctor listened to him with a curious eagerness. Probably Sir Philip and Lady Morland impressed him as an odd couple; he would be anxious to learn what sort of relative this was who had traveled from London to see them.

Philip was in small humor for conversation. He looked forward to an exceedingly unpleasant interview, when his lips would utter consoling words to which he must strive to impart a genuine and heartfelt ring; that would need an effort, to say the least.

The road wound its way through pines and heather, but ever

142

upward, until the trees yielded to an unbroken range of open mountain, and the farms that nestled in nooks of the hillside disappeared wholly.

Glimpses of the sea were caught where a precipitous valley tore a cleft in the land. On a lofty brow in front Philip saw a solitary and half-dismantled building.

"Is that the Grange House?" he inquired.

"Yes."

"Why on earth did two old people, one of them an invalid, select such a lonely residence?"

"That has been puzzling me for days."

"How long have they been here?"

"I cannot say. I was only called in four days ago."

They passed a policeman patrolling his country beat. The doctor gave him an affable smile. The man saluted promptly, but looked after them with a puzzled air. He continued to watch them at intervals until they reached the Grange House.

Anson noticed that the track, it was a gate-guarded bridle path now, mounted steadily to the very threshold.

"The place stands on the edge of a cliff," he said.

"Yes. It was built by some recluse. The rock falls sheer, indeed slopes inwards to some extent, for three hundred feet."

"Some day, I suppose, it will fall into the sea?"

"Probably, but not in our time. Here we are. Just allow me to hitch the reins to the gatepost."

He jumped lightly out of the dogcart.

"Are there no servants?"

"Only an old woman and her daughter. They are busy at this hour."

Philip understood that a meal might be in preparation. He hoped not; personally, he could not eat there.

Dr. Williams pressed the latch of an old-fashioned door. He whispered:

"Be as quiet as possible. He may be asleep; if he is, it will not be for long, poor fellow."

Indeed the doctor himself betrayed some slight agitation now. He perspired somewhat, and his hand shook.

Anson followed him into a somber apartment, crudely furnished, half dining room, half kitchen. Though the light of a June evening was clear enough outside, the interior of the house was gloomy in the extreme. There were some dark curtains shrouding a doorway.

"Lady Morland is in there," murmured the doctor, brokenly. "Will you go to her?"

Philip obeyed in silence. He passed through the curtains. It was so dark that he imagined he must be in a passage with a door at the other end.

"Can't I have a light?" he asked, partly turning toward the room he had just quitted.

In the neglected garden at the landward front of the Grange House the horse stood patiently on three legs, ruminating, no doubt, on the steepness of hills and the excellence of pastures.

Nearly an hour passed thus, in solemn quietude. Then a boy on a bicycle, red-faced with exertion, pedaled manfully up the hill, and through the gate.

"I hope he's here," thought he. "It's a long way to coom for nothin'."

Around his waist was a strap with a pouch bearing the king's monogram. He ran up to the door and gave a couple of thunderous knocks, the privileged rat-tat of a telegraph messenger.

There was a long delay. Then a heavy step approached, and a man opened the door, a big, heavy-faced man, with eyes that stared dreadfully, and a nose damaged in life's transit.

"Philip Anson, Esquire," said the boy, briskly, producing a buff-colored envelope.

The man seemed to swallow something.

"Yes; he's here. Is that for him?"

"Yes, sir. Any reply?"

The man took the telegram, closed the door, and the boy heard his retreating footsteps. After some minutes he returned.

"It's too late to reply to-night, isn't it?" he inquired.

"Yes, sir. It coom'd after hours, but they'd paid t' porterage i' Lunnon, so t' postmistress said ye'd mebbe like to hev it at yance. I've ridden all t' way frae Scarsdale."

Late that evening, when the protracted gloaming of the north was fast yielding to the shadows of a cloudy night, the big man from the Grange House drove into Scarsdale. He pulled up at the Fox and Hounds public house. He wanted Mr. Green.

Anson's valet came.

"Your master says you are to bring his portmanteau to the Grange House to-night. He intends remaining there. You must get the landlord to sit up until you return. It will take you an hour and a half to drive both ways."

Green was ready in five minutes. He learned that a stable boy must crouch at their feet to bring the dogcart back. It was the property of the Fox and Hounds' proprietor.

Very unwillingly the horse swung off again toward the moor. There was little conversation. The driver was taciturn, the Londoner somewhat scared by the dark loneliness.

At the Grange House they were met by Philip Anson. He stood in the open doorway. He held a handkerchief to his lips and spoke in a husky voice, the voice of one under the stress of great agitation:

"That you, Green? Just give my bag to the driver and return to the village. Here is a five-pound note. Pay your bill and go back to London by the first train to-morrow. I stop here some few days."

The astonished servant took the note. Before he could reply, his master turned, crossed a room feebly lighted by a dull lamp, and passed through a curtained doorway.

Green was staring perplexedly at the house, the kitchen, his ill-favored companion carrying Philip's portmanteau within, when he heard his master's voice again, and saw him standing between the partly drawn curtains, with his face quite visible in the dim rays of the lamp.

"Green?"

"Yes, sir."

"Here are my keys. Unlock the bag and take the keys with you. You remember the small portmanteau in my safe at Park Lane?"

"Yes, sir."

"Open the safe, get that bag, and send it to me to-morrow night by train to the Station Hotel, York."

"To-morrow night, sir?"

"Yes."

The keys were thrown with a rattle onto a broad kitchen table. Evidently Mr. Anson would not brook questions as to his movements, though his few words sounded contradictory. Green got down, unfastened the portmanteau and went back to the dogcart.

"They're queer folk i' t' grange," said the stable boy, as they drove away. "There's a barrow-night and a lady as nobody ever sees, an' a dochtor, an' a man—him as kem for ye."

"Surely they are well known here?"

"Not a bit of it. On'y bin here about a week. T' doctor chap's very chirpy, but yon uther is a rum 'un."

Green was certainly puzzled very greatly by the unexpected developments of the last few minutes, but he was discreet and well trained.

He liked his young master, and would do anything to serve his interests. Moreover, the ways of millionaires were not the ways of other men. All he could do was to hear and obey.

He slept none the less soundly because his master chose voluntarily to bury himself, even for a little while, in such a weirdly tumbledown, old mansion as the Grange House.

Chapter XVIII

"Revenge is Mine; I Will Repay"

"Can't I have a light?" said Philip, with head screwed round to ascertain if the doctor were following him.

Some sense, whether of sight or hearing he knew not, warned him of movement near at hand, an impalpable effort, a physical tension as of a man laboring under extreme but repressed excitement.

He paid little heed to it. All the surroundings in this weird dwelling were so greatly at variance with his anticipations that he partly expected to find further surprises.

Dr. Williams did not answer. Philip advanced a halting foot, a hesitating hand groping for a door.

Instantly a stout rope fell over his shoulders, a noose was tightly drawn, and he was jerked violently to the stone floor of the passage. He fell prone on his face, hurting his nose and mouth. The shock jarred him greatly, but his hands, if not his arms, were free, and, with the instinct of self-preservation that replaces all other sensations in moments of extreme peril, he strove valiantly to rise.

But he was grasped by the neck with brutal force, and some one knelt on his back.

"Philip Anson," hissed a man's voice, "do you remember Jocky Mason?"

So he had fallen into a trap, cunningly prepared by what fiendish combination of fact and artifice he had yet to learn. Jocky Mason, the skulking criminal of Johnson's Mews. Was he in that man's power?

Under such conditions a man thinks quickly. Philip's first ordered thought was one of relief. He had fallen into the clutches of an English brigand. Money would settle this difficulty, if all other means failed.

"Yes, yes," he gurgled, half-strangled by the fierce pressure on his throat.

"You hit me once from behind. You can't complain if I do the same. You sent me to a living hell for ten years—not your fault that it wasn't forever. Lie still! Not all your money can save you now. I am judge and jury, and hell itself. You are dying—dying—dead!"

And with the final words drawled into his ears with bitter intensity, Philip felt a terrible blow descend on his head. There was no pain, no fear, no poignant emotion at leaving all the world held so dear to him. There was an awful shock. A thundercloud seemed to burst in his brain, and he sank into the void without a groan.

Now, in falling, the hard, felt hat he wore dropped in front of his

146

face. The first wild movement of his head tilted it outward, but the savage jerk given by his assailant brought the rim slightly over his skull again.

In the almost complete darkness of the passage, Mason could not see the slight protection this afforded to his victim, and the sledge-hammer blow he delivered with a life-preserver—that murderous implement named so utterly at variance with its purpose—did not reveal the presence of an obstacle.

He struck with a force that would have stunned an ox; it must have killed any man, be he the hardest-skulled aborigine that ever breathed. But the stout rim of the hat, though crushed like an eggshell, took off some of the leaden instrument's tremendous impact. Philip, though quite insensible, was not dead. His sentient faculties were annihilated for the time, but his heart continued its life-giving functions, and he breathed with imperceptible flutterings.

Mason rose, panting with excitement, glutted with satisfied hate. He lifted his victim's inert form with the ease of his great strength.

"Come on!" he shouted, and strode toward a door which he kicked open.

A step sounded haltingly in the passage. Grenier, the soi-disant doctor, livid now and shaking with the ague of irretrievable crime, stumbled after his more callous associate. Unconsciously he kicked Philip's hat to one side. He entered the room, an apartment with a boundless view of the sea.

Here there was more light than in the kitchen. The windows faced toward the northwest, and the last radiance of a setting sun illumined a wall on the right.

"Not there!" he gasped. "In this chair; his face—I must see his face!"

Mason, still clasping his inanimate burden, laughed with a snarl.

"Stop that," he roared. "Pull yourself together. Get some brandy. I've done my work. If you can't do yours, let me finish it."

"Oh, just a moment! Give me time! I hate the sight of blood. Get a towel. Bind it round his neck. His clothes! They will be saturated. And wipe his face. I must see his face."

Grenier was hysterical; he had the highly strung nervous system of a girl where deeds of bloodshed were concerned. While Mason obeyed his instructions he pressed his hands over his eyes.

"Bring some brandy, white-liver. Do you want me to do everything?"

This gruff order awoke Grenier to trembling action. He went to a cupboard and procured a bottle. Mason, having placed Anson in a chair and steadied his head against the wall, seized half a tumblerful of the neat spirit and drank it with gusto. The other, gradually recovering his self-control, was satisfied with a less potential draught.

"It will be dark soon," growled Mason. "We must undress him first, you said."

"Yes. If his clothes are not blood-stained."

"Rot! He must go into the water naked in any case. The idea is your own."

"Ah! I forgot. It will soon be all right. Besides, I knew I should be upset, so I have everything written down here—all fully thought out. There can be no mistake made then."

He produced a little notebook and opened it with uncertain fingers. He glanced at a closely written page. The words danced before his vision, but he persevered.

"Yes. His coat first. Then his boots. Clothes or linen stained with blood to be burned, after cutting off all buttons. Now, I'm ready. I will not funk any more."

His temperament linked the artistic and criminal faculties in sinister combination, and he soon recovered his domination in a guilty partnership. It must have been the instinct of the pickpocket that led him to appropriate Philip's silver watch, with its quaint shoelace attachment, before he touched any other article.

"Queer thing," he commented. "A rich man might afford a better timekeeper. But there's no accounting for tastes."

Mason, satiated and stupefied, obeyed his instructions like a ministering ghoul. They undressed Philip wholly, and Grenier, rapidly denuding himself of his boots and outer clothing, donned these portions of the victim's attire.

Then the paint tubes and the other accessories of an actor's make-up were produced. Grenier, facing a mirror placed on a table close to Philip, began to remodel his own plastic features in close similitude to those of the unconscious man. He was greatly assisted by the fact that in general contour they were not strikingly different.

Philip's face was of a fine, classical type; Grenier, whose nose, mouth and chin were regular and pleasing, found the greatest difficulty in controlling the shifty, ferret-like expression of his eyes. Again, Philip had no mustache. The only costume he really liked to wear was his yachting uniform, and here he conformed to the standard of the navy. The shaven lip, of course, was helpful to his imitator. All that was needed was an artistic eye for the chief effect, combined with a skilled use of his materials. And herein Grenier was an adept.

But the light was growing very uncertain.

"A lamp," he said, querulously, for time sped and he had much to do; "bring a lamp quickly."

Mason went toward the front kitchen. Grenier did not care about being left alone, face to face with the pallid and naked form in the chair, but he set his teeth and repressed the tendency to rush after his confederate.

The latter, in returning, halted an instant.

148

"Hello!" he cried. "Here's his hat."

After placing the lamp on the table beside the mirror, he went back to the passage.

Grenier was so busy with the making-up process that he did not notice what his companion was doing. His bent form shrouded the light, and Mason placed the hat carelessly on a chair. He chanced to hold it by an uninjured part of the rim, and never thought of examining it.

At last Grenier declared himself satisfied.

"What do you think of the result?" he demanded, facing about so that the other could see both Anson and himself.

"First-rate. It would deceive his own mother."

A terrific rat-tat sounded on the outer door.

A direct summons to the infernal regions could not have startled both men more thoroughly. Grenier, with the protecting make-up on forehead and cheeks, only showed his terror in his glistening eyes and palsied frame. Mason, whom nothing could daunt, was, nevertheless, spellbound with surprise.

What intruder was this who knocked so imperatively? They were a mile and a half from the nearest habitation, four miles from a village. What fearful chance had brought to their door one who thus boldly demanded admission? Had their scheme miscarried at this vital moment? Had Anson suspected something and arranged that he should be followed by rescuers—avengers?

The sheer agony of fear restored Grenier's wits. He was not Grenier now, but Philip Anson, a very shaky and unnerved Philip Anson, it was true, but sufficiently likelife to choke off doubting inquiries.

He clutched Mason's arm and pointed a quivering finger toward Philip.

"Out with him! This instant! The tide is high!"

"But his face! If he is found—"

Mason reached for the life-preserver with horrible purpose.

"No, no. No more noise. Quick, man. You must go to the door. Only summon me if necessary. Oh, quick!"

He rushed to another door and opened it. There was a balcony beyond. It overhung the very lip of the rock. Far beneath, the deep blue of the sea shone, and naught else.

Mason caught up Anson's limp form and ran with him to the balcony. With a mighty swing he threw him outward, clear of the cliff's edge. For a few tremulous seconds they listened. They thought they heard a splash; then Mason turned coolly to Grenier:

"Is there any blood on my coat?"

"I can see none. Now, the door! Keep inside!"

With quaking heart he listened to Mason's heavy tread along the passage and across the kitchen. He clinched the back of a chair in the effort to calm himself by forcible means. Then he heard the unbolting of the door and the telegraph messenger's prompt announcement:

"Philip Anson, Esquire."

Mason came to him carrying the telegram.

Grenier subsided into the chair he held. This time he was prostrated. He could scarce open the flimsy envelope.

"Abingdon counsels caution. Says there is some mistake. Much love.

"Evelyn."

That was all, but it was a good deal. Grenier looked up with lack-luster eyes. He was almost fainting.

"Send him away," he murmured. "There is nothing to be done. In the morning—"

Mason saw that his ally was nearly exhausted by the reaction. He grinned and cursed.

"Of all the chicken-hearted—"

But he went and dismissed the boy. Grenier threw himself at full length on a sofa.

"What's up now?" demanded Mason, finding him prone.

"Wait—just a little while—until my heart stops galloping. That confounded knock! It jarred my spine."

"Take some more brandy."

"How can I? It is impossible. I haven't got an ox-head, like you."

Mason placed the lamp on a central table. Its rays fell on Philip's hat. Something in its appearance caught the man's eye. He picked up the hat and examined it critically.

"Do you know," he said, after a silence broken only by Grenier's deep breathing, "I fancy I didn't kill him, after all."

"Not—kill him? Why—he was dead—in that chair—for an hour."

"Perhaps. I hit hard enough, but this hat must have taken some of it. When you were busy, I thought his chest heaved slightly. And just now, when I carried him outside, he seemed to move."

"Rot!"

"It may be. I struck very hard."

Grenier sat up.

"Even if you are right," he muttered, "it does not matter. He fell three hundred feet. The fall alone would kill him. And, if he is drowned, and the body is picked up, it is better so. Don't you see! Even if he were recognized he would be drowned, not—not—Well, his death would be due to natural causes."

He could not bring himself to say "murdered"—an ugly word.

"If you were not such a milksop, there would be no fear of his being recognized."

But Grenier laughed a hollow and unconvincing laugh; nevertheless, it was a sign of recovery.

"What nonsense we are talking. A naked man, floating, dead, in the North Sea. Who is he? Not Philip Anson, surely! Philip Anson is gayly gadding about England on his private affairs. Where is Green? Hunter, go and tell Green to bring my traps here instantly. I wish him to return to town on an urgent errand."

There was a glint of admiration in Mason's eyes. Here was one with Anson's face, wearing Anson's clothes, and addressing him in Anson's voice.

"That's better," he chuckled. "By G—d, you're clever when your head is clear."

"Now be off for Green. You know what to say."

"You will be alone. Will you be afraid?"

The sneer was the last stimulant Grenier needed.

"If you were called on to stand in Philip Anson's boots during the next week or ten days, my good friend," he quietly retorted, "you would be afraid sixty times in every hour. Your job has nearly ended; mine has barely commenced. Now, leave me."

Nevertheless, he quitted that chamber of death, carrying with him all that he needed, and hurrying over the task while he could yet hear the dogcart rattling down the hill.

He commenced with an inventory of Philip's pockets.

His eyes sparkled at the sight of a well-filled pocketbook, with a hundred pounds in notes stuffed therein, cards, a small collection of letters, and other odds and ends. Among Philip's books was Evelyn's hurried note of that morning, and on it a penciled memorandum:

"Sharpe left for Devonshire yesterday. Lady M. wrote from Yorkshire."

"That was a neat stroke," thought Grenier, with a smile—when he smiled he least resembled Philip. "Being a man of affairs, Anson promptly went to the Morlands' solicitors. I was sure of it. I wonder how Jimmie arranged matters with Sharpe. I will know to-morrow at York."

A check book in another pocket added to his joy.

"The last rock out of my path," he cried, aloud. "That saves two days. The bait took. By Jove! I'm in luck's way!"

There was now no need to write to Philip's bank for a fresh book, which was his first daring expedient.

He seated himself at a table and wrote Philip's signature several times to test his hand. At last it was steady. Then he put a match to a fire all ready for lighting, and burned Philip's hat, collar, shirt and underclothing; also the blood-stained towel.

When the mass of clothing was smoldering black and red he threw a fresh supply of coal on top of it. The loss of the hat did not trouble him; he possessed one of the same shape and color.

He was quietly smoking a cigar, and practicing Philip's voice between the puffs, when Mason returned with the valet.

The scene, carefully rehearsed by Grenier in all its details, passed off with gratifying success. Purring with satisfaction, the chief scoundrel of the pair left in the Grange House by the astonished servant, began to overhaul the contents of Philip's bag.

It held the ordinary outfit of a gentleman who does not expect to pay a protracted visit—an evening dress suit, a light overcoat, a tweed suit, and a small supply of boots and linen. A tiny dressing case fitted into a special receptacle, and on top of this reposed a folded document.

Grenier opened it. Mason looked over his shoulder. It was headed:

"Annual Report of the Mary Anson Home for Destitute Boys."

Mason coarsely cursed both the home and its patron. But Grenier laughed pleasantly.

"The very thing," he cried. "Look here!"

And he pointed to an indorsement by the secretary.

"For signature if approved of."

"I will sign and return it, with a nice typewritten letter, to-morrow, from York. Abingdon is one of the governors. Oh, I will bamboozle them rarely."

"This blooming charity will help you a bit, then?"

"Nothing better. Let us go out for a little stroll. Now, don't forget. Address me as 'Mr. Anson.' Get used to it, even if we are alone. And it will be no harm should we happen to meet somebody."

They went down the hill and entered the rough country road that wound up from Scarsdale to the cliff. Through the faint light of a summer's night they saw a man approaching.

It was a policeman.

"Absit omen," said Grenier, softly.

"What's that?"

"Latin for a cop. You complained of my want of nerve. Watch me now."

He halted the policeman, and questioned him about the locality, the direction of the roads, the villages on the coast. He explained pleasantly that he was a Londoner, and an utter stranger in these parts.

"You are staying at the Grange House, sir?" said the man, in his turn.

"Yes. Come here to-day, in fact."

"I saw you, sir. Is the gentleman who drove you from Scarsdale staying there, too? I met you on the road, and he seemed to know me."

Grenier silently anathematized his carelessness. Policemen in rural Yorkshire were not as common as policemen in Oxford Street. It was the same man whom he had encountered hours ago.

"Oh, he is a doctor. Yes, he resides in the Grange House."

"You won't find much room for a party there, sir," persisted the constable. "I don't remember the gentleman at all. What is his name?"

"Dr. Williams. He is a genial sort of fellow—nods to anybody. Take a cigar. Sorry I can't ask you to go up and have a drink, but there is illness in the place."

The policeman passed on.

"Illness!" he said, glancing at the gloomy outlines of the farm. "How many of 'em are in t' place. And who's yon dark-lookin' chap, I wonder? My, but his face would stop a clock!"

Chapter XIX

Philip Anson Redivivus

Next morning Mason trudged off to Scarsdale at an early hour. He ascertained that Green had quitted the Fox and Hounds Inn in time to catch the first train.

He returned to Grange House with the dogcart and drove Grenier to Scarsdale with his luggage, consisting of Philip's portmanteau and his own, together with a hatbox.

He touched his cap to Grenier, when the latter smiled affably on him from the luxury of a first-class carriage, and he pocketed a tip with a grin.

A porter was also feed lavishly, and the station master was urbanity itself as he explained the junctions and the time London would be reached.

Left to himself, Mason handed over the dogcart to the hostler at the inn, paid for its hire, and again walked to the deserted farm. He surveyed every inch of the ground floor, carefully raked over the ashes in the grate, scrubbed the passage with a hard broom and water, packed some few personal belongings in a small bag, and set out again, after locking the door securely, for a long tramp over the moor. Nine miles of mountain road would bring him to another line of railway. Thence he would book to London, and travel straight through, arriving at the capital late at night, and not making the slightest attempt to communicate with Grenier en route.

There was little fear of comment or inquiry caused by the disappearance of the inhabitants of the Grange House.

He and "Dr. Williams" were the only residents even slightly known to the distant village. Such stores as they needed they had paid for. The house was hired for a month from an agent in the county town, and the rent paid in advance. It was not clear who owned the place. The agent kept it on his books until some one should claim it.

As the murderer walked and smoked his reflections were not quite cheerful, now that he could cry "quits" with Philip Anson.

His experiences of the previous night were not pleasant. Neither he nor Grenier went to bed. They dozed uneasily in chairs until daylight, and then they admitted that they had committed Anson's body to the deep in a moment of unreasoning panic.

He might be found, and, even if he were not identified, that confounded policeman might be moved to investigate the proceedings of the curious visitors to Grange House.

That was the weak part of their armor, but Grenier refused to admit the flaw.

"A naked man found in the sea—and he may never be found—has not necessarily been thrown from a balcony three hundred feet above sea level. The notion is grotesque. No constabulary brain could conceive it. And who is he? Not Philip Anson; Philip Anson is alive. Not Dr. Williams; any Scarsdale man will say that. And your best friend, Mason, would not take him for you."

But Mason was not satisfied. Better have buried the corpse on the lonely farm—in the garden for choice. Then they would know where he was. The sea was too vague.

Of pity for his victim he had not a jot. Had Philip Anson pitied him, or his wife, or his two children? They, too, were dead, in all probability. While in London he had made every sort of inquiry, but always encountered a blank wall of negation. John and William Mason, even if they lived, did not know he was their father. They were lost to him utterly.

Curse Philip Anson. Let him be forgotten, anyway. Yet he contrived to think of him during the nine weary miles over the moor, during the long wait at the railway station, and during the slow hours of the journey to London.

On arriving at York, Grenier secured a palatial suite at the Station Hotel, entering his name in the register as "Philip Anson."

He drove to the post office and asked if there was any message for "Grenier."

Yes. It read:

"Family still at Penzance. Persuaded friend that letter was only intended to create unpleasantness with uncle. He took same view and returned to town. Will say nothing."

Unsigned, it came from a town near Beltham. Grenier was satisfied. He lit a cigarette with the message.

At a branch post office he dispatched two telegrams.

The first to Evelyn:

"Will remain in the North for a few days. Too busy to write to-day. Full letter to-morrow. Love.

"Philip."

The second, to Mr. Abingdon:

"Your message through Miss Atherley noted. Please suspend all inquiries. Affair quite unforeseen. Will explain by letter.

Address to-day, Station Hotel, York.

"Anson."

Then he entered a bank and asked for the manager.

"My name may be known to you," he said to the official, at the same time handing his card.

"Mr. Anson, Park Lane—the Mr. Anson."

"I suppose I can flatter myself with the definite article. I am staying here some few days, and wish to carry out certain transactions requiring large sums of money. I will be glad to act through your bank, on special terms, of course, for opening a short account."

"We will be delighted."

"I will write a check now for five thousand pounds, which kindly place to my credit as soon as possible. Shall we say—the day after to-morrow?"

"That is quite possible. We will use all expedition."

"Thank you. You understand, this is merely a preliminary. I will need a much larger sum, but I will pay in my next check after hearing from London. I am not quite sure about the amount of my private balance at the moment."

The bank manager assured him there would be no difficulty whatever under such conditions.

Grenier obtained his passbook and check book, after writing a check on London before the other man's eyes.

For a small amount, an introduction would have been necessary. In the case of Philip Anson, the millionaire, a man who handled thousands so readily, it was needless. Moreover, his procedure was unexceptionable—strictly according to banking business.

Grenier rushed off to the station, caught a train for Leeds, went to the bank of a different company with different London agents, and carried through the same maneuver.

He returned to York and secured the services of the hotel typist. He wrote to Philip's bankers:

"I am transacting some very important private business in the North of England, and have opened temporary accounts with the — Bank in York and the — Bank in Leeds, and I shall need a considerable sum of ready money. Possibly I may also open accounts in Bradford and Sheffield. To-day I have drawn two checks for five thousand pounds each. Kindly let me know by return the current balance to my credit, as I dislike overdrafts and would prefer to realize some securities."

The next letter ran:

"My Dear Abingdon: Excuse a typewriter, but I am horribly

156

busy. The Morlands' affair is a purely family and personal one; it brings into activity circumstances dating far back in my life and in the lives of my parents. Sir Philip is not dying, nor even dangerously ill. Lady Louisa is in Yorkshire, and I am making arrangements which will close a long-standing feud.

"Write me here if necessary, but kindly keep back all business or other communications, save those of a very urgent character, for at least a week or perhaps ten days.

"Sorry for this enforced absence from town. It simply cannot be avoided, and I am sure you will leave a detailed explanation until we meet. I have signed the inclosed annual report of the home. Will you kindly forward it to the secretary? Yours sincerely,

"Philip Anson."

Grenier dictated this epistle from a carefully composed copy. He understood the very friendly relations that existed between Philip and his chief agent, and he thought that in adopting a semi-apologetic, frankly reticent tone, he was striking the right key.

The concluding reference to the Mary Anson Home was smart, he imagined, while the main body of the letter dealt in safe generalities.

Naturally, he knew nothing of the conversation between the two men on this very topic a couple of months earlier.

But Langdon's ample confessions had clearly revealed Philip's attitude, and the unscrupulous scoundrel was willing now to dare all in his attempt to gain a fortune.

While he was dining a telegram was handed to him:

"You forgot to send your address, but Mr. Abingdon gave it to me. So grieved you are detained. What about blue atom?

"Evelyn."

Did ever woman invent more tantalizing question than that concluding one? What was a blue atom? No doubt, creation's scheme included blue atoms, as well as black ones and red ones. But why this reference to any particular atom? He tried the words in every possible variety of meaning. He gave them the dignity of capitals. BLUE ATOM. They became more inexplicable.

In one respect they were effective. They spoiled his dinner. He had steeled himself against every possible form of surprise, but he was forced to admit that during the next three days he must succeed in persuading Evelyn Atherley that Philip Anson was alive, and engaged in important matters in Yorkshire. That was imperative—was his scheme to be wrecked by a blue atom?

157

Moreover, her query must be answered. His promise to write was, of course, a mere device. It would be manifestly absurd to send her a typewritten letter, and, excellently as he could copy Philip's signature, he dared not put his skill as a forger to the test of inditing a letter to her, no matter how brief. Finally he hit upon a compromise. He wired:

"Stupid of me to omit address. Your concluding sentence mixed up in transmission. Meaning not quite clear. Am feeling so lonely.

"Philip."

Then he tried to resume his dinner, but his appetite was gone.

In postal facilities, owing to its position on a main line, York is well served from London. At 9 P. M. two letters, one a bulky package and registered, reached him.

The letter was from Mr. Abingdon. It briefly acknowledged his telegram, stated that a man in the Athenæum, who knew Sir Philip Morland, had informed him, in response to guarded inquiries, that the baronet was exceedingly well off, and called attention to some important leases inclosed which required his signature.

The other note was from Evelyn. It was tender and loving, and contained a reference that added to the mystification of her telegram.

"In the hurry of your departure yesterday," she wrote, "we forgot to mention Blue Atom. What is your opinion? The price is high, certainly, but, then, picture the joy of it—the only one in the world!"

And, again, came another message:

"I referred to Blue Atom, of course. What did the post office make it into?

"Evelyn."

Blue Atom was assuming spectral dimensions. He cursed the thing fluently. It was high priced, a joy, alone in solitary glory. What could it be?

He strolled into the station, and entered into conversation with a platform inspector.

"By the way," he said, casually, "have you ever heard of anything called a blue atom?"

The man grinned. "Is that another name for D. T.'s, sir?"

Grenier gave it up, and resolved to postpone a decision until the next morning.

By a late train Philip's portmanteau arrived. It was locked, and the key reposed in the safe. Green, it ultimately transpired, solemnly opened the safe in the presence of the housekeeper and butler, locked it again without disturbing any of the other contents, and handed the key to the butler, who placed it in the silver pantry.

In the solitude of his room, Grenier burst the lock. The rascal received one of the greatest shocks of his life when he examined the contents—a quantity of old clothing, some worn boots, a ball of twine, a bed coverlet, a big, iron key, the tattered letters, and a variety of odds and ends that would have found no corner in a respectable rag shop.

He burst into a fit of hysterical laughter.

"Ye gods and little fishes!" he cried. "What a treasure! The Clerkenwell suit, I suppose, and a woman's skirt and blouse. Old-timers, too, by their style. His mother's, I expect. He must have been fond of his mother."

At that moment Jocky Mason, beetle-browed and resentful, was reading a letter which reached his lodgings two hours before his arrival, in an envelope bearing the ominous initials—O. H. M. S.

It was from the Southwark Police Station.

"Sir: Kindly make it convenient to attend here to-morrow evening at 8 P. M. Yours truly,

"T. Bradley, Inspector."

The following day it was Mason's duty to report himself under his ticket-of-leave, but it was quite unusual for the police to give a preliminary warning in this respect. Failure on his part meant arrest. That was all the officials looked after.

"What's up now?" he muttered. "Anyway, Grenier was right. This gives me a cast-iron alibi. I'll acknowledge it at once."

His accomplice, hoping to obtain sleep from champagne, consumed the contents of a small bottle in his bedroom, while he scanned the columns of the local evening papers for any reference to a "Seaside Mystery" on the Yorkshire coast.

There was none. Anson's body had not been recovered yet.

Before going to bed, he wound Philip's watch. He examined it now with greater interest than he had bestowed on it hitherto.

Although silver, it appeared to be a good one. He opened the case to examine the works. Inside there was an inscription:

"Presented to Philip Anson, aged fifteen years, by the officers and men of the Whitechapel Division of the Metropolitan Police as a token of their admiration for his bravery in assisting to arrest a notorious burglar."

159

Beneath was the date of Mason's capture.

"Where was I ten years ago?" he mused.

He looked back through the soiled leaves of a sordid record, and found that he was then acting in a melodrama entitled "The Wages of Sin."

And the wages of sin is death! The drama insisted on the full measure of Biblical accuracy. Altogether, Grenier lay down to rest under unenviable conditions.

He dreamed that he was falling down precipices, and striking sheets of blue water with appalling splashes. Each time he was awakened by the shock.

But he was a hardy rogue where conscience was concerned, and he swore himself to sleep again. Rest he must have. He must arise with steady head and clear brain.

He was early astir. His first act was to send for the Yorkshire morning papers. They contained no news of Philip Anson dead, but the local sheet chronicled his arrival at York.

This was excellent. The banker would see it. A few printed lines carry great weight in such matters.

Then he signed the leases, dispatched them in a typewritten envelope and telegraphed:

"Documents forwarded this morning. Please meet wishes expressed in letter."

"Surely," he reflected, "Abingdon will not give another thought to my proceedings. Philip Anson is not a boy in leading strings."

He wired to Evelyn:

"Sorry for misunderstanding. Blue Atom must wait until my return."

Here was a way out. Whatever that wretched speck of color meant, it could be dealt with subsequently.

But Evelyn's prompt reply only made confusion worse confounded:

"Delay is impossible. The man has put off the duchess two days already."

So a man, and a duchess, and a period of time were mixed up with a blue atom. He must do something desperate; begin his plan of alienation sooner than he intended. He answered:

"Too busy to attend to matter further. Going to Leeds to-day. Letters here as usual."

160

And to Leeds he went. Residence in York was a fever—a constant fret. In Leeds he was removed from the arena. He passed the afternoon and evening in roaming the streets, consumed with a fiery desire to be doing, daring, braving difficulties.

But he must wait at least another day before he could lay hands on any portion of Philip Anson's wealth save the money stolen from his pockets.

At the hotel there was only one letter and no telegrams.

The London bankers wrote:

"We beg to acknowledge yours of yesterday. Your cash balance at date is twelve thousand four hundred and ten pounds nine shillings one penny. Your securities in our possession amount to a net value at to-day's prices of about nine hundred and twenty thousand pounds, including two hundred and fifty thousand pounds Consols at par. We will forward you a detailed list if desired, and will be pleased to realize any securities as directed.

"Kindly note that instructions for sale should be given in your handwriting, and not typed."

There was joy, intoxicating almost to madness, in this communication, but it was not unleavened by the elements of danger and delay.

His signature had been accepted without demur; he could control an enormous sum without question; these were the entrancing certainties which dazzled his eyes for a time.

But it was horribly annoying that a millionaire should keep his current account so low, and the concluding paragraph held a bogey, not wholly unforeseen, but looming large when it actually presented itself.

The memorandum in Philip's handwriting on Evelyn's letter was now thrice precious. He hurriedly scrutinized it, and at once commenced to practice the words.

"Devonshire" and "Sharpe" gave him the capitals for "Dear Sirs." He was at a loss for a capital "C," but he saw that Philip used the simplest and boldest outlines in his caligraphy, and he must risk a "C" without the upper loop. In "Lady M.," too, he had the foundation of the "£" to precede the requisite figures. Soon he framed a letter in the fewest words possible:

"Yours of to-day's date received. Kindly sell Consols value one hundred and fifty thousand pounds, and place the same to my credit."

He copied it again and again, until it was written freely and carelessly, and every letter available compared favorably with the original in his possession. Then he posted it, thus saving a day, according to his calculations.

With this missive committed irrecoverably to the care of his majesty's mails, Victor Grenier's spirits rose. Now, indeed, he was in the whirlpool. Would he emerge high and dry in the El Dorado of gilded vice which he longed to enter, or would fortune consign him to Portland again—perchance to the scaffold? He could not say. He would not feel safe until Philip Anson was a myth, and Victor Grenier a reality, with many thousands in the bank.

Already he was planning plausible lies to keep Mason out of his fair share of the plunder. A few more forged letters would easily establish the fact that he was unable to obtain a bigger haul than, say, fifty thousand pounds.

And what did Mason want with twenty-five thousand pounds? He was a gnarled man, with crude tastes. Twenty, fifteen, ten thousand would be ample for his wants. The sooner he drank himself to death the better.

With each fresh cigar Mason's moiety shrank in dimensions. The murder was a mere affair of a vengeful blow, but this steady sucking of the millionaire's riches required finesse, a dashing adroitness, the superb impudence of a Cagliostro.

But if his confederate's interests suffered, the total fixed in Grenier's original scheme in nowise became affected.

He meant to have a hundred thousand pounds, and he firmly decided not to go beyond that amount. His letter to the bankers named one hundred and fifty thousand pounds, and he calculated that by stopping short at two-thirds of the available sum he would not give any grounds for suspicion or personal inquiry.

Yet he would shirk nothing. Mr. Abingdon and Miss Atherley must be avoided at all events; others he would face blithely. He took care to have ever on the table in his sitting room a goodly supply of wines and spirits.

If anyone sought an interview, it might be helpful to sham a slight degree of intoxication. The difference between Philip drunk and Philip sober would then be accounted for readily.

But rest—that was denied him. It was one thing to harden himself against surprise; quite another to forget that disfigured corpse swirling about in the North Sea.

He wished now that Philip Anson had not been cast forth naked. It was a blunder not to dress him, to provide him with means of identification with some unknown Smith or Jones.

When he closed his eyes he could see a shadowy form wavering helplessly in green depths. Never before were his hands smeared with blood. He had touched every crime save murder.

162

Physically, he was a coward. In plotting the attack on Philip, he had taxed his ingenuity for weeks to discover some means where he need not become Mason's actual helper. He rejected project after project. The thing might be bungled, so he must attend to each part of the undertaking himself, short of using a bludgeon.

He slept again and dreamed of long flights through space pursued by demons. How he longed for day. How slowly the hours passed after dawn, until the newspapers were obtainable, with their columns of emptiness for him.

A letter came from Evelyn. It was a trifle reserved, with an impulse to tears concealed in it.

"I asked mother for fifty pounds," she wrote, "so the Blue Atom incident has ended, but I don't think I will ever understand the mood in which you wrote your last telegram. Perhaps your letter now in the post—I half expected it at mid-day—will explain matters somewhat."

He consigned Blue Atom to a sultry clime, and began to ask himself why Mr. Abingdon had not written. The ex-magistrate's reticence annoyed him. A letter, even remonstrating with him, would be grateful. This silence was irritating; it savored of doubt, and doubt was the one phase of thought he wished to keep out of Mr. Abingdon's mind at that moment.

As for Evelyn, she mistrusted even his telegrams, while a bank had accepted his signature without reservation. He would punish her with zest. Philip Anson's memory would be poisoned in her heart long before she realized that he was dead.

Chapter XX

Nemesis

Philip was thrown into the sea on a Tuesday. Jocky Mason reached London on Wednesday, and kept his appointment with Inspector Bradley on Thursday evening.

The inspector received him graciously, thus chasing from the ex-convict's mind a lurking suspicion that matters were awry. There is a curious sympathy between the police and well-known criminals. They meet with friendliness and exchange pleasantries, as a watchdog might fraternize with a wolf in off hours.

But Mason had no responsive smile or ready quip.

"What's up?" he demanded, morosely. "You sent for me. Here I am. I would have brought my ticket sooner if you hadn't written."

"All right, Mason. Keep your wool on. Do you remember Superintendent Robinson?"

"Him that was inspector in Whitechapel when I was put away? Rather."

"Well, some friends of yours have been inquiring from him as to your whereabouts. He sent a message round, and I promised that you should meet them if you showed up. I was half afraid you had bolted to the States."

"Friends! I have no friends."

"Oh, yes, you have—very dear friends, indeed."

"Then where are they?"

He glared around the roomy police office, but it was only tenanted by policemen attending to various books or chatting quietly across a huge counter.

His surly attitude did not diminish the inspector's kindliness.

"Don't be so doubtful on that point, Mason. Have you no children?"

Something in the police officer's eyes gave the man a clew. His swarthy face flushed and his hands clinched.

"Yes," he said, huskily. "I left two boys. Their mother died. They were lost. I have looked for them everywhere."

Inspector Bradley pointed to a door.

"Go into that room," he said, quietly, "and you will find them. They are waiting there for you."

Mason crossed the sanded floor like one walking in his sleep. He experienced no emotion. He was a man stunned for the nonce.

He opened the door of the waiting room, and entered cautiously. He might have expected a hoax, a jest, from his attitude.

Two stalwart young men were standing there talking. Their chat ceased as he appeared. For an appreciable time father and sons looked at each other with the curiosity of strangers.

He knew them first. He saw himself, no less than their unfortunate and suffering mother, in their erect figures, the contour of their pleasant faces.

To them he was unknown. The eldest boy was ten years old, the younger eight, when they last met. But they read a message in the man's hungering eyes, and they were the first to break the suspense.

"Father!" cried John.

The other boy sprang to him without a word.

He took them in his arms. He was choked. From some buried font came long-forgotten tears. He murmured their names, but not a coherent sentence could he utter.

They were splendid fellows, he thought, so tall and well knit, so nice-mannered, so thoroughly overjoyed to meet him.

That was the best of it. They had sought him voluntarily. They knew his record, and were not ashamed to own him. During the long days and nights of ceaseless inquiry he was ever tormented by the dread lest his children, if living, should look on him as accursed, a blot on their existence.

He half hoped that he might discover them in some vile slum, where crime was hallowed, and convicts were heroes. He never pictured them as honest, well-meaning youths, sons of whom any father might be proud, for in that possibility lurked the gnawing terror of shame and repudiation.

Mason's heart was full. He could not thank God for His mercy—that resource of poor humanity was denied him, and, to his credit be it said, he was no hypocrite.

His seared soul awoke to softer feelings, as his eyes, his ears, his very heart, drank in fuller knowledge of them. But he was tormented in his joy by an agonized pang of remorse. Oh, that he could have met them with hands free from further crime!

In some vague way he felt that his punishment for Philip Anson's death would be meted out by a sterner justice than the law of the land. He was too hard a man to yield instantly. He crushed back the rising flood of horror that threatened to overwhelm him in this moment of happiness. He forced himself again to answer their anxious inquiries, to note their little airs of manliness and self-reliance, to see with growing wonder that they were well dressed and wore spotless linen.

A police station was no place for confidences. Indeed, both boys were awed by their surroundings.

They passed into the outer office, and Mason went to thank Inspector Bradley.

"Don't forget your ticket," whispered the pleased officer.

The reminder jarred, but it was unavoidable. Mason got his ticket indorsed, the lads looking on shyly the while, and the three regained the freedom of the street.

"Let us find some place to sit down and have a drink," suggested Mason.

"No, father," said John, with a frank smile. "Neither of us takes drink. Come home with us. We have a room ready for you."

"I have lodgings—"

"You can go there to-morrow, and get your belongings."

"Yes. Jump into this cab," urged Willie. "We live in Westminster. It is not very far."

Mason was fascinated by the boys' pleasant assumption of authority. They spoke like young gentlemen, with the accent that betokens a good education. He yielded without a protest.

They sat three abreast in a hansom, and the vehicle scurried off toward the Westminster Bridge Road.

Mason was in the center. His giant form leaned over the closed doors of the cab, but he turned his head with interested eagerness as one or other of his sons addressed him.

"I suppose, father, you are wondering how we came to meet in such a place," said John.

"It might puzzle me if I found time to think."

"Well, the superintendent arranged everything. Unfortunately, he was away on his holidays when—when you were released—or we would have met you then, and his deputy was not aware of the circumstances. As soon as the superintendent returned he wrote to the governor, and was very much annoyed to find that you had slipped away in the meantime."

"He wouldn't be so annoyed if he was there himself," growled Mason, good-humoredly.

"Oh, John didn't mean that, father," broke in Willie. "The annoyance was his, and ours. You see, we had not known very long where you were. We didn't even know you were alive."

"Of course, of course. Somebody has been looking after you well. That's clear enough. They wouldn't be always telling a pair of boys that their father was in Portland."

"It gave us such a shock when we heard the truth," said downright John.

"But we were so glad to hear that our father was living, and that we should soon see him," explained the younger.

"When did you hear first?"

"About four months ago. Just before we took our present situations. We are saddlers and ornamental leather workers. Between us we earn quite a decent living. Don't we, John?"

"In fifteen weeks we have saved enough to pay for half our furniture, besides keeping ourselves well. There's plenty to eat, dad. You won't starve, big as you are."

They all laughed. The cab was passing St. Thomas' Hospital. Across the bridge a noble prospect met their eyes. London had a glamour for Mason that night it never held before.

"So Robinson wrote to Bradley, knowing that I would report myself to-day, and Bradley arranged—"

"Who is Robinson, father?" interrupted John.

"The superintendent, to be sure. He used to be inspector at Whitechapel."

"He is not the man we mean. We are talking of Mr. Giles, superintendent of the Mary Anson Home."

The two boys felt their father's start of dismay, of positive affright. They wondered what had happened to give him such a shock. Peering at him sideways from the corners of the hansom, they could see the quick pallor of his swarthy face.

"You forget, John," put in the adroit William, "that father knows as little about our lives as we knew about his until very recently. When we reach our flat we must begin at the beginning and tell him everything."

"There isn't much to tell," cried John. "When poor mother died, we were taken care of by a gentleman whom Mr. Philip asked to look after us. When the Mary Anson Home was built we were among the first batch of inmates. If ever a young man has done good in this world, it is Mr. Philip Anson. See what he did for us. Mother was nursed and tended with the utmost kindness, but her life could not be saved. We were rescued from the workhouse, taught well and fed well, and given such instruction in a first-class trade that even at our age we can earn five pounds a week between us. And what he has done for us he does for hundreds of others. God bless Philip Anson, I say!"

"Amen!" said his brother.

The voices of his sons reached Mason's tortured brain like sounds heard, remote but distinct, through a long tunnel. His great frame seemed to collapse. In an instant he became an old man. He set his teeth and jammed his elbows against the woodwork of the cab, but, strive as he would, with his immense physical strength and his dogged will, he shook with a palsy.

"Father!" cried John, anxiously, little dreaming how his enthusiastic speech had pierced to the very marrow of his hearer, "are you ill? Shall we stop?"

"Perhaps, John, a little brandy would do him good," murmured Willie.

"Father, do tell me what is the matter. Willie, reach up and tell the man to stop."

Then Mason forced himself to speak.

"No, no," he gasped. "Go on. It is—only—a passing spasm."

He must have time, even a few minutes, in which to drive off the awful specter that hugged him in the embrace of death. He dared not look at his sons. If he were compelled to face them on the pavement in the flaring gaslight, he would run away.

His anguish was pitiable. Great drops of sweat stood clammy on his forehead. He passed a trembling hand across his face, and groaned aloud unconsciously:

"Oh, God forgive me!"

It was the first prayer that had voluntarily left his lips for many a day.

The boys heard. They interpreted it as an expression of sorrow that his own career should have been so cut off from their childhood and joyous youth.

"Well, cheer up, dad, anyhow," cried the elder, much relieved by this conclusion. "We are all together again, and you can face the world once more with us at your side."

No dagger of steel could have hurt so dreadfully as this well-meant consolation. But for the sake of his sons the man wrestled with his agony, and conquered it to some outward seeming.

When the cab stopped outside a big building he was steady on his feet when he alighted, and he managed to summon a ghastly smile to his aid as he said to John:

"I am sorry to set you a bad example. But that is nothing new, is it? I must have some spirit, strong spirit, or I can't keep up."

"Certainly, father. Why not? It is all right as medicine. Willie, you go and get some brandy while I take father upstairs."

Their flat was on the second floor. It was neatly furnished, fitted with electric light, and contained five rooms.

John talked freely, explaining housekeeping arrangements, the puzzle as to their father's size, for the first bed they bought was a short one, their hours of work, the variety of their employment, any and every cheering topic, indeed, until Willie came with a bottle.

Both of them glanced askance at the quantity Mason consumed, but they passed no comment. He tried to smoke, and sat so that the light should not fall on his face. And then he said to them:

"Tell me all you know about Philip Anson. It interests me."

Snap! The hard composition of his pipe was broken in two.

"What a pity!" cried Willie. "Shall I run and buy you a new one?"

"No, my boy, no. I can manage. Don't mind me. I can't talk, but I will listen. May the Lord have mercy on me, I will listen!"

He suffered that night as few men have suffered. Many a murderer has had to endure the torments of a haunted conscience, but few can have been harrowed by hearing their own sons lauding to the sky the victim's benefactions to themselves and to their dead mother.

He was master of his emotions sufficiently to control his voice. He punctuated their recital by occasional comments that showed he appreciated every point. He examined with interest specimens of their work, for they understood both the stitching and the stamping of leather, and once he found himself dully speculating as to what career he would have carved out for himself were he given in boyhood the opportunities they rejoiced in.

But throughout there was in his surcharged brain a current of cunning purpose. First, there was Grenier, away in the North, robbing a dead man and plotting desolation to some girl. He must be dealt with.

Then he, the slayer, must be slain, and by his own hand. He would spare his sons as much pain as might be within his power.

He would not merely disappear, leaving them dubious and distressed. No. They must know he was dead, not by suicide, but by accident. They would mourn his wretched memory. Better that than live with the abiding grief of the knowledge that he was Philip Anson's murderer.

He was quite sure now that the dead would arise and call for vengeance if he dared to continue to exist. Yes, that was it—a life for a life—a prayer that his deeds might not bear fruit in his children—and then death, speedy, certain death.

Some reference to the future made by Willie, the younger, who favored his mother more than the outspoken John, gave Mason an opportunity to pave the way for the coming separation.

"I don't want you two lads to make any great changes on my account," he said, slowly. "It is far from my intention to settle down here, and let all your friends become aware that you are supporting a ticket-of-leave father. Yes, I know. You are good boys, and it won't be any more pleasant for me to—to live away from you, than it would be for you—under—other conditions—to be separated from me. But—I am in earnest in this matter. I will stop here to-night just to feel that I am under the same roof as you. It is your roof, not mine. Long ago I lost the right to provide you with a shelter. To-morrow I go away. I have some work to do—a lot of work. It must be attended to at once. Of course, you will see me, often. We can meet in the evening—go out together—but live here—with you—I can't."

His sons never knew the effort that this speech cost him. He spoke with such manifest hesitation that Willie, who quickly interpreted the less-pronounced signs of a man's thoughts, winked a warning at his brother.

He said, with an optic signal:

"Not a word now, John. Just leave things as they are."

Under any ordinary conditions he would be right. He could never guess the nature of the chains that encircled his father, delivering him fettered to the torture, bound hand and foot, body and soul.

At last they all retired to their rooms, the boys to whisper kindly plans for keeping their father a prisoner again in their hands; Mason to lie, open-eyed, dry-eyed, through the night, mourning for that which might not be.

The rising sun dispelled the dark phantoms that flitted before his vision.

He fell into a fitful slumber, disturbed by vivid dreams. Once he was on a storm-swept sea at night, on a sinking ship, a ship with a crew of dead men, and a dead captain at the helm.

Driving onward through the raging waves, he could feel the vessel settling more surely, as she rushed into each yawning caldron. Suddenly, through the wreck of flying spindrift, he saw a smooth harbor, a sheltered basin, in which vessels rode in safety. There were houses beyond, with cheerful lights, and men and women were watching the doomed craft from the firm security of the land.

But, strain his eyes as he would, he could see no entrance to that harbor; naught save furious seas breaking over relentless walls of granite.

Even in his dream he was not afraid.

He asked the captain, with an oath:

"Is there no way in?"

And the captain turned corpselike eyes toward him. It was Philip Anson. The dreamer uttered a wild beast's howl, and shrank away.

Then he awoke to find Willie standing by his bedside with soothing words.

"It is all right, father. You were disturbed in your sleep. Don't get up yet. It is only five o'clock."

At that hour a policeman left his cottage in a village on the Yorkshire coast, and walked leisurely toward the Grange House.

He traversed four miles of rough country, and the sun was hot, so he did not hurry. About half-past six he reached the farm. There were no signs of activity such as may be expected in the country at that hour.

He examined three sides of the building carefully—the sea front was inaccessible—and waited many minutes before he knocked at the door. There was no answer. He knocked again more loudly. The third time his summons would have aroused the Seven Sleepers, but none came.

He tried the door, and rattled it; peered in at the windows; stood back in the garden, and looked up at the bedrooms.

"A queer business," he muttered, as he turned unwillingly to leave the place.

"Ay, a very queer business," he said, again. "I must go on to Scarsdale, an' mak' inquiries aboot this Dr. Williams afore I report to t' super."

Chapter XXI

The Rescue

When Philip's almost lifeless body was flung over the cliff it rushed down through the summer air feet foremost. Then, in obedience to the law of gravity, it spun round until, at the moment of impact with the water, the head and shoulders plunged first into the waves.

At that point the depth of the sea was sixty feet at the very base of the rock. At each half-tide, and especially in stormy weather, an irresistible current swept away all sand deposit, and sheered off projecting masses of stone so effectually, that, in the course of time, the overhanging cliff must be undermined and fall into the sea.

High tide or low, there was always sufficient water to float a battleship, and the place was noted as a favorite nook for salmon, at that season preparing for their annual visit to the sylvan streams of the moorland valleys.

The lordly salmon is peculiar in his habits. Delighting, at one period of the year, to roam through the ocean wilds, at another he seeks shallow rivers, in whose murmuring fords he scarce finds room to turn his portly frame.

And the law protects him most jealously.

In the river he is guarded like a king, and when he clusters at its mouth, lazily making up his mind to try a change of water, as a monarch might visit Homburg for a change of air, he can only be caught under certain severe restrictions.

He must not be netted within so many yards of the seaward limit of the estuary; he may not be caught wholesale; the nets must have a maximum length of four hundred feet; they must not be set between 7 P. M. on a Friday and 7 A. M. on a Monday.

Viewed in every aspect, the salmon is given exceptional chances of longevity. His price is high as his culinary reputation, and the obvious sequel to all these precautions is that certain nefarious persons known as poachers try every artifice to defeat the law and capture him.

A favorite dodge is to run out a large quantity of nets in just such a tideway as the foot of the cliff crowned by Grange House. None can spy the operations from the land, while a close watch seaward gives many chances of escape from enterprising water bailiffs, who, moreover, can sometimes be made conveniently drunk.

When Philip hurtled into the placid sea his naked body shone white, like the plumage of some gigantic bird.

Indeed, a man who was leisurely pulling a coble in a zigzag course— while two others paid out a net so that its sweeping curves might embarrass any wandering salmon who found himself within its

171

meshes—marked the falling body in its instantaneous passage, and thought at first that some huge sea fowl had dived after its prey.

But the loud splash startled the three men. Not so did a cormorant or a white-winged solan plunge to secure an unwary haddock.

The net attendants straightened their backs; the oarsman stood up. The disturbance was so near, so unexpected, that it alarmed them. They looked aloft, thinking that a rock had fallen; they looked to the small eddy caused by Philip's disappearance to see if any sign would be given explanatory of an unusual occurrence.

Were Philip thrown from such a height when in full possession of his senses, in all likelihood such breath as was in his lungs at the moment of his fall would have been expelled by the time he reached the water.

He must have resisted the rush of air, uttered involuntary cries, struggled wildly with his limbs.

But, as it chanced, Mason's rough handling in carrying him to the balcony made active the vital forces that were restoring him to consciousness.

He was on the very threshold of renewed life when he fell, and the downward flight helped rather than retarded the process. Indeed, the rush of air was grateful. He drank in the vigorous draught, and inflated his lungs readily. His sensations were those of a man immersed in a warm bath, and the shock of his concussion with the surface of the sea in nowise retarded the recuperative effect of the dive.

Of course he was fortunate, after falling from such a height, in striking the water with his right shoulder. No portion of the human body is so fitted to bear a heavy blow as the shoulders and upper part of the back. Had he dropped vertically on his head or his feet he might have sustained serious injury. As it was, after a tremendous dive, and a curve of many yards beneath the sea, he bobbed up inside the salmon net within a few feet of the boat.

Instantly the fishermen saw that it was a man, an absolutely naked man, who had thus dropped from the sky.

They were amazed, very frightened indeed, but they readily hauled at the dragging net and brought Philip nearer the boat. Even at this final stage of his adventure he incurred a terrible risk.

Unable to help himself in the least degree, and swallowing salt water rapidly now, he rolled away inertly as the net rose under the energetic efforts of his rescuers. There was grave danger that he should drop back into the depths, and then he must sink like a stone.

Wearing their heavy sea boots, none of the fishermen, though each was an expert swimmer, dared to jump into the water. But the oarsman, being a person of resource, and reasoning rapidly that not the most enthusiastic salmon bailiff in England would pursue him in such manner, grabbed a boathook and caught Philip with it beneath the arm.

He only used the slight force needful to support him until another could grasp him.

Then they lifted the half-drowned man on board, turned him on his face to permit the water to flow out of his lungs, and, instantly reversing him, began to raise his elbows and press them against his sides alternately.

Soon he breathed again, but he remained unconscious, and a restored circulation caused blood to flow freely from the back of his head.

Of course the men were voicing their surprise throughout this unparalleled experience.

"Whea is he?"

"Where did he coom frae?"

"Nobbut a loony wad hae jumped off yon crag."

"He's neaked as when he was born."

At last one of them noticed his broken scalp. He pointed out the wound to his companions.

"That was never dean by fallin' i' t' watter," he said.

They agreed. The thing was mysteriously serious. Philip's youth, his stature, his delicate skin, the texture of his hands, the cleanliness of his teeth and nails, were quick tokens to the fisherman that something quite beyond the common run of seaside accidents had taken place. The oarsman, a man of much intelligence, hit on an explanation.

"He was swarmin' doon t' cliff after t' birds," he cried. "Mebbe fotygraffin' 'em. I've heerd o' sike doin's."

"Man alive," cried one of his mates, "he wouldn't strip te t' skin for that job."

This was unanswerable. Not one gave a thought to the invisible Grange House.

They held a hasty consultation. One man doffed his jersey for Philip's benefit, and then they hastily covered him with oilskin coat and overalls.

It was now nearly dark, so they ran out a marking buoy for their net, shipped oars, and pulled lustily to their remote fishing hamlet, three miles away from the outlet of the river which flowed through Scarsdale.

Arrived there, they carried Philip to the house of one who was the proud owner of a "spare" bed.

And now a fresh difficulty arose. A doctor, and eke a policeman, should be summoned. A messenger was dispatched at once for the nearest medical man—who lived a mile and a half away, but the policeman, who dwelt in the village, was a bird of another color.

These men were poachers, lawbreakers. At various times they had all been fined for illegal fishing. The policeman was of an inquiring turn of mind. He might fail to understand the mystery of the cliff, but he would most certainly appreciate every detail of their presence in that particular part of the sea which lapped its base.

173

So they smoked, and talked, and tried rough remedies until the doctor arrived.

To him they told the exact truth; he passed no comment, examined his patient, cut away the hair from the scalp wound, shook his head over it, bound it up, administered some stimulant, and sat down to await the return of consciousness.

But this was long delayed, and when, at last, Philip opened his eyes, he only rallied sufficiently to sleep.

The doctor promised to come early next day, and left.

Throughout Wednesday and Thursday Philip was partly delirious, waking at times to a vague consciousness of his surroundings, but mostly asking vacantly for "Evelyn."

Often he fought with a person named "Jocky Mason," and explained that "Sir Philip" was not in Yorkshire at all.

The wife of one of his rescuers was assiduous in her attentions. Most fortunately, for these fisherfolk were very poor, that lure spread beneath the cliff inveigled an unprecedented number of salmon, so she could afford to buy eggs and milk in abundance, and the doctor brought such medicines as were needed.

Gradually Philip recovered, until, at nine o'clock, on Thursday night, he came into sudden and full use of his senses.

Then the doctor was sent for urgently; Philip insisted on getting up at once. He was kept in bed almost by main force.

With the doctor's arrival there was a further change. Here was an educated man, who listened attentively to his patient's story, and did not instantly conclude that he was raving.

He helped, too, by his advice. It was utterly impossible to send a telegram to London that night. No matter what the sufferings of anxious friends concerning him, they could not be assuaged until the morning.

Yes, he would find money and clothes, accompany him, if need be, on the journey if he were able to travel to-morrow—attend to all things, in fact, in his behalf—for millionaires are scarce birds in secluded moorland districts. But, meanwhile, he must take a drink of milk and beef essence, rest a little while, take this draught, in a small bottle indicated, and sleep.

Sleep was quite essential. He would awake in the morning very much better. The knock on the head was not so serious as it looked at first sight. Probably he would not even feel it again if he wore a soft cap for some days. The broken skin was healing nicely, and concussion of the brain had as many gradations as fever, which ranges from a slight cold to Yellow Jack.

In his case he was suffering from two severe shocks, but the crisis was passed, and he was able, even now, to get up if it could serve any possible purpose.

All this, save the promise of help, the doctor said with his tongue in his cheek. He had not the slightest intention of permitting Philip to travel next day. It was out of the question. Better reason with him in the morning, and, if needful, bring his friends to Yorkshire rather than send him to London.

But—the police must be informed at once. It was more than likely the criminals had left the Grange House soon after the attempted murder. Yet, if Philip did not object, a policeman should be summoned, and the tale told to him. The man should be warned to keep the story out of the papers.

The arrival of the constable at a late hour created consternation in the household. But the doctor knew his people.

"Have no fear, Mrs. Verril," he whispered to the fisherman's wife, "your husband caught a fine fish when he drew Mr. Anson into his net. He will not need to poach salmon any more."

The doctor sat by Philip's bed while the policeman made clumsy notes of that eventful Tuesday night's occurrences.

Then, in his turn, he amazed his hearers.

He described his encounter with another Philip Anson in the highroad, at an hour when the real personage of that name was unquestionably being attended to by the doctor himself in the fisherman's cottage.

"Ay," he said, in his broad Yorkshire dialect, "he was as like you, sir, as twea peas, on'y, now that I see ye, he wasn't sike a—sike a gentleman as you, an' he talked wi' a queer catch in his voice. T'uther chap 'ud be Jocky Mason, 'cordin' te your discription; soa it seems to me 'at this 'ere Dr. Williams, 'oo druv' you frae t' station, must ha' took yer clothes, an' twisted his feace te luke as mich like you as he could."

The doctor cut short further conversation. He insisted on his patient seeking rest, but in response to Philip's urgent request, he wrote a long telegram, which he promised would be handed in when the Scarsdale telegraph office opened next morning.

And this was Philip's message to Evelyn:

"I have suffered detention since Tuesday night at the hands of Jocky Mason, whose name you will recollect, and another man, unknown. I am now cared for by friends, and recovering rapidly from injuries received in a struggle. I return to London to-day." The doctor smiled, but said nothing. "My only fear is that you must have endured terrible uncertainty, if by any chance you imagined I was missing. Tell Abingdon.
"Philip Anson."

And then followed his address, care of the doctor.

"Is that all?" said Anson's new-found friend.

Philip smiled feebly, for he was very weak.

175

"There is one matter, small in many ways, but important, too. You might add: 'I hope you have not lost Blue Atom by this mischance.'"

He sank back exhausted.

It was on the tip of the doctor's tongue to ask:

"What in the world is a Blue Atom?"

But he forbore. The sleeping potion was taking effect, and he would not retard it. He subsequently wrote a telegram on his own account:

"Mr. Anson is convalescing, but a journey to-day is impossible. A reassuring message from you will save him from impatience, and help his recovery. He has been delirious until last night. Now all he needs is rest and freedom from worry."

His man waited at Scarsdale post office until a reply came next day. Then he rode with it to the village where Philip was yet sleeping peacefully. Indeed, the clatter of hoofs without aroused him, and he opened his eyes to find the doctor sitting as though he had never quitted his side.

Evelyn's message must have caused much speculation as to its true significance in the minds of those telegraphic officials through whose hands it passed.

It read:

"Am absolutely bewildered. Cannot help feeling sure that news received to-day really comes from you. In that case, who is it who has been wiring repeatedly, in your name, from Station Hotel, York? Do not know what to think. Am going immediately to Abingdon. Please send more information. Suspense unbearable.

"Evelyn."

If ever there was need for action it was needed now. Anson's strenuous energy brought forth the full strength of his indomitable will. The pallor fled from his cheeks, the dullness from his eyes.

"Dr. Scarth," he cried, "you must not keep me here in view of that telegram from the woman I love. Believe me, I will be worse, not better, if you force me to remain inactive, chained almost helpless in this village, and miles away from even a telegraph office. Help me now, and you will never regret it. I ask you—"

The doctor cut short his excited outburst.

"Very well," he said. "Whatever you do, try and cease from troubling yourself about circumstances which a few hours will put right. I must return to my dispensary for one hour. Then I will come for you, bring some clothes and the necessary money, and we will leave Scarsdale for York at 2.30 P. M. That is the best I can promise. It must satisfy you."

He gave hasty directions as to his patient's food, and left him.

176

Another telegram arrived, with it the policeman, in the dogcart of the Fox and Hounds Inn.

"Abingdon went to Devonshire yesterday. His wife says he suspected that something had gone wrong. Unhappily we do not know his address, but he wires that he is not to be expected home to-day. Do ask Dr. Scarth to send further news if unable yourself.
"Evelyn."

Philip hesitated to be explicit as to the real nature of the outrage inflicted on him by Jocky Mason and his unknown accomplice. He hastily determined that the best assurance he could give to the distracted girl was one of his immediate departure from the village.

The policeman helped him as to local information, and he wrote the following:

"Leaving Scarsdale at 2.30 P. M. Passing through Malton at four o'clock, and reach York five-ten. Dr. Scarth permits journey, and accompanies me. Send any further messages care of respective station masters prior to hours named. Accept statement implicitly that I will reach London to-night. Will wire you from York certain; earlier if necessary. As for identity, you will recall May 15th, Hyde Park, near Stanhope Gate, four o'clock."

Evelyn and he alone knew that at that spot on the day and hour named, they became engaged.

The policeman valiantly lent the few shillings necessary, and the sturdy horse from the Fox and Hounds tore back to Scarsdale.

But the constable was of additional value. His researches in Scarsdale provided a fairly accurate history and description of the two denizens of the Grange House.

Philip himself had, of course, seen "Dr. Williams" in broad daylight and undisguised—not yet could he remember where he heard that smooth-tongued voice. Jocky Mason he only pictured hazily after the lapse of years, but the policeman's details of his personal appearance coincided exactly with Philip's recollection, allowing for age and the hardships of convict life.

At last came the doctor, with a valise.

"I am sorry," he laughed, "but all the money I can muster at such short notice is twelve pounds."

"I began life once before with three halfpence," was the cheery reply.

The few inhabitants of the hamlet gathered to see them off, and the fisherman's wife was moved to screw her apron into her eyes when Philip shook hands with her, saying that she would see him again in a few days.

"Eh, but he's a bonny lad," was her verdict. "'Twas a fair sham' te treat him soa."

At Scarsdale and at Malton again came loving words from Evelyn. Now she knew who it was who telegraphed to her.

And the mysterious Philip Anson at York remained dumb.

"The wretch!" she said to her mother. "To dare to open my letter and send me impudent replies."

More than once she thought of going to York to meet her lover, but she wisely decided against this course. Mr. Abingdon was out of town, and Philip might need some one he could trust to obey his instructions in London.

At ten minutes past five Anson and Dr. Scarth arrived in York.

A long discourse in the train gave them a plan. They would not appeal at once to the police. Better clear the mist that hid events before the aid of the law was invoked. There were two of them, and the assistance of the hotel people could be obtained if necessary.

They hurried first to the station master's office. Anything for Anson? Yes. Only a few words of entreaty from Evelyn to avoid further risk.

Then to the hotel. They sought the manager.

"Is there a man staying here who represents that his name is Philip Anson?"

The question was unusual in its form, disturbing in its innuendo. The man who asked it was pale, with unnaturally brilliant brown eyes, a gentleman in manner, but attired in ill-fitting garments, and beneath his tweed cap he wore a surgical bandage.

And Philip Anson, the millionaire, of whom he spoke thus contemptuously, was staying in the hotel, and paying for its best rooms.

But the manager was perfectly civil. The presence of Dr. Scarth, a reputable-looking stranger, gave evidence that something important was afoot. Mr. Anson was in his rooms at the moment. Their names would be sent up.

Dr. Scarth, quick to appreciate the difficulties of the situation, intervened quietly.

"Is he alone?"

"Yes."

"Then it will be better if you accompany us in person. An unpleasant matter can be arranged without undue publicity."

This was alarming. The manager went with them instantly. They paused at the door indicated.

"Come with me," said Philip, turning the handle without knocking.

Grenier, intent on the perusal of a letter he had just written, looked up quickly.

He was face to face with Philip Anson.

Chapter XXII

A Settlement of Old Scores

The one man stood, the other sat, gazing at each other in a silence that was thrilling.

Dr. Scarth and the hotel manager entered noiselessly, and closed the door behind them. Grenier, adroit scoundrel that he was, was bereft of speech, of the power to move. He harbored no delusions. This was no ghost coming to trouble his soul in broad daylight. It was Philip Anson himself, alive, and in full possession of his senses, a more terrible apparition than any visitor from beyond the grave. His presence in that room meant penal servitude for life for Victor Grenier, a prison cell instead of palatial chambers, bread and skilly in place of Carlton luncheons.

No wonder the scoundrel was dumb, that his tongue was dry. He went cold all over, and his eyes swam.

Philip advanced toward him. Grenier could not move. He was glued to his chair.

"Who are you?" said Anson, sternly.

No answer. As yet the acute brain refused to work. Lost—ruined—no escape—were the vague ideas that jostled each other in chaos.

"Can you not speak? Who are you that dares to usurp my name, after striving to murder me?"

No answer. The shifty eyes—the eyes of a detected pickpocket—wandered stupidly from Philip's set face to that of the perplexed hotel manager, and the gravely amused doctor.

Philip never used strong language, but he was greatly tempted at that moment.

"Confound you!" he shouted. "Why don't you answer me?"

"I—I—my name is Philip Anson. The manager—the—bank."

As a spent fox will vainly try the last despairing device of climbing a tree in full sight of the hounds, so did Victor Grenier evolve the desperate scheme that perhaps—perhaps—he might carry out a feeble pretense of self-assertion.

If only he could get away, into the crowded station, into the streets, slink into obscurity while the chase swept past, he might yet endeavor to escape.

"You Philip Anson! You vile impostor! I am sorely inclined to wring your neck!"

Philip came nearer. In sheer fright lest the other might give effect to his words Grenier again backed his chair violently. It caught against a thick rug and he fell headlong. For an instant they all thought he had hurt himself seriously.

179

The doctor and manager ran to pick him up, but he rose to his knees and whined:

"I will tell everything. I mean, there is some mistake. Look at my letters, my bank books. They are Philip Anson's. Indeed, there is a mistake."

On the table were many documents and a pile of bank notes. Everything was in order, neatly pinned and docketed. A number of telegrams, of which the topmost was signed "Evelyn," caught Philip's eye. He took them up. Not only were his betrothed's messages preserved, but copies of Grenier's replies were inserted in their proper sequence.

And Evelyn's letters, too, lay before him. He flushed with anger as he read.

"Oh," he cried, in a sudden blaze, "if I talk with this scoundrel I shall do him an injury. Send for the police. They will know how to deal with him."

The mere mention of the police galvanized Grenier into the activity of a wild cat. He had risen to his feet and was standing limply between the doctor and manager when that hated word electrified him.

With one spring he was free of them, rushing frantically to the door. After him went all three, the manager leading.

Grenier tore the door open and got outside. It was a hopeless attempt. He would be stopped by hotel porters at the foot of the stairs by the manager's loud-voiced order. Yet he raced for dear liberty, trusting blindly to fate.

And fate met him more than halfway.

A tall man, coming upstairs with a page boy, encountered Grenier flying downward. He grabbed him in a clutch of iron and cried sardonically:

"No, you don't! A word with me first, if the devil was at your heels!"

Intent on his prize, he paid no heed to others.

"Which is his room?" he said to the boy.

"No. 41, sir!" stammered the youngster, who thought that millionaires should be treated with more ceremony than this wolf-eyed stranger bestowed on the great Mr. Anson.

"Go on, then! I'll bring him."

"It is Jocky Mason," murmured Philip to Dr. Scarth. With the manager they had halted in the corridor. Mason strode past them, with eyes only for the cowering Grenier, who was making piteous appeals to be set free.

The stronger ruffian threw his confederate into Room 41, and was about to close the door when he saw Philip, close behind him.

He stepped back a pace, mute, rigid, seeking with glaring eyes to learn whether or not he was the victim of hallucination.

Philip knew him instantly. The voice he heard on the stairs, the policeman's rough but accurate picture, the recollection of the captive of Johnson's Mews, all combined to tell him that in truth Jocky Mason stood before him.

More than that, the would-be murderer handled his accomplice in a way that promised interesting developments. Now, perchance, the truth might be ascertained. Escape was out of the question for either of them. The manager's cry had brought four strong porters pellmell to the spot.

"You and I will enter," said Anson to Dr. Scarth. "You," to the manager, "might kindly remain here with your men for a few minutes."

"Shall I summon the police?"

"Not yet. I want to clear matters somewhat. They are dreadfully tangled."

Mason, spellbound, but fearless as ever, heard the dead man speak, saw him move. He could not refuse the evidence of eyes and ears. As Philip advanced into the room, the giant put his hands wildly to his head, and sobbed brokenly:

"Thank God! Thank God! For my boys' sake, not for mine!"

His extraordinary attitude, his no less extraordinary words, amazed at least two of his hearers. Grenier, rendered callous now by sheer hopelessness, was pouring out some brandy and lighting a cigarette. The revulsion of feeling at the sight of Mason had calmed him. He would make the most of the few minutes that were left before he was handcuffed.

Dr. Scarth took the precaution of locking the door, and putting the key into his pocket. It is doubtful if he would have done this had he known Mason's violent character. But, unknown to Philip, he carried a revolver, which he whipped forth when Grenier bolted, and as rapidly concealed when it was not needed.

"You did not kill me, you see," said Philip, sinking into a chair, for the excitement was beginning to tell on him.

The big man slowly dropped his hands. His prominent eyes seemed to be fascinated by the sight of one whom he threw apparently lifeless into the sea.

"I could lick your boots," he said, thickly.

The queer idea sounded ludicrous. Yet it conveyed a good deal. It smacked of remorse, repentance.

"Tell me," began Philip, but a loud knocking without interrupted him.

"Who is there?" said Dr. Scarth.

"Abingdon. I want to see Mr. Anson," was the reply, in a voice that Philip hailed joyfully.

Mr. Abingdon was admitted. His astonishment was extreme at the nature of the gathering, but he instantly noticed Philip's wan appearance, and the bandage on his head.

"My dear, dear boy," he cried, "what has happened?"

Philip told him briefly. As the ex-magistrate's glance rested on

Mason and Grenier it became very chilly. It brought Portland Prison near to the soul of one of them. He poured out more spirit.

The respite given by Mr. Abingdon's arrival gave Mason time to focus his thoughts. The man had lived in an inferno since he slipped away from his sons that morning on a plea of urgent business in order to catch a fast train for York in the afternoon.

He knew that Grenier would make the Station Hotel his headquarters, and his sole desire was to stop that enterprising rogue from committing further crimes which might be damaging to Anson's estate, and disastrous to the peace of mind of the girl he loved.

In no way did he hold Grenier responsible for urging him to commit murder. The journey to York was undertaken in the first place to save Philip's memory from the slur which was intended to be cast upon it, and, secondly, to afford a plausible pretext for a platform accident whereby his own life should be dashed out of him by an engine.

He would stumble over a barrow, fall helplessly in front of an incoming train, and end his career far from London, far from inquiry and published reports which might be injurious to his sons.

It might, perhaps, be necessary to use forcible means to persuade Grenier to abandon his tactics. They would be forthcoming; he gave earnest of that on the stairs.

Of course, the discovery that Philip lived gave a fresh direction to his purpose. A great load of guilt was lifted off his conscience, but the position remained little less serious personally.

So when, at last, he began to tell his story, there was a brutal directness, a rough eloquence, that silenced all questioning.

At first his hearers thought he was rambling and incoherent as he described his release from jail, his visit to the Mary Anson Home, his long and fruitless search for the lost boys.

He told of his meeting with Grenier, the espionage they both practiced on Anson's movements, and the plot hatched with Langdon, whose relationship with Sir Philip and Lady Morland now first became known to Philip.

He was quite fair to Grenier, giving him full credit for having stopped him more than once from murdering Philip when opportunities presented themselves. He dealt ruthlessly with the scene in the Grange House, even smiling dreadfully as he described Grenier's squeamishness over the suggestion that Philip's face should be battered into a shapeless mass.

Then followed his journey to London, the meeting with his two sons at Southwark Police Station, and the torturing knowledge, coming too late, that he had slain the benefactor of his wife and children.

There was an overwhelming pathos in his recital of the boys' kindness to him. He gave a lurid picture of his feelings during the previous night as he listened to their praises of Philip Anson, and their pleasant plans for their father's future. He only winced once, and that was at the remembrance of the parting a few hours ago.

And he finished by a pitiful appeal for mercy, not for himself, but for Grenier!

"I put the whole thing into his mind, Mr. Anson," he said. "He would never have thought of robbing you but for me. Let him go, make him leave the country. He will never trouble you again. As for me, when I go from this room, I walk to my death. You can't stop me. I will not lay hands on you, I promise, but not all the men in waiting there outside can hold me back. In five minutes, or less, I will be dead. It will be an accident. No one will be the wiser, and my boys will be spared the knowledge that their father tried to kill the man to whom they owe everything."

This amazing stipulation, backed up by a fearless threat, be it noticed, drew an indignant protest from Mr. Abingdon. Philip said nothing.

"Oh, very well," growled Mason. "There is another way."

His right hand dived into a pocket, and Dr. Scarth again fingered his revolver.

But Philip cried imperiously:

"Sit still, Mason. I have heard all that you have to say. Be quiet, I tell you. Wait until I refuse your request."

"My dear boy," interrupted Mr. Abingdon, who knew Philip's generous impulses, "you will never think of condoning—"

"Forgive me! Let me carry matters a stage further. Now you, Grenier. What have you to say?"

"Very little!" was the cool response. "My excellent friend has made a clean breast of everything. You didn't die, and so spoiled the finest coup that ever man dreamed of. I had no difficulty in concocting the requisite epistles from Sir Philip and Lady Morland. Your London bank accepted my signatures with touching confidence. I have opened two accounts in your name, one in York and one in Leeds, five thousand pounds each. This morning I heard from London that one hundred and fifty thousand pounds of your Consols had been realized, and placed to your current account. Just to be feeling the pulse of the local money market, I drew out two thousand pounds to-day. It is there, in notes, on the table. You will also find the check books and passbooks in perfect order. Oh, by the way, I told your man Green to open your safe and send me your mysterious portmanteau. It is in my bedroom. That is all, I think. I am sorry if I worried the young lady—"

"You unutterable scamp," cried Philip.

"Well, I had to keep her quiet, you know. As it was, she suspected me. I suppose my messages hadn't the proper ring in them. And—what the deuce is a Blue Atom?"

Dr. Scarth was even more interested than ever, if possible.

"Blue Atom! Blue Atom is a nobler specimen of a dog than yourself. He is a prize toy Pomeranian; you are a mongrel."

Grenier, for an instant, grew confused again. He sighed deeply.

"A dog!" he murmured. "A blue Pomeranian! Who would have guessed it?"

Philip turned to Mason.

"If I leave you here alone with this man, Grenier, will you keep him out of mischief?"

Jocky gave his associate a glance which caused that worthy to sit down suddenly.

"And yourself? Promise that you will remain as you are until I return?"

"I promise."

Anson led his friends from the room. He thanked the manager for the assistance he had given, and told him the affair might be arranged without police interference.

Long and earnestly did he confer with Mr. Abingdon. It was a serious thing to let these men off scot-free. Grenier's case was worse, in a sense, than that of Mason.

There were three banks involved, and, forgery, to a bank, is a crime not to be forgiven. There was a dubious way out. Philip might accept responsibility for Grenier's transactions. If the London bank accepted Grenier's signature for his, surely the local institutions would accept his for Grenier's.

Mr. Abingdon was wroth at the bare suggestion.

"You will be forging your own name," he protested, vehemently.

"Very well, then. He shall write checks payable to self or order, indorse them, and I will pay them into my account."

"I dare not approve of any such procedure."

So Philip, though sorely tried, again labored his arguments that the trial of Grenier would be a cause célèbre in which his, Anson's, name would be unpleasantly prominent. Evelyn would be drawn into it, and Abingdon himself. There would be columns of sensation in the newspapers.

Moreover, it was quite certain that Jocky Mason would commit suicide unless they captured him by a subterfuge, and then the whole story would leak out.

It ended by Philip gaining the day, for, at the bottom of his heart, Abingdon was touched by Mason's story—thoroughpaced ruffian though he was.

They re-entered No. 41. The pair were sitting as they were left; Grenier was not even smoking. The affair of the Blue Atom had deeply wounded his vanity.

Philip walked straight to Mason, and took him by the shoulder.

"Now, listen to me," he said. "I gave you one crack on the head, and you have given me one. Shall we say that accounts are squared?"

"Do you mean it, sir?"

"Yes, absolutely."

"Then, all I can say is this, sir. During the rest of my life I'll make good use of the chance you have given me. God bless you, for my boys' sake, more than my own."

"And you," went on Philip, turning to the disconsolate Grenier. "Will you leave England and make a fresh start in a new land? You are young enough, and clever enough, in some respects, to earn an honest living."

"I will, sir. I swear it."

The utter collapse of his castle in Spain had sobered him. The gates of Portland were yawning open for him, and the goodness of the man he had wronged had closed them in his face. Never again would he see their grim front if he could help it.

He readily gave every assistance in the brief investigation that followed. Mr. Abingdon looked on askance as he wrote checks for three thousand pounds and five thousand pounds on the York and Leeds banks respectively, but even Philip himself gave an astonished laugh when he saw his own signature written with quiet certainty and accuracy.

"Oh, that's nothing," cried Grenier, in momentary elation. "I took in Mr. Abingdon, and sent a complete letter to the London bank."

"You did not take me in," growled Abingdon. "You made one fatal mistake."

"And what was that, sir?"

"You alluded to the annual report of the 'Home.' Everyone connected with that establishment, from the founder down to the latest office boy, invariably calls it the 'Mary Anson Home.' Mr. Anson would never write of it in other terms."

Grenier was again abashed.

"Have you any money in your pocket?" said Philip, when the forger had accounted for every farthing.

For one appreciable instant Grenier hesitated. Then he flushed. He had resisted temptation.

"Yes," he said, "plenty. Langdon supplied me with funds."

"How much?"

"Two hundred and fifty pounds. I have over seventy left."

"I will arrange matters with him. Come to my West End office next Monday, and you will be given sufficient to keep you from poverty and crime until you find your feet in Canada. Remember, you sail on Wednesday."

"No fear of any failure on my part, sir. I can hardly credit my good— or, what I want to say is, I can never thank you sufficiently."

"Pay Mason's fare to London. Better stay with him. His sons may have a good influence on you, too."

Mason rose heavily.

"I'll find him a job, sir. He can pack your bag."

The words recalled to Philip the knowledge of his incongruous attire. Soon he wore his own clothes. He refused to allow Grenier to divest himself of the garments he wore, but he was glad to see his old watch again.

Dr. Scarth bade them farewell and returned to Scarsdale by the last train.

Philip and Abingdon arrived in London at 2.15 A.M. On the platform, accompanied by her mother, was Evelyn.

She wept all the way to Mount Street, where Philip would be accommodated for the night. She cried again when she saw his poor, wounded head; but she laughed through her tears when she ran off to fetch a very small and very sleepy dog, with long blue hair falling in shaggy masses over his eyes and curling wonderfully over his tiny body.

Mr. James Crichton Langdon was imperatively summoned to London, and given such a lecture by Mr. Abingdon that he so far abandoned the error of his ways as to strive to forget that such a person as Evelyn Atherley existed.

The ex-magistrate had seen him in Devonshire, and was so skeptical of his statements concerning the whereabouts of Sir Philip and Lady Morland that he traveled direct to York, via Gloucester and Birmingham, to clear up with Philip in person a mystery rendered more dense by the curious letter and telegram he received in London.

One day, in August, the Sea Maiden dropped anchor off the Yorkshire coast not far from the gaunt cliff on which stood Grange House.

Dr. Scarth entertained Mr. and Mrs. Anson in his house for the night, and some of the men were allowed ashore.

They came back full of a story they had heard, how the "skipper" had met with a mishap on the big point to s'uth'ard, was rescued by three fishermen, and had bought for each man the freehold of the house in which he lived, besides presenting them jointly with a fine smack.

"He's a rare good sort, there's no doubt about that," said the chief narrator, "an', of course, 'e can afford to do that sort of thing, bein' the King o' Diamonds."

"He's more than the King of Diamonds; he's the King of Trumps," observed a gigantic, broken-nosed stoker, who listened to the yarn, not being one of the shore-going men.

"You've known him this long time, haven't you, Mason?" said the first speaker.

"Yes—ever since he was a bit of a boy. Ten years it must be. But we lost sight of each other—until I met him the other day. Then he gave me a job—for the sake of old times!"

THE END

186